The Heart
of Play

Jay Palmer

All Books by Jay Palmer

The VIKINGS! Trilogy:
>DeathQuest
>The Mourning Trail
>Quest for Valhalla

The Egyptians! Trilogy:
>SoulQuest
>Song of the Sphinx
>Quest for Osiris

Jeremy Wrecker, Pirate of Land and Sea

The Grotesquerie Games

The Magic of Play

The Heart of Play

The Seneschal

Viking Son

Viking Daughter

Dracula – Deathless Desire

>The Heart of Play Cover Artist: Jay Palmer
>Website: JayPalmerBooks.com

The Heart of Play

To our amazing niece,
Heather,
from her loving Aunt Karen
and Uncle Jay.

Chapter 1

Hilary

The last bell finally rang. Before I left the classroom I paused to look at Audrey's empty chair. Audrey had been absent from school all week. I didn't care; we hadn't spoken in two months, not since school had started. With a deep-throated growl audible only to me, I picked up my book-bag and followed the line of students into the crowded hall, wending my way toward the main doors.

Whatever had happened to Audrey wasn't my problem. We weren't friends anymore. Audrey had given to me, and then stolen, my greatest opportunity; she'd taken me to Arcadia, a magic world where living dolls danced and sang. I'd proven to be a great magician, chanting and flipping my jump rope with a mastery even Audrey couldn't claim. Together we'd defeated Punch and freed the baby dolls.

Then Audrey had done the unthinkable; Audrey had banished me from Arcadia.

How could anyone forgive such a betrayal?

Arcadia was incredible, a place where all my dreams could come true. Wealth, fame, and power ... everything magic could conjure was mine ... and then Audrey had crushed my dreams.

Audrey had never really been my friend. Looking back over our five-year friendship, I could see now that everything Audrey had ever said hid secret meanings; dark, unkind, and downright insulting.

Audrey and I had never been alike. I was cool and popular while Audrey was quiet and shy. I liked the newest, loudest jammin' music while Audrey liked old songs whose lyrics were clear and romantic. I loved gold jewelry and fancy clothes while Audrey dressed plain, not caring about fashions or labels. My skin was as brown as Hershey's chocolate while Audrey was white as cream. But our biggest difference was ambition; I wanted everything life had to offer while Audrey seemed content with whatever she got. Our differences would've eventually driven us apart so I really hadn't lost very much ...

... except Arcadia.

Audrey had tried to talk to me several times since school started, but Audrey's expelling me from Arcadia was the act of an eternal enemy. I wouldn't listen. I could never trust her again, and whatever was keeping her out of school all week, I hoped it was painful.

In the sunlight I walked past rows of parked school busses lining the busy lot and the driveway lined with parents waiting to collect their kids. I joined the familiar crowd who walked home, which used to include Audrey. Step by step, three blocks passed amid pointless babble, and other kids slowly broke off to head to their homes, until I was alone.

Carrying my book-bag, I passed a large, fancy gray car, almost a limousine, parked outside my building, and then I ascended the elevator to my condo.

I inserted my key and turned it in the lock, but felt no resistance; *the front door of my condo hadn't been locked ...!*

I paused and stepped back, wary: *Mother never forgot to lock our door!* This was unheard of ... and a serious potential threat. We always locked our door. If Mother had come home from work early, then she still would've locked the door. *Had we been robbed? What if the robbers were still inside?*

What should I do?

Pocketing my key, I grasped the doorknob lightly, and as gently and silently as possible I slowly twisted it.

Peering into the narrow gap, I saw most of our living room unchanged, nothing out of place. I inched the door open slightly wider and spied a clear view of our hallway and kitchen. Nothing seemed missing or disheveled and no strange noises reached my ears. I stepped inside and glanced about.

Sitting quietly upon our couch was the last person I expected to ever see again.

"Great Aunt Virginia ...!" I exclaimed.

"Hello, Hilary Agatha Martin," Great Aunt Virginia said.

Great Aunt Virginia looked the same as always, austere, aged, with bright silver hair like chrome wire spun about her head, each strand uniformly rigid and perfectly in place. She had sea-green eyes, was very thin, and wore a long, full dress; a tight bodice above ballooning skirts, under which only the toes of highly-polished, sharp-pointed shoes could be seen. Her dress appeared to be entirely of embroidered black silk with traces of white lace puffing out at her collar and cuffs ... I'd always wondered if she'd sewn it herself. A broach on her collar showed a natural golden leaf trapped in a dark-glass oval, but it was of no plant that Audrey or I knew. Beside her rested a thick cane, leaning against a large carpet-bag purse, both of which were probably antiques and worth a fortune. Her cane seemed to be made entirely of ebony, like the black keys on a piano, but it was smooth, intricately carved, and two small red gems gleamed from its handle like watchful eyes.

"A pleasure to see you again, sweet child," Great Aunt Virginia said.

"I ... didn't think you ... wanted to see me anymore," I said.

"Children take the slightest grain of evidence and make mountainous assumptions," Great Aunt Virginia said. "Do you have any evidence that I disliked your company?"

"Well, no ...," I said.

"And yet you'd be insulted if I called you a child," Great Aunt Virginia said.

I bit my lip and said nothing.

"Hilary, I need you to come to Arcadia," Great Aunt Virginia said.

"But ... Audrey said I could never go there again ...!" I said.

"Audrey is also a child," Great Aunt Virginia said. "She made a false assumption."

"Can we go now?" I asked.

"No, we must wait for your mother," Great Aunt Virginia said. "I can't let you face this risk without her permission. Another threat has arisen ... far greater than Punch."

"Can't Audrey handle it?" I asked.

"Audrey can't help anyone," Great Aunt Virginia said. "Audrey has been captured, and without a jumper, I've no means to free her."

I pressed Great Aunt Virginia for details, but she put me off, insisting it was only polite to wait for my mother. I asked about Princess Gracely, Hiram, and Muskay; Great Aunt Virginia assured me they were all fine, and that the dolls of Arcadia were safe, and would be happy if not for the new threat. I wanted to ask about Audrey but I couldn't; I was still angry with her, so an awkward silence fell.

I felt excited and terrible. I wanted to return to Arcadia more than anything. I couldn't miss this chance! Yet I didn't want to see Audrey again. Audrey didn't deserve me coming to rescue her. But I didn't think I could leave anyone, even Audrey, in the hands of something worse than Punch. I felt like a hypocrite, like I was telling a lie even though I'd said nothing. I was keeping the fact that Audrey and I weren't speaking unsaid. *I was letting Great Aunt Virginia believe in something that wasn't true to get something that I wanted.* No matter how justified my anger, I was being untruthful.

"Hilary!" Mom scolded as she opened the door. *"You didn't lock ...!"*

"Mom!" I interrupted her. "We ... have company."

Mom stepped inside, glanced into our living room and almost dropped her laptop.

"Virginia ...!" Mom exclaimed, surprised.

"Forgive me, Madge," Great Aunt Virginia said. "I hope I'm not intruding."

"No, forgive me," Mom recovered quickly, and she set her computer bag down. "Always a pleasure ...!"

"You're wondering what I'm doing here," Great Aunt Virginia said. "To be honest, I need help Hilary's help."

"Arcadia ...?" Mom asked.

"There's trouble," Great Aunt Virginia said.

"Is Audrey all right?" Mom asked.

"Yes and no," Great Aunt Virginia said. "An old enemy has returned and we can't fight her."

"Why not?" Mom asked.

"Because the enemy we'd have to fight ... is Audrey," Great Aunt Virginia said.

Chapter 2

Our Enemy Revealed

"Charlotte ...?" Mom said into her phone. "Yes. I know. Can you come over? Charlotte, you need to come. Virginia ... is here."

Mom paused and we could hear Audrey's mother over the speaker.

"No, Audrey's fine ... I think. Charlotte, you stay there. We'll come right over."

Mom hung up.

"Virginia, would you mind?" Mom asked. "I don't think she should be driving ..."

"Of course," Great Aunt Virginia said. "My driver is downstairs."

A uniformed driver in a gray suit, but without the small-billed hat, was standing beside the fancy gray car as we emerged from my building. I wasn't surprised; Great Aunt Virginia didn't carry a cell phone or beeper, but strange things always happened around her. The driver took Great Aunt Virginia's carpet bag and opened and held the door as Mom entered first, then me, and lastly Great Aunt Virginia, and the driver quickly motored us to Audrey's apartment.

Mrs. Darby opened the door at our first knock. Her eyes were red, her skin pale, and she looked like she hadn't slept in days.

"Charlotte," Mom said, and they briefly hugged, and then Great Aunt Virginia came in.

"So good to see you!" Mrs. Darby said.

"Charlotte, I won't pretend this isn't serious," Great Aunt Virginia said. "An ancient enemy has returned to Arcadia ... and she's captured Audrey."

"Is she safe?" Mrs. Darby asked.

"Physically, no one has harmed her ... or is likely to harm her," Great Aunt Virginia said. "It's Audrey who's doing the harm."

"Audrey ...?" Mrs. Darby asked.

"Perhaps we should sit down," Great Aunt Virginia said. "I need to tell you everything."

We all took seats, leaving the large recliner for Great Aunt Virginia. She set her carpet-bag purse upon the floor, opened it widely, and out of it she lifted a silver tray with four tall, frosted glasses, each filled with ice, which she set upon the coffee table. Then she lifted out a glass pitcher of iced tea, which was too large to have fit inside her purse, had no lid, and would certainly have spilled. Mrs. Darby, Mom, and I exchanged glances, surprised but not questioning.

After she poured and handed each of us a glass of iced tea, she took a drink from the last glass, then set it down and sat upon the recliner.

"It began very quietly," Great Aunt Virginia said softly, her hands folded in her lap. "An unsettled feeling slowly pervaded Arcadia. A hand puppet refused to build his assignment. He insisted on working on a secret project of his own, ignoring Boss Fist. Two troll dolls got into a violent, angry fight and had to be forcibly separated. One paper doll purposefully ripped another. The rag dolls began snipping at each other and several marionettes got their strings in a knot. Rumors began, suspicions of the cause of the disquiet, each doll blaming others. A seething unrest overwhelmed every village.

"Then the queen of Arcadia went mad and began imprisoning dolls, even ordering their executions. The king tried to calm her but to no avail. Many dolls were locked in the deepest dungeon of the castle and false reports were given to the queen that the dolls had been destroyed. Finally, the queen ordered the tin soldiers to attack the stuffed animals and drive them from Arcadia. With no other recourse, the king refused, and he finally ordered the queen to be chained in her tallest tower ... until her insanity could be cured.

"Then the king went mad, even worse than the queen. All stuffed animals were banished, and the hand puppets were ordered to make terrible weapons and devices of torture. At this point I interceded and demanded an explanation ... and the king ordered me exiled. I was forced to flee, yet I returned in secret and sought out Mr. Magee, Judy, and the ancient ones ... anyone who could tell me what was happening. Yet no one knew.

"The paper dolls found our answer. In an old filing cabinet, they found a reference to an ancient evil that had plagued Arcadia almost a century ago, and not been seen since."

Great Aunt Virginia closed her eyes and sighed deeply.

"A voodoo doll," Great Aunt Virginia said. "A voodoo doll has come to work evil upon Arcadia."

"A voodoo doll ...?" Mom asked, raising her eyebrows and glancing at me. "That can't be! Voodoo isn't real!"

"The magic of play works both ways," Great Aunt Virginia said. "The innocent dream of goodness, but the ambitious dream of power. Anything can be real in a dream."

"What did you do?" Mrs. Darby asked.

"I snuck into the tallest tower to see the queen," Great Aunt Virginia said. "No one dared defy the king and only she could refuse him. I found her still imprisoned in her tower, weeping for the terrible things she'd done. Yet I couldn't free her, not without a jumper, and so I left her to seek the source of the madness that had claimed her.

"While Princess Gracely spied for us, Hiram, Muskay, and I helped the paper dolls make a timetable of all the dolls and people who'd gone mad. Eventually we realized that at no time had two dolls or people gone mad simultaneously. That's the one weakness of a voodoo doll; it can only possess one individual at a time. Remember that, Hilary; the voodoo doll can only possess one doll ... or person ... at one time."

I nodded my head but said nothing.

"I went to each of the doll villages," Great Aunt Virginia said. "I ordered all the dolls to pair up, to join into small groups of two, three, or four. Each doll had to know the others, and give an alarm if anyone suddenly started acting strangely. Together we marched against the king, but without a jumper I couldn't subdue him. That's the worst weapon of the voodoo doll; we can assault those she's possessed, but until we find her, we can't stop her from possessing others. Within an hour, she can abandon one victim and take over another.

"For this reason I surrendered my spare jump rope to Princess Gracely, who swore she'd hide it where I'd never find it," Great Aunt Virginia said. "Although my jumping years are over, a jump rope would make me too powerful, and if the voodoo queen took me and my jump rope then her powers would be unlimited. Unarmed, we sent teams of scouts to scour every inch of Arcadia. We had the stuffed animals with wings soar across the hills and valleys, looking for her ship.

"According to the notes of the paper dolls, the last time a voodoo doll invaded was before I was born. Back then, Great Aunt Annie was the jumper of Arcadia, and she and the dolls tracked and located the voodoo doll aboard a wooden boat docked in the shadows of the great swamp.

"All of Arcadia marched against her. One after another, many dolls became possessed and had to be restrained. Finally, Great Aunt Annie became her pawn and ordered the hunt to end, but Muskay recognized that she was possessed, refused, and Hiram held Great Aunt Annie helpless while Muskay led the final attack."

Great Aunt Virginia sighed and shook her head.

"They found her boat and searched it, but the voodoo doll had fled," Great Aunt Virginia said. "Released by the voodoo doll, Great Aunt Annie had her whole boat carried back to the king and queen, and they ordered it burned. As it went up in flames, the dolls cheered and peace was restored to Arcadia."

"But ... she's back," Mom said.

"This could be a different voodoo doll, but I think not," Great Aunt Virginia said. "This time, they, he or she, went for the greatest power in Arcadia they knew of

11

... me, as all the dolls knew I was the jumper who'd replaced Great Aunt Annie. Finally I was possessed by the voodoo doll. Under her influence, I ordered the dolls to do terrible things.

"Audrey stopped me. The voodoo doll didn't know about her, and when Audrey confronted me, the voodoo doll didn't know who she was. Audrey instantly realized that I was being manipulated ... or maybe she thought I'd gone mad. Either way, she used her magic to bind me, and when the madness of the voodoo doll ended, I told Audrey all I knew."

Great Aunt Virginia hung her head in shame.

"I should've guessed," Great Aunt Virginia said. "I should've suspected ...!"

"What?" I asked.

"Unbeknownst to me, as soon as Audrey next arrived, she was possessed by the voodoo doll," Great Aunt Virginia said. "Foolishly, I told Audrey, who was really the voodoo doll, everything. I described all about how Great Aunt Annie had once defeated the voodoo doll, and how it was her duty as the new jumper to find and banish, or destroy, if possible, this ancient threat to Arcadia.

"Then Audrey smiled, a terrible, wicked grin, and I realized what had happened, but what could I do? I couldn't physically fight Audrey, and even if I could, my victory would do nothing to the voodoo doll. Audrey took three steps backwards, lifted her jump rope, began jumping ... and she banished me from Arcadia."

"You were banished ...?" I asked, astounded.

"I was," Great Aunt Virginia said. "But don't fear; Arcadia is always open to those whose hearts are light. I can return to Arcadia at any time ... but I dare not go alone."

"You want Hilary to enter Arcadia and fight Audrey ...?" Mom asked.

"Only if she must," Great Aunt Virginia said. "The voodoo doll is our true enemy. We must enter quietly ... and find her lair. She knows we'll be coming. She knows we're looking for her. We'll need help ... from the other dolls ... yet that's our greatest threat. Arcadia is too big for us to search alone, but the voodoo doll could become anyone ... at any time. We could be talking to her for hours, or journey with her, and we'd never know. We can't afford to trust anyone ... not even each other."

"This sounds dangerous," Mom said.

"Very," Great Aunt Virginia said. "That's why I need you, Madge, and Charlotte, if you'll come."

"*Us* ...?" Mom and Mrs. Darby asked.

"No one knows, and can identify, your daughters like you," Great Aunt Virginia said. "This time, we can't abandon our jump rope, because the voodoo doll has one, too. We must work together to find and stop the voodoo doll ... or Arcadia ... and Audrey ... will be doomed."

Chapter 3

Our Mission Begins

Mom made several phone calls, first to Dad, explaining that Audrey was missing and she was taking Mrs. Darby to Baltimore to look for her. She told dad she was also taking me, and he'd have to take care of Michael, my little brother, while we were gone. Then she called a babysitter to be there when Michael got home from baseball practice, and the school to inform them that the babysitter would be waiting outside our condo for Michael to arrive. Mrs. Darby changed clothes while Mom made her phone calls, and then we went back to our condo. Mom and I changed out of our school and work clothes into jeans and jackets, and I put on my favorite necklace and grabbed my weapon: my jump rope.

I couldn't wait to do magic again!

Great Aunt Virginia's driver drove us all to Baltimore. We seldom spoke, each lost in our troubled thoughts. I was still angry with Audrey, not that I wanted her possessed by a voodoo doll, but I'd still not forgiven her for banishing me from Arcadia ... or for telling me I was banished. Rescuing her would be the price I paid for returning to the land where I could do magic. Also, I'd be doing it to save the dolls, to save Arcadia ... so I could enjoy it again. Perhaps I could learn to bring its magic back to the real world ... where real magic could make all my dreams come true.

"Great Aunt Virginia, can I ask a question?" I asked as we cruised the freeway.

"Of course," Great Aunt Virginia said.

"After ... I was banished, and we went home, I tried to do magic," I said. "I took my jump rope to the park and jumped until my feet hurt. I tried all the chants. Nothing worked."

"Did you try hard?" Great Aunt Virginia asked. "Did you try to do magic ... seriously?"

"Yes," I said.

"The magic is in the play," Great Aunt Virginia explained. "You can't use magic to ... do your homework ... or babysit your brother. Those needs are real. When in Arcadia, you were so unaccustomed to talking dolls that everything seemed unreal ... everything seemed like a game. You can't do magic seriously ... you have to be lost in the magic of play."

Listening, Mom and Mrs. Darby exchanged glances, but I sat back and said nothing. I should've guessed what I was doing was wrong. All these months I could've been doing magic, but I'd been attempting it seriously ... my heart overflowing with anger at Audrey. Magic didn't come from my jump rope ... or my chants. Magic came from me, the jumper ... not from my mind but from my heart.

Audrey had told me this but I'd resented her so

16

much I'd forgotten. Anger had been my real enemy, keeping me from getting everything I wanted.

Looking back, I'd been angry for months. Every time I'd watched TV, whenever I saw the face of someone important, I'd thought *'that could be me, on TV, being rich and famous'.* Every time I listened to music or saw something I couldn't afford, I'd silently growled, blaming Audrey for what I didn't have. Yet Audrey had told me everything Great Aunt Virginia had just said. Anger had blocked my mind ... like loud earphones block normal hearing.

Earphones are easier to remove than anger.

Normally, long car rides bored me but I sat excited ... and a little scared. I couldn't wait to get back to Arcadia, but ... what did they expect me to do? How could I fight an enemy I couldn't find? Worse, what would I do if I had to fight Audrey?

What if I tried to fight Audrey ... and failed?

We didn't take the elevator. Great Aunt Virginia led us up three flights of stairs, and then we entered her small apartment. It looked unchanged, like a museum of antiques. Faded wallpaper of dull-pinstripes covered every wall. Crystals hung from ancient lampshades, resembling tiny chandeliers, and dark-stained wooden chairs and couches bore affixed red velvet cushions. Bric-a-brac cluttered the apartment and faded paintings of strange people, dressed in fashions not worn for a century, stared from wooden frames.

Rather than a coffee table, before the couch stood a short wooden table that seemed to be made for a child of another age. Around it sat four tiny chairs, only one empty. The other three held Hiram, the red-plaid jacketed teddy bear with black-button eyes, Princess

Gracely, the very old porcelain doll with long blonde hair, wearing a flowing, lacey white dress, and Muskay, the cloth-sewn jester doll, checkered red and black, as they existed here ... in the real world. All sat before a miniature pink and blue china tea set, carefully-arranged upon a spotless white lace tablecloth. I smiled at the magic tea set, eager to enter Arcadia again.

"Have you ever made tea?" Great Aunt Virginia asked me.

"No, ... well, hot tea ... with teabags," I said.

All three of the adults smiled, and Great Aunt Virginia took me into her beautiful but antiquated kitchen. There she lit a wooden match and ignited an old gas stove, upon which she placed a large metal teapot filled with water. On the counter was a ceramic teapot whose distinctive markings matched the magic tea set.

Great Aunt Virginia looked at my jeans and tutted.

"Proper clothing helps, but we're not embarking upon a social visit," Great Aunt Virginia sighed, and she opened a great wooden cabinet that sat upon her kitchen counter; inside it were many tan-colored clay jars. "Now, these are your herbs and spices, and this ..." she tapped a thick, heavy green marble bowl that had a matching stone handle sticking out of it, which ended in a plain, rough, rounded bottom. "... this is a mortar and pestle. You fill the pestle with tea leaves and then grind them with the mortar."

At her direction, and with Mom and Mrs. Darby watching, I took out two large sprigs of chamomile, half a dandelion leaf, three berries of sumach, and five blossoms of sweet balm. I dropped each into the pestle, and then Great Aunt Virginia let me choose three other ingredients. I didn't know most of them, but I found peppermint, red clover, and rose petals. I added only a little of each, and then I began grinding them all into powder. This wasn't as easy as I'd expected, and Mom scolded me when I'd tried to pound them. Mrs. Darby showed me how to circle the heavy mortar around the bottom of the pestle very swiftly, letting the scrapes of each pass grind the dried herbs, berries, and petals into a fine powder.

The pungent aroma tickled my nose and I had to resist the urge to sneeze. As the ancient kettle began to whistle, Great Aunt Virginia turned off the stove and pronounced my grinding 'satisfactory', although she looked at my tea disdainfully. When it began to whistle, she lifted her boiling kettle, filled her ceramic teapot with steaming water, and then had me hold my palms together as she spooned the powdered herbs and spices into my bare hands.

"Now, gently breathe upon it, and then cast it into the water," Great Aunt Virginia said.

As if it were a game, I did as I was told. This was the play, I knew, where the magic would be found.

"Now we have to let the tea steep," Great Aunt Virginia said. "Let's sit in the parlor."

Carrying the hot teapot with a potholder to the tiny doll's table, Mom, Mrs. Darby, and Great Aunt Virginia sat side-by-side on the antique couch, whose red velvet cushions looked hard and uncomfortable, not deep and soft. As I stood looking at them, Great Aunt Virginia glanced at me and then at the empty chair before the magic tea set, and I understood her meaning. Although the chair was far too small, I squeezed between its wooden arms and sat at the table with her three favorite dolls.

Great Aunt Virginia opened an aged wooden box which began to tinkle a slow, merry tune.

"I'm very excited," Mom told Great Aunt Virginia. "I always wanted to see Arcadia."

"I just want to find Audrey," Mrs. Darby said.

"We can't find Audrey right away," Great Aunt Virginia said. "If we do, and the voodoo doll is possessing her, then she'll know where we are ... and that we have Hilary."

"Where are we going?" Mom asked.

"We need help," Great Aunt Virginia said, a bitter regret filling her voice. "We don't know who we can trust, so we dare not go to Bambole."

"Bambole ...?" Mom asked.

"Bambole is the capital city of Arcadia," Mrs. Darby said. "Audrey told me of it."

"Bambole is Italian for dolls," Mom said.

"That's true," Great Aunt Virginia said. "The thrones of Arcadia are called Oyuncak and Bebekler, which is Turkish for dolls. Turkey is the nation where St. Nicolas lived, so our thrones were named to honor him. Most of our oldest place names are translations of the word 'dolls'."

"What's Bambole like ...?" Mom asked. "What kind of dolls live there?"

"The nursery of the baby dolls lies in Bambole," Great Aunt Virginia said. "However, the city isn't built for dolls. While Hiram, Muskay, and Princess Gracely are dolls in this world, they have human forms in Arcadia, and they need houses and apartments to live in, just like we do."

"The humans in Arcadia take care of the baby dolls," Mrs. Darby said.

"Yes, but the other dolls didn't want to live in the shadows of humans," Great Aunt Virginia said. "That's why they each founded villages for their kind."

"So ... why aren't we going to Bambole?" I asked.

All three adults turned to look at me.

"We'd be seen," Great Aunt Virginia stated as if it were obvious.

"Yes, but we'd blend in," I said. "Four people in a city of people don't stand out. In a city of dolls, we'll be apparent to any who sees us ... even from a distance."

Mom and Mrs. Darby looked shocked, but Great Aunt Virginia smiled.

"Hilary knows how to play," Great Aunt Virginia said, looking from Mom to Mrs. Darby. "If you two can't join in the play, as she has, then no magic will take you to Arcadia."

"I'm ready, but I'm still worried about Audrey," Mrs. Darby said.

"The game she's trapped in is serious, but it's still just a game," Great Aunt Virginia reminded her.

"Don't worry," Mom said to Mrs. Darby. "We're joining in the game, and we won't quit playing until Audrey is safe and with us."

"... Until all the dolls are safe," I amended.

Great Aunt Virginia smiled.

"Time to drink our tea," Great Aunt Virginia said.

Great Aunt Virginia let Mom pour the tea for her, for herself, and for Hiram. Then the teapot was passed to Mrs. Darby, who poured for herself and Princess Gracely. Then the teapot was passed to me, and I filled my cup, then poured for Muskay, who sat on the opposite side of the table from the adults. After I set the teapot back on its padded rest, we all lifted our teacups and Great Aunt Virginia paused.

"Princess Gracely, you do indeed look lovely today," Great Aunt Virginia said, looking at the porcelain bride doll. Then she nodded to Mom.

"Hiram," Mom smiled, taking her cue. "You appear handsomely bearish!"

Mrs. Darby smiled and looked at the cloth jester.

"Muskay, are you being mischievous?" Mrs. Darby asked. "Not everyone appreciates your wry sense of humor, you know."

All three adults looked at me, and I turned to each doll at the table.

"Princess Gracely, Hiram, and Muskay; it's so good to see you again!" I said. "I hope you like the tea. It's my first attempt and I pray I got it right."

We all drank ... at least, the humans did. The three dolls, Princess Gracely, Hiram, and Muskay, sat as always, without moving, but I tried not to dwell upon that; such realizations weren't part of the game. I sat back and took another sip of my tea, blowing on it first to cool it. It smelled heady; the peppermint beckoned while the rose petals added an aroma of elegance. It tasted sweet, and I could distinguish the richness of the red clover under the more powerful flavors.

"Drink deeply and slowly," Great Aunt Virginia whispered softly. "We may have to be away for quite a while."

We sat, sipping our hot tea, much longer than usual. Several more times Great Aunt Virginia urged us to talk to the dolls, and we each took our turn, laughing and sharing compliments. The tea slowly cooled and became easier to drink without burning our tongues, and its vapors added to our game. Its comforting scents filled our nostrils, relaxed us, and helped us enter the world of play. Then we refilled our cups, and Great Aunt Virginia gave each of us a cinnamon stick. She had us stir our tea clockwise three times and drink again. I felt like a witch casting a spell, yet I carefully stirred and drank.

The tingling sensation finally came, accompanied by dizziness, but both were expected. They signaled that our game held all the magic it needed. With my fuzzy sight, I glanced at the dolls; Hiram and Princess Gracely, who were holding their teacups to their lips, drinking in small sips, and Muskay, who was holding his cup high, as if toasting, and with a grin he lifted his saucer and set it on top of his plush, tri-pointed red-and-black jester's cap, making all three of his little bells jingle.

We all laughed, and then Great Aunt Virginia's living room, with all her antiques, vanished.

Chapter 4

Reunited with Friends

Bright sunlight filtered down through leafy branches. I was sitting on a rock looking up at tall trees. Beside me lay a fallen log upon which Great Aunt Virginia, Mom, and Mrs. Darby were sitting. We were outdoors, in a forest, and on both sides of one thin tree trunk we could easily see the red plaid edges of Hiram's jacket.

"Hiram, if you're going to hide behind a tree, then you need to choose one wider than you," Great Aunt Virginia giggled.

Out from behind the thin tree poked the black-haired, bushy-bearded face of Hiram.

"Are you ... yourself?" Hiram asked.

"I am," Great Aunt Virginia said. "Are you?"

"He is," came the velvety voice of Princess Gracely, and she rose up from behind a thick bush, looking as beautiful as ever.

"He's as much himself as he usually is, I'm sorry to

say," Muskay said, and we all looked up to see Muskay, in his jester's costume, perched on a branch above our heads. "Alas ... more's the pity!"

With amazing dexterity, Muskay jumped off the limb, performed a flip, and landed right before us.

"Ta-da!" he sang, holding his arms straight out.

"Enough of that," Great Aunt Virginia scolded him. "Where's Audrey?"

"We don't know," Hiram said. "We've been hiding out since Audrey banished you."

"We were so worried for you," Princess Gracely said, sounding as if she were holding back tears, and she hurried forward and hugged Great Aunt Virginia tightly.

"I'm fine, no need to worry," Great Aunt Virginia comforted her. "I've brought help."

"We need it," Muskay said. "We dared not go back, and Falcon won't come out of hiding."

"Is Falcon hiding in the Hall of the Trolls again?" I asked.

"We think so, but we couldn't go looking," Princess Gracely said.

"Everyone knows we're your friends, so they're sure to be watching for us," Hiram said. "We saw no reason to lead them to Falcon."

"I saw a reason!" Muskay argued. "It would be obvious if Falcon were possessed; he'd have a backbone for the first time!"

"We'll need Falcon eventually," Great Aunt Virginia said. "For now, we have two new friends you must meet."

"Two lovely ladies ...!" Muskay insisted with a smile, and Great Aunt Virginia cuffed him lightly.

"Mind your manners," Great Aunt Virginia said. "This is Charlotte, Audrey's mother, and this is Madge,

Hilary's mother. You all remember Hilary."

"Hard to forget the jumper that helped us defeat Punch," Hiram said.

"Indeed, and we are honored to welcome Charlotte and Madge, the mothers of our two jumpers," Princess Gracely said with a smile and a slight curtsey. "I'm only sorry you didn't arrive to find Arcadia at its best."

"It's a pleasure to meet you," Mrs. Darby said to Hiram, Princess Gracely, and Muskay. "Audrey has told me all about you."

"Thank you, I'm delighted to finally ...," Mom began, but then she stopped, her eyes wide.

We followed her line of sight. On the ground, peeking out from a pile of leaves, was a little pink unicorn looking warily at us.

"Oh, he's just a friend," Princess Gracely said, and she bent and held out a hand to the pink unicorn. "Come, little one! Come out and play!"

Slowly the unicorn emerged. It looked like a carnival prize, no bigger than a large kitten, and it was made of pink fake fur with a stitched gold lame horn and hooves and glued-on fabric eyes, white with large blue pupils outlined in black. Princess Gracely picked it up, carried it to Mom, and placed it in her arms. Mom cradled the baby unicorn like she would an infant. The living stuffed animal blinked, smiled, and snuggled warmly against her.

"The stories are true," Mom said. "I believed them, since I watched you fade, but ... to see them ... to hold them ...!"

"They're really alive," Mrs. Darby said, her eyes fixed on the tiny pink unicorn as if she, too, had doubted.

"We'll see lots of stuffed animals," I said. "We need

to rescue Audrey."

"The only rescue for Audrey is to find the cursed token of her and destroy it," Hiram said. "Without that token, the voodoo doll can't control her."

"Those tokens must be in the lair of the voodoo doll," Great Aunt Virginia said. "Her last boat was full of them; that's why they burned it. Have any new vessels or structures appeared?"

"No boats," Muskay said.

"No new houses, either," Princess Gracely said.

"The Factory is empty," Hiram said. "That's where we've been hiding."

"Who isn't possessed?" Great Aunt Virginia asked.

"We've no way of knowing," Princess Gracely said. "But Muskay came up with a way for us to test each other ..."

Princess Gracely held up one thin finger, then lifted it to her lips and kissed it. Then Hiram clapped his hands twice, and Muskay stuck his thumbs into his ears and waved his hands.

"Those are our secret signs," Princess Gracely said. "We each have our own, and only we know about them. Whenever one of us does ours, the others do theirs, and so we know we're not possessed."

"The voodoo doll doesn't know them, so she wouldn't be able to do the right sign," Muskay said.

"Good thinking," Great Aunt Virginia said. "Charlotte, Madge, Hilary; we should each make up one so we can prove we're not possessed."

Great Aunt Virginia lifted one finger, then touched her forehead with it. Mom curled both of her forefingers and hooked them, and Mrs. Darby interlocked her fingers and turned her palms down, facing the ground. I twirled both my hands at my sides, as if I was flipping my jump rope.

"Excellent," Great Aunt Virginia said. "Now, we must all remember our priority: if any of us look possessed, even for a second, we do our signs and raise the alarm."

"With all due respects, if Hilary looks possessed then we should take her jump rope," Hiram said. "Begging your pardon, young jumper, but if you became possessed ...!"

I nodded gravely. *We couldn't let the voodoo doll control two jumpers!*

"This is our advantage," Great Aunt Virginia said to us. "Audrey thinks Hilary was banished and that their mothers can't come to Arcadia. The voodoo doll will be looking for Princess Gracely, Hiram, Muskay, and I. She won't be looking for you."

"We should start with the rag dolls," Muskay said.

"Why?" Hiram asked.

"Because they're the most proper," Princess Gracely said. "It'd be easy for the voodoo doll to mimic the forwardness of the hand puppets, the officiousness of the tin soldiers, or the vacant expressions of the troll dolls, but we'll know at once if a rag doll doesn't act with strict politeness."

"The marionettes would be equally obvious," I said. "All of them are masterful dancers ... that's not a skill you can learn without practice."

"True, but to learn that, you'd have to get them to dance," Muskay said. "Not that any marionette has ever refused to dance ..."

"All for the best," Great Aunt Virginia said. "We'll seek Mistress Flax first, and then Master Strand."

"Let's just hope neither of them are possessed," Hiram said.

"Let's hope Hilary hasn't forgotten how to jump rope," Muskay said.

Every eye turned to look at me.

"I can jump," I said, hoping I was right.

"It's time to prove that," Great Aunt Virginia said. "There's a thin woods near the village of the rag dolls. You need to jump us there."

Trying to hide the lump in my throat, I lifted my jump rope. Fighting tremulations, I separated and gripped each wooden handle and dropped and stepped over my braided blue cord. This hadn't worked since I'd fought beside Audrey against Punch, and if it didn't work now then all our plans ... and my dreams ... would fail. They all stepped back to give me room, staring expectantly; *I'd be a terrible disappointment if I couldn't ...!*

With a deep breath I flipped my jump rope. Behind me, my cord flew up, and instinctively I jumped as it descended. Easily I double-jumped and began inventing a chant.

> *"To the charming village*
> *Of the rag dolls.*
> *To their tiny homes and shops ..."*

I stopped ... *what rhymed with dolls?*

"To their little halls ...," Muskay suggested.

I blushed and started again.

> *"To the charming little village*
> *Of the rag dolls.*
> *To their tiny homes and shops.*
> *To their little halls.*
> *Take us all,*
> *Take us all,*
> *Swift as swift can be.*
> *Take us all,*

To Mistress Flax,
My dearest friends and me. "

In my mind I imagined the nearby woods I recalled seeing when Audrey had taken me there, before we'd challenged Punch. As the others circled around me, just outside the range of my whipping jump rope, I repeated my chant again and again, and finally felt the strain of magic tingle within my chest. To my delight, gold and silver sparkles began to brighten the blue cord of my jump rope.

I was doing it ...!
I was doing magic again ...!

Slowly, my sparkling sphere of magic expanded to engulf all of us ... and then we began to fade.

Chapter 5

The Village of the Rag Dolls

Greater than I recalled, the strain of magic tore at me, tiring, almost painful, as if a spectral hand was pulling all my energy out of my chest. Yet I recalled the enormity of the magic I was doing, transporting not only myself but six adults ... *a feat unto itself.*

The world changed. With each pass of my sparkling blue rope before my eyes the tree trunks thinned and changed colors, from rough, dark gray to smooth, pale brown, their leaves became darker, and the trees shifted positions. The light grew brighter as the sun was suddenly filtered by a lesser canopy. I jumped until the strain of the magic lessened, and then I slowed my rope and my gold and silver sparkles faded.

We were again amid trees but wholly different, in another forest. From our hidden vantage, peering between the low branches, we spied the distant village of the rag dolls.

Outside our woods lay an old-world village of

charming cottages and shops. Under numerous rising brick chimneys and assorted tiny weather vanes lay the sharp-peaked, red-tiled roofs of two and three-story buildings, mostly painted white, yet equally brown with ornate, stained frames and lattices, as if each house was wrapped in a dark-wooden lace. Railed balconies hung over awnings to shelter narrow sidewalks that lined small cobblestone streets. No building was larger than a doll house, and many rag dolls walked upon streets barely wide enough for Hiram's shoes. These dolls were cloth-bodied, and a few looked identical; I recognized some of them from TV commercials that aired only before Christmas. All were soft and cloth-sewn, some with yarn hair, others more realistic, and a few looked handmade. Some had faces painted on hard ceramic or plastic heads over soft bodies, while others had beautiful faces made by needlepoint, masterfully-sewn.

"It's wondrous," Mrs. Darby said, staring at the tiny village.

"Well done, Hilary," Great Aunt Virginia congratulated me.

"We shouldn't all go," Muskay said, looking at all the dolls wandering through the village. "We'll be recognized."

"Charlotte and I aren't known," Mom said, and Mrs. Darby startled.

"Pretend to be new dolls," Princess Gracely told them.

"If any ask, say you're 'newly arrived' and exploring Arcadia's countryside," Great Aunt Virginia said. "Ask for the Madame of the Weavers; that should be Mistress Flax."

"Confirm her identity before you ask her to follow you," Hiram said. "The real Mistress Flax's last owner was named Dorothy."

"Whatever you do, don't pick her up or speak disrespectfully," Muskay warned. "In Arcadia, dolls don't like to be treated like toys."

"We'll be careful," Mom promised. "Ready, Charlotte?"

"I'll go along with the game," Mrs. Darby said.

"Don't step on a house!" Hiram warned. "They're more fragile than they seem."

"Your clumsiness isn't a quality they share," Muskay snided.

Mom and Mrs. Darby stepped out of the greenery and walked into the open. We watched anxiously, and Mrs. Darby's words, and the constant, tremulous tone of her voice, haunted me. She was clearly worried about Audrey, and would be so until we found her. But ... if I was forced to fight Audrey ... *would I have to fight Mrs. Darby, too?*

Most of the dolls seemed frightened of Mom and Mrs. Darby, but a few stayed and spoke to them, and soon we saw them literally step into the city and walk down the only street wide enough for humans, especially adults. I recognized the textile mill, their largest building, where the rag dolls wove new fabrics upon wide looms. There, Mom and Mrs. Darby paused and seemed to be speaking to someone, and finally both turned around and walked back ... so slowly I wondered what was delaying them. Only as they approached us could I see why they walked so slowly; Mistress Flax was leading their way.

Mistress Flax was an old but masterfully-stitched rag doll, made of cream-colored silk, and her face was both stitching and paint; her lips were sewn with bright red thread and her eyes were tiny green stitches, while her cheeks were pinked like faded red stains.

"Mistress Flax, you look lovely!" Princess Gracely said, and she curtsied as Mistress Flax walked into the woods.

"Always a pleasure, Princess Gracely," Mistress Flax said. "Virginia the Grand! So good to see you! We were all worried by your abrupt departure."

"Departure ...?" Great Aunt Virginia asked. "Mistress Flax, I ... I know you welcome jumpers at any time, as nothing disrupts your workers ..."

"Virginia, there's no need to test me," Mistress Flax scolded. "Tight deadlines are the bane of my existence, but I'd miss them all to be rid of the voodoo doll."

"Our apologies, Mistress Flax, but we must be cautious," Hiram said.

"Tell me, Mistress Flax," Muskay pushed forward. "What are bodice stays?"

"Mr. Muskay," Mistress Flax glared at him disapprovingly. "If you wish to be a jester that is your business, but unless you intend to start wearing a corset, bodice stays are none of your concern."

"That's her," Muskay grinned.

"Mistress Flax, we desperately need your help," Great Aunt Virginia said.

"Introductions first, if you please," Mistress Flax interrupted. "If these two are new dolls then I'm a pair of pinking shears."

"Mistress Flax, may I introduce Madge and Charlotte," Princess Gracely said. "These are the mothers of Hilary and Audrey."

"At your service," Mrs. Darby said.

"An honor to meet you," Mom said.

"Indeed a pleasure," Mistress Flax said with a slight bow, and then she turned to me. "Welcome back,

Jumper Hilary. I trust you are well."

"Yes, thank you," I said.

"We have little time," Great Aunt Virginia said.

"Rag dolls travel slowly, but we get where we need to be," Mistress Flax said. "However, you need the speediest dolls. We can't use the stuffed animals as Great Aunt Annie the Grand did. All stuffed animals have been outlawed, especially the birds. Your best hope lies in Sparkle City."

"Sparkle City ...?" I asked.

"It's new," Hiram said. "Boss Fist assigned all of his crew to building it."

"It's the new home of the glamour dolls," Princess Gracely explained. "They needed a place to live; they refused to stay in the Factory."

"It's the best doll-home in Arcadia!" Muskay smiled, and Great Aunt Virginia cuffed him again.

"It's a shameful place," Mistress Flax said. "Still, they're our only hope. We rag dolls will do what we can, and send word, if we find anything."

"Do you know anything about Audrey?" I asked.

"Yes," Mistress Flax said. "Audrey and the voodoo doll are sitting on the thrones of Oyuncak and Bebekler in Bambole. Audrey is wearing the queen's crown and no one knows what happened to the king."

"Has anything else happened?" Great Aunt Virginia asked.

"In the last few days, the tin soldiers were ordered to hunt all the stuffed animals, and round them up, if they can," Mistress Flax said. "Their orders came straight from General Walnut, curse his solid wooden head. I hope he was being possessed as the order was ridiculous."

"What about Master Strand?" Hiram asked.

"You won't find him anywhere," Mistress Flax said. "Master Strand marched to Bambole and demanded that Audrey show him where she was hiding the king and queen. We suspect that she did; he vanished and didn't return. However, his chief assistant, Miss Hangly, is a trustworthy young woman. If you want to address the marionettes, I suggest you begin with her. However, be sure to ask if any of her people are missing."

"Missing ...?" Princess Gracely asked.

"Yes," Mistress Flax said. "For weeks we've been having dolls not show up for work, and when we go looking, there's no trace of them."

"No one saw them leave ...?" Muskay asked.

"The voodoo doll must've taken them," Hiram said.

"But ... why ...?" Mistress Flax asked. "And ... where are they now ...?"

"Your wisdom is invaluable," Princess Gracely said to Mistress Flax. "We'll do as you ask and seek the missing dolls."

"Thank you for everything," Great Aunt Virginia said.

"You're welcome, but I leave you with one last caution," Mistress Flax said. "Virginia, you may be older now, and wiser, than Great Aunt Annie was when we last fought the voodoo doll, but so is she. The voodoo doll's complete takeover of Arcadia was managed in days, whereas Punch tried and failed after a year of preparation. That implies a dangerous level of cunning and determination. We can't underestimate this enemy; you've already failed once. If you fail a second time you won't get a third attempt."

"What does she want?" I asked. "What does the voodoo doll hope to accomplish?"

"The greatest danger of an intelligent enemy is that they don't reveal the natures of their games," Mistress

Flax said. "Chances are, when we do learn her plan, what she's really after, it may be too late."

We all nodded. Mistress Flax spoke like a general commanding troops ... and none of us dared argue with her.

The Heart of Play

Chapter 6

The Stages of the Marionettes

We waited until long after Mistress Flax had vanished into the streets of her village lest anyone know she'd been talking to us. Sudden flashes of gold and silver, coming from the woods she was walking away from, would reveal our meeting to anyone watching, and we couldn't afford for the voodoo doll to discover to whom we were talking. We might be able to evade Audrey for a while, but Mistress Flax would be vulnerable to Audrey's jump rope, and her absence would leave the other rag dolls helpless.

"It's time we visited Theater City, the stages of the marionettes," Great Aunt Virginia said.

I was glad we'd waited, for I'd needed time to rest. I stood up and lifted my jump rope and everyone gathered around me in a wide circle.

This time the gold and silver sparkles came much easier.

"To the marionette's home

Wide flat stages
On the wooden-wheeled carts ..."
I stuttered, for I couldn't think of a rhyme.
"Used for ages!" Muskay said.
I nodded my thanks to him, and began again.
"To the marionette's home
Wide flat stages
On the wooden-wheeled carts
Used for ages
Carry us, carry us
To see their prancing
Carry us, carry us
To delighted dancing."
I'd repeated my chant for the fourth time before I felt
the strain of the magic pull its hardest, and then I almost
staggered under the strain. Yet I kept going and soon
the woods vanished and changed to a small sunny glen,
an open space between a forest of oaks and a wall of
thick evergreens.

Amid the trees we spied four large, box-shaped,
wooden horse-drawn carriages, minus the horses; their
leather harnesses lay empty upon the ground. A large
table, like a wooden picnic table in the park, stood
uncluttered between the large, boxy covered carts. On
the sides facing the table, each wooden cart had a huge,
rectangular, heavily-decorated window draped with thick
velvet curtains, drawn apart, each displaying a wide,
miniature theatrical stage. Upon one stage hung dozens
of stringed marionettes dancing in perfect
synchronization, clapping their wooden hands and
stomping their shiny boots.

These marionettes were men and women, painted in
matching purple and silver outfits, with tall hats, each
with a fluffy white dove's feather in front, wearing

gleaming black boots. Each appeared to be about fifteen inches tall, hanging from strings stretched to the ceiling of their cart-borne stage, with brightly-painted eyes of white half-spheres dotted with brown-painted pupils and glued to their polished natural-wood faces. In unison, their arms lifted and their little black boots slammed down onto the wooden floors of their stages.

"We are the marionettes, the dancers and the singers!
We delight and amaze! We are the joy-bringers!
We are the dolls that make Arcadia fun!
When entertaining is needed we are the one!
We make the other dolls smile, laugh, and sing!
Each to their happiest we always bring!
We can dance any dance! We never fail or fall!
We are the marionettes, the best dolls of all!"

When their song and dance concluded, Mom and Mrs. Darby repeated their mission. Both walked forward and pretended to be new dolls, but this time we were close enough to hear their conversation.

"That was wonderful!" Mrs. Darby said.

"What are you doing here? Who are you? This is a private rehearsal!" said a high-pitched woman's voice with a southern accent.

"We apologize," Mrs. Darby said. "We didn't mean to intrude."

"We're new arrivals ... exploring for the first time," Mom said. "We'll leave so that you can continue your practice."

"Before we go, is there a Miss Hangly here?" Mrs. Darby asked.

"I'm Miss Hangly," said the same woman's voice.

"Someone in Bambole asked us to give you a message," Mrs. Darby said.

"A private message for your ears only," Mom said.

43

"Before we leave, would you mind ...?"

Moments later, Mom and Mrs. Darby came walking back out of the woods. Behind them, pushing through the tall grasses, came a wooden doll with a silver hat topped with a white feather, and a purple-painted bodice the same color as her knee-length purple silk skirt. Long black strings came from her hands, boots, knees, and the top of her hat behind the feather. These strings were coiled up and attached to a wooden crossbrace she carried slung over her shoulder.

"Is this about Master Strand?" Miss Hangly whispered as soon as they were out of hearing range of the other dolls.

Mom bent low and whispered.

"You should ask Great Aunt Virginia," she murmured, and she pointed to us.

Miss Hangly's painted eyes widened, and then she rushed forward.

"Virginia!" she exclaimed. "You're safe!"

"I can't bend that low," Great Aunt Virginia whispered. "Just this once, would you mind ...?"

"By all means!" Miss Hangly said, and she lifted up her crossbrace.

With a nod from Great Aunt Virginia, Mom reached down, took the crossbrace, and lifted it high, until the smiling marionette was even with everyone's heads.

"You know about the voodoo doll ...?" Great Aunt Virginia asked.

"Arcadia won't be safe until we hornswoggle her!" Miss Hangly said.

"That's what we're trying to do," Great Aunt Virginia said. "Unfortunately, we can't be everywhere, and we don't know who to trust."

"Speaking of which, do you know what a puppeteer

44

calls a marionette's crossbrace?" Muskay asked.

"It's called a 'control'," Miss Hangly said. "We don't use that term, as dolls in Arcadia are controlled only by themselves."

"Thank you," Great Aunt Virginia said. "We can't be too careful."

"Is Master Strand safe?" Miss Hangly asked.

"No one will be safe until we banish the voodoo doll," Hiram said.

"When we can, we'll rescue him," Great Aunt Virginia said. "Until then, saving him would only expose the rest of us."

"But she has Audrey!" Miss Hangly said. "How can we fight against a jumper?"

"This is Hilary, the jumper who helped us defeat Punch," Great Aunt Virginia said. "This is her mother and Audrey's mother."

"If the voodoo doll learns you're here ...," Miss Hangly warned.

"You mustn't tell," Princess Gracely said.

"We'll tap-dance around any questions," Miss Hangly promised. "Is there anything else we can do?"

"We need volunteers to help us scout," Great Aunt Virginia said. "Search for any strange boats or dwellings. Send all messengers to us."

"Where will you be?" Miss Hangly asked.

"We're hiding in the empty Factory ... or at The Palace," Great Aunt Virginia said.

"We'll do it," Miss Hangly said.

"Search carefully ... and quietly," Great Aunt Virginia said. "Try not to be seen."

"We'll quick-step through the shadows," Miss Hangly said. "If she's anywhere near us, we'll find her."

"We have to ask ...," Princess Gracely said. "Are any

marionettes missing?"

Miss Hangly's eyes widened.

"How did you know?" Miss Hangly asked. "Over half of our troop is gone, and more seem to vanish every day."

"The rag dolls reported the same," Great Aunt Virginia said. "Try to keep your people calm. While we look for the voodoo doll, we're also searching for the missing dolls."

Gratitudes exuded in whispers, and Mom lowered Miss Hangly down to the ground, then handed her the crossbrace. With practiced ease, she coiled her strings, tossed her crossbrace over her shoulder, and headed back, pushing through the grass with a determined walk.

With silent nods, we walked to the farthest edge of the clearing, behind tall backs of the wooden carts that blocked us from view of the marionettes. I stepped out to where I could flip my jump rope.

"Sparkle City," Great Aunt Virginia whispered to me.

I hesitated over a minute until I had a chant in mind, and then I began flipping my rope and jumping, whispering my words.

> *"To Sparkle City, take us there!*
> *In Sparkle City we may share!*
> *Wisdom and secrets with our friends!*
> *To Sparkle City, there us send!"*

My chant was simple so it took a while to work, but finally gold and silver sparkles trailed my blue cord. I felt the heavy magical strain weaken me, and then we were gone.

Chapter 7

The Hall of the Glamor Dolls

The loud music struck our ears before the wooden
carts of the marionettes had fully faded. The surprise of
it almost caused me to trip and foul my magic, but I
Single-jumped to catch my balance and forced myself to
keep going. Despite the strain that was beginning to
hurt, I kept pushing, chanting, and jumping until the
pain lessened. Before I stopped jumping I was gasping
for breath and felt exhausted.

The loud music wasn't a modern song but it clearly
had a fast beat, a deep thumping base, and a man's voice
singing over a strumming electric guitar. It sounded like
a disco song, repetitive dance music, spritely and lively. I
turned to see the source of the music ... and almost
laughed.

Sparkle City was a large shining ball, ten feet tall,
covered in little mirrors, with six long, thin rectangular
buildings reaching out from its base like the low arms of
an octopus. Lights of many colors flashed inside the

small, round windows of the mirrored sphere. Sharing glances, we stepped close and peered into the tiny windows.

The whole mirrored-ball was a dance hall, made of six levels of balconies over a wide floor, all of which were covered with glamour dolls dancing to the loud music. Winged glamour dolls were flying in the open air in the center, and several long brass poles reached from the top to the bottom, and some glamour dolls were clinging to them, dancing on the poles. The dolls were great dancers, although some moved only at their articulated joints.

Smiling, I stared in through the window at the flashing colored lights, wondering if any of these dolls had once been mine. The glamour dolls were all smiling, looking like they were having a wonderful time. I'd never been to a real dance, but I'd always wanted to ... a true rave where I could dress up fancy and flashy and dance in front of a live band.

"Can we help you?" came a voice.

To our surprise, we glanced down at the lower, rectangular buildings only to find feminine faces in almost every window, and several glamour dolls had stepped out of a door that opened by our feet.

"Hello," Great Aunt Virginia said, looking down.

Princess Gracely knelt before the dolls.

"Sorry, but with the music so loud we didn't hear you," Princess Gracely said.

"It's a party," said a glamour doll with long black hair wearing an Asian dress decorated with Chinese characters. "Anyone is welcome."

"Even a voodoo doll ...?" Muskay asked.

"We never turn away anyone," the glamour doll replied haughtily.

"Who's in charge of Sparkle City?" Great Aunt Virginia asked.

"We're a party, not a business," the glamour doll replied. "We don't need someone in charge."

"Can we talk to the glamour dolls with wings?" I asked.

"I know you," said another glamour doll, a blonde wearing a yellow pantsuit. "You were one of the jumpers ... you helped free us from the slavery of Punch."

"Yes, and now I need your help," I said.

"I'll get them," the blonde glamour doll said.

"Please do so discretely," Great Aunt Virginia said. "We're trying to help others, but we need to do it quietly."

"We'll wait for the winged glamour dolls over by those trees," I said. "We don't want to ... step on ... anything ... by accident."

"I'll send them," the glamour doll promised, and she went back inside.

"Could you tell us something?" Princess Gracely asked the remaining dolls. "Are any of the glamour dolls missing?"

"Missing ...?" one glamour doll asked. "No one's been reported missing ..."

"No one's been looking, either," a red-haired glamour doll said.

"Have you noticed anyone missing?" Hiram asked.

"No, but glamour dolls are free to come and go as they please," the doll said. "It's a party."

We thanked them, then walked away toward the trees.

"So much for secrecy," Mom muttered.

"They didn't seem to understand what a voodoo doll is," Mrs. Darby said.

"They may not know," Great Aunt Virginia said.

"Vacuous ... like the trolls," Muskay sneered.

"Muskay, that's not nice," Princess Gracely said.

"New dolls are created for a specific purpose, and it's hard to break free of your origin," Great Aunt Virginia said. "Jesters have been around for two thousand years; they started in Ancient Egypt and reached their height of popularity in Middle Ages Europe, so they've had centuries to mature. Yet the first jesters were comical fools and buffoons."

"Now ... that's not nice!" Muskay said.

"Glamour dolls do seem fixated on appearances," Hiram said.

"I played with glamour dolls when I was a girl," Mrs. Darby said.

"So did I," Mom said.

"I still have some," I said. "They're exactly what I expect them to be ... the way that little girls play with them."

Many sparkling flecks flew out of the giant mirrored ball and winged toward us. The flying glamour dolls appeared as I remembered them, only unarmed by scalpels, which they'd carried when entranced by Punch. Each was a different color and fashion; the violet fairy had purple hair, thickly bound in a ponytail, with familiar tiny, thin, painted eyebrows, plastic lips smiling, an inhumanly-perfect figure, long, unbending legs, and a violet skirt that exactly matched her buzzing wings, both layered with heavily-glittered scraps of purple lace. The pink flying glamour doll had intricately coutured blonde hair, pink wings, and under a furry bodice, her skirt consisted of glitter-coated strips of fabric hanging from her tiny sewn waistband. One flying fairy was green, with a dress and circlet made of tiny cloth leaves, and another fairy had a light-blue dress and matching wings. The red fairy wore the shortest skirt, the midnight-blue fairy wore a deeply-plunged neckline with a hem that reached to her ankles, and the sparkling black fairy's tight skirt had the longest slit. The other two fairies seemed to be of every color, like small, flying rainbows.

"Hello," Great Aunt Virginia said.

"Hello," they chorused in harmony, as if with one voice.

"We're friends who helped free you from Punch," Great Aunt Virginia said. "We need an important favor from you. Another evil enemy, like Punch, has invaded Arcadia, and they've already taken many dolls."

This revelation spawned horrified expressions on all the flying glamour dolls.

"To drive them away we need to find them," Great Aunt Virginia said. "We need trustworthy friends who can fly all over Arcadia and report back to us. We need to know if there are any new structures, houses, huts, carriages, or boats anywhere in Arcadia."

"We can do that," the pink glamour doll said. "But ... where's our jumper, Audrey the Great?"

"Audrey can't be here," Great Aunt Virginia said. "We're trying to search secretly so that our enemy doesn't know we're looking. We need you to be quick, quiet, and very discrete."

"If you spot anything, bring news to the Factory ...," Hiram said.

"We don't go near the Factory," the red fairy said. "No glamour doll will enter there ... ever again."

"Then take your reports to Mr. Magee ... at The Palace," Princess Gracely said.

"That we can do," the light-blue glamour doll said.

"Don't tell anyone what you're looking for ... or why,"

Muskay said. "If our enemy learns about us then they may possess us, as Punch did to you."

"We'll be cautious," the black glamour doll promised.

"Wait," I said. "When we fought Punch, there were a dozen of you, and now there's only nine ..."

"Where are the other winged fairies?" Muskay asked.

The glamour dolls looked confused, glancing at each other.

"We don't know," the green glamour doll said.

"They could be anywhere," the blue glamour doll agreed.

"Well, you have our thanks," Great Aunt Virginia said to the flying glamour dolls. "Now, fly off in different directions, to the farthest corners of Arcadia, and return as fast as you can."

"Then tell Mr. Magee about everything you see," Princess Gracely said.

"Search everywhere and notice every new dwelling ...," Muskay warned, "... or the glamour dolls may become possessed again."

With worried glances, the winged glamour dolls all flew away, flying with ease high into the sky, and then they split apart and vanished over the treetops in different directions, trailing only sparkles of many colors, glitter floating in the sky. With them traveled our hopes; if we couldn't find the lair of the voodoo doll then we were all doomed to be possessed.

Chapter 8

A Restful Retreat

"We should leave," Hiram said, looking at all the windows in Sparkle City. "Too many glamour dolls can see us."

I sighed heavily and Great Aunt Virginia noticed.

"Getting tired, Hilary?" Great Aunt Virginia asked.

"Only a little," I lied.

"We need to call it a day," Great Aunt Virginia said. "Hilary, jump us back to the Factory, and there we'll rest."

I nodded, stood up, gathered my strength, and thought of a rhyming chant. Anticipating the relief of rest, I lifted my jump rope and began.

> *"To the Factory*
> *We must go.*
> *To the Factory*
> *Our magic throw.*
> *To the Factory*
> *Which we know.*

To the Factory ...."

"Winds us blow," Muskay added when my rhyming
skills failed.

I repeated my chant five times before my rope began
to sparkle. I felt slightly embarrassed. I knew all the
tricks of jumping rope and was better than Audrey, but
she was better at making up and remembering chants.
Of course, I'd never admit that ...

"Concentrate!" Great Aunt Virginia ordered.

My sparkles were growing dimmer so I forgot my spat
with Audrey and focused on my jumping, ignoring the
streams of sweat trickling down my cheeks. Soon my
sparkles grew again and my circle expanded. Just before
I collapsed, before the squeezing strain finally subsided,
we were suddenly standing before the Factory. Weary, I
almost fell as the sparkles faded, and my jump rope
dropped from my hands. Muskay caught me before I
fell and Hiram hurried to help support me.

The Factory was a great, rectangular gray-stone castle,
a life-sized medieval fortress. It had many chimneys,
none of which were belching smoke. It looked like a toy
castle blown to adult size, but built of real stone, with
turrets, battlements, and towers, but it seemed to be all
one building, not a great hall surrounded by a thick wall.
The Factory stood in a wide clearing, surrounded by hills
topped with trees. No one seemed to be inside; the
Factory appeared to be deserted.

"I'll go first," Princess Gracely said.

We entered right behind Princess Gracely. The
familiar, first large hall had the same high ceiling and tall
windows, missing only the baby dolls whom Punch had
forced to labor for him. We crossed the empty hall and
entered the second, inner hall, where Audrey and I had
fought Punch. There I glanced at the dark doorway that

led to the lightless basement, where I'd descended to drive back the shadow puppets long enough to free Judy, Punch's imprisoned wife. Only by her might were we able to triumph over Punch, but my memories of those shadow puppets were still frightening. I didn't want to descend those dark steps into that basement ever again.

"Hilary, lend me your jump rope, please," Great Aunt Virginia said.

"Wait ...!" Muskay said as I started to lift my jump rope, and then he stuck his thumbs into his ears and waved his hands. Catching on, we each repeated our signs, and when it was my turn, I twirled my hands as if I were jumping rope.

"Well, none of us are possessed," Muskay said.

Reassured, I handed Great Aunt Virginia my jump rope. She reached up onto a shelf and pulled down three tall candles. With a whispered voice, she chanted.

"Fire light,
Fire bright,
Spark a flame,
Drive back the night."

She tapped the top of one candle with one handle of the jump rope and the candle burst aflame. Then she returned my jump rope to me. Hiram took the lit candle, and Princess Gracely and Muskay each took one of the other candles and lit them from Hiram's.

"Now, do you need anything else for the night?" Great Aunt Virginia asked.

"No, we'll be fine," Princess Gracely said. "There's food, beds, and blankets aplenty in the basement."

"Get some rest," Muskay said, and to my surprise, he and Great Aunt Virginia hugged tightly. "We'll be here in the morning."

"We'll be late, arriving long after breakfast," Great

Aunt Virginia said, and she looked at Mom, Mrs. Darby, and I. "Take hands and stand close together."

I hung my jump rope over my shoulders and took Mom's right hand and Great Aunt Virginia's left. They both took hold of Mrs. Darby's hands.

"We will come back ...?" Mrs. Darby asked.

"Until we free Audrey ... and can take her home, we're not going anywhere," Great Aunt Virginia assured her. "Now, we all need to think deeply ... about our desire to go home."

I didn't want to go home but I was too tired to do more magic, and I'd never sleep in that dark basement. With a sigh, I thought about sleeping in my warm, safe bed ... and then I blinked. As if the lights suddenly changed direction the shadows shifted to a different angle, the Factory faded out, and Great Aunt Virginia's apartment appeared. We were standing beside the small table with the magic tea set and the three dolls resting in their chairs.

"Until we know where our enemy is, the best we can do for Audrey is to stay hidden," Great Aunt Virginia said. "We might as well make ourselves comfortable. I'll start dinner."

Mrs. Darby cried a few tears, but Mom took her back into a small bedroom ... while Great Aunt Virginia and I pretended not to notice. By her reckoning, Audrey had been missing almost a week, and her distress was obvious. If my Mom had vanished for a week, with no clue to where she was, I'd be frantic.

Great Aunt Virginia busied herself in her kitchen, but I didn't want to get in her way or admit I knew nothing about cooking. I never expected I'd have to cook anything. All my plans for my future ended with me being rich and famous, and then I could hire people to cook and clean for me. All I needed to do was focus on my goals, my ambitions to be rich and famous, and everything else would work itself out, so I left Great Aunt Virginia to putter alone in her kitchen. I explored the shelves in her living room.

Old dolls, photos, and books filled Great Aunt Virginia's apartment. The furniture was all antiques and gave off a scent of great age and furniture polish. The musty smells of old books also filled the living room, but not a hint of dust showed. Every wood-framed photo was black-and-white, as if colors didn't exist in the dreary, pre-technology age. The countless white doilies looked hand-made and I wouldn't be surprised if Great Aunt Virginia had crocheted them all, as they looked as clean and old as the furniture. The same books sat on her shelves, in the same places I'd seen them the last time I'd been here, before Audrey had tricked and cheated me out of Arcadia ... or so we'd both thought.

Some of these books I had, and others we had videos of, but I'd never heard of Anne of Green Gables, Pippi Longstockings, or The Secret Garden; perhaps if I googled them then I could learn more of Great Aunt Virginia's secrets. Yet I secretly regretted not having a TV or computer, something with a lighted screen to help me pass the time.

Mrs. Darby, her eyes dry but red, and mom offered to help Great Aunt Virginia in her kitchen, which was too small for three cooks. Of course, Great Aunt Virginia didn't need help, and within half-an-hour we sat crowded around her small kitchen table before China plates.

"Don't fret," Great Aunt Virginia said to Mrs. Darby. "If we'd found Audrey while she's possessed then we'd have been forced to confront her."

"Couldn't you ... force her back here?" Mrs. Darby asked. "Wouldn't that break her hold ...?"

"I don't know, but I wouldn't want to risk it," Great Aunt Virginia said. "Punch learned about our world, this world, and used his knowledge to cause great evil. I wouldn't want the voodoo doll to know of this world ... or have access to modern devices."

"The dolls don't know about ... reality ...?" Mom asked. "I mean ... this world?"

"Some do, but most dolls don't believe in this world, which is just another legend to them," Great Aunt Virginia said. "Some call this world 'Birtharia', that this world is where dolls exist before they're born. Others call this 'Humanaria' and don't believe dolls exist here. One legend says the jumpers live in a land of love, where all dolls are cared for, and others say that jumpers escaped from a land of tormentors, where evil children make slaves of dolls. Most don't believe in either, and many call humans 'Forgetters', for dolls are loved by human children, but forgotten when most become adults. Since dolls don't grow old or die, they don't understand our world. It takes them a long while to understand our ways."

"Wouldn't it be better for them ... to know the truth?" Mrs. Darby asked.

"Truth consists of provable evidence," Great Aunt Virginia said. "Despite all I know, I carry no evidence that Arcadia is real. In Arcadia, I've no proof that the human world exists."

"But dolls don't exist in Arcadia until they're made here ...," Mom argued.

"I know that, but I can't prove it when I'm there," Great Aunt Virginia said. "The ancient ones tell a story that's thousands of years old, that predates every civilization that still exists on Earth ... that describes how the first dolls created a rugged land of jumpers to provide them with strong protectors."

We exchanged nervous glances, none of us willing to argue.

"Can ... can we meet the ancient ones?" Mrs. Darby asked.

"I hope to ... tomorrow," Great Aunt Virginia said. "They're in Bambole, in the Hall of the Ancient Ones, and it's always best to seek their wisdom. Yet there's only one pair of dolls in Arcadia that's as powerful as a jumper, and we need to find them, too."

"We're going to Bambole tomorrow?" I asked.

"Yes," Great Aunt Virginia said. "We go to meet the ancient ones ... and then ... to seek an audience with the king and queen of Arcadia."

Great Aunt Virginia's steamy chicken stew tasted as if it had been simmering all day, poured over soft brown rice, with buttery rolls of cornbread on which we liberally spread fruity jams. Mom, Mrs. Darby, and Great Aunt Virginia discussed everything all over again, but it was an exact repeat, so I ate without adding any comments. That's the problem with grownups; adults hash and rehash the same details over and over again until your eyes start to roll and yawns begin. Children are better at conversation; everything we talk about is new.

After dinner the same conversation repeated, and I picked up a doll wearing a complex gown that seemed to be made of tiny pearl beads. She was very pretty but old fashioned. I'd never want hair as long as hers, but her gown was elegant, such as a movie star might wear to the Oscars. I imagined myself wearing a gown like that, showing up for an awards show ... with reporters shoving microphones at me and plying me with questions ...

while my fans cheered.

"Hilary, put that doll back, and thank Great Aunt Virginia for letting you play with her," Mom finally said. "We've got to get to Arcadia early tomorrow, so it's time for bed."

"Thank you, Great Aunt Virginia," I said, and I carefully put the doll back on its shelf.

"Thank you," Great Aunt Virginia said to me. "There's nothing so kind to a doll as to play nicely with it."

We followed Great Aunt Virginia as she led us to her narrow hallway, which looked bigger than I recalled. Seven closed doors faced us and Great Aunt Virginia opened one door for each of us, leading to a tiny, antique bedroom filled with dolls. My door creaked and opened upon a tiny room crammed with a narrow bed covered in stuffed animals. Framed pictures of horses decorated its faded lily-wallpaper and a chest of drawers stood shoved in one corner. An old steel radiator rested under its only narrow window, which was heavily-curtained. No closet door showed. Frowning, I took my jump rope, stepped inside, and found a folded pink nightshirt laying on the edge of my bed. Around the nightshirt curled a long red snake, a coil of soft velvet, red on top and white on its belly, which looked like it would be five feet long if stretched straight. Within a few minutes I was wearing the pink nightshirt and pulling the thick blankets overtop me; if I'd be expected to jump rope everyone around Arcadia again then I wanted to be well-rested.

Chapter 9

The Words of the Wise

The sound of splashing water awoke me and Mom came into my bedroom.

"Great Aunt Virginia is cooking breakfast," Mom said. "Mrs. Darby is taking a bath, and then I will, and then you. We need to be quick and get dressed and ready in time to eat."

Mom set some clean clothes on my bed, a fancy pink dress I'd never seen before, and then she kissed me and left. Pushing back the covers, I found the long snake wrapped around me and many soft dolls and stuffed animals crowded beside me, most resting on my pillow beside my head. I yawned and blinked, looking at them.

"I hope I get to see all of you in Arcadia," I said to them.

When it was my turn I sat in my bath, listening to the grownups talking in the kitchen ... probably rehashing the same conversation they'd had at least four times last night. Afterwards, I put on the pink dress mother had left for me, left my dirty clothes in a pile on the floor, and went to join the women. We breakfasted on oatmeal, scones, jam, and orange juice. I finished first, then went back to my bedroom to fetch my jump rope. As I opened the door I almost shrieked; my dirty clothes lay neatly folded on the foot of my bed surrounded by the snake and stuffed animals.

"Thank you," I said to the dolls before I closed the door, carrying my jump rope with me.

While we waited for Great Aunt Virginia to bathe and get ready, I wondered how the dolls had folded my clothes, let alone picked them up off the rug where I'd left them. Most of the dolls were too small to jump from the floor up onto the bed. Silently, I imagined the dolls holding tight onto the tail of the snake, letting it reach down and pull up each item in its mouth, up onto the bed, where they worked as a team to fold it ... and then I recalled being banished from Arcadia ... for trying to force reality into the play of make-believe. Quickly I forgot the whole thing. I wanted to understand the magic of the dolls but not so badly that I'd risk being banned from Arcadia again.

Over an hour we waited, and when Great Aunt Virginia came out to join us she looked exactly the same, as prim and proper as ever. I offered to make tea but Great Aunt Virginia shook her head.

"We're late," Great Aunt Virginia said. "Besides, your mother and Mrs. Darby are still new to Arcadia. They need to experience it properly to understand it, and so do you, although you've already accepted much. This morning we're drinking imaginary tea ... it may take us a bit longer but this is a delicate stage."

We sat as before, Great Aunt Virginia on the red couch between Mom and Mrs. Darby, and I squeezed into the tight chair at the dolls' table, before the magic china tea set. We passed around the empty teapot, and poured as if it were real, and then we added imaginary sugar and cream, and finally lifted our cups to our lips. To my surprise Mom blew upon her imaginary tea, and then carefully pretended to drink. We each complimented Princess Gracely upon her incredible beauty, Hiram upon his rugged manliness, and Muskay upon his cleverness and wit. We also complimented each other and lavished flowery praises upon every doll watching us until we were all smiles. Great Aunt Virginia poured more imaginary tea after our tea cups seemed empty. We laughed and enjoyed our tea, pretending to drink more.

Slowly the tingling sensation stole over us.

Arcadia appeared as bright beams of light streaming down from high, thin windows. We appeared in a circle of seven chairs, in which Hiram and Princess Gracely were patiently sitting, awaiting our arrival. Muskay was pacing around the outside of the chairs.

"Good morning, and welcome back," Princess Gracely said.

"We've nothing new to tell you," Hiram said.

"If those flying glamour dolls had found something, Mr. Magee would've found a way to tell us," Muskay said.

"We'll have to visit the Palace as soon as we can, but first we've got more pressing needs," Great Aunt Virginia said. "We need to sneak into Bambole, and to do that, we need all our friends."

"Where to ...?" Princess Gracely asked.

"To get Falcon," Great Aunt Virginia said.

Hiram and Muskay pulled back the chairs and Great

Aunt Virginia recited a jump rope chant for me to use, and I began to chant as I flipped my rope and jumped over it.

> *"Troll Hill! Troll Dolls!*
> *Trouble to us calls!*
> *Trouble here! Trouble there!*
> *Magic take us everywhere!*
> *Over valley! Over sea!*
> *Where the trolls are*
> *Let us be!*
> *Trouble now! Trouble still!*
> *Take us now to Troll Hill!"*

The bright morning sun shone down upon a wide, grassy hill brightly colored by beautiful flowers. Two magnificent marble doors, three feet tall, lay built into the very side of the great hill, with a miniature stone stairs leading up to them. Many wide, white-framed windows with matching shutters dotted the hillside near the marble doors, all of which were open. Troll Hill also had, in seemingly random order, countless tiny, dark, round, overgrown windows beside small openings that looked like caves tunneled into its sides.

Running about among the vibrant flowers and tall grasses were hundreds of tall tufts of shockingly-colored hair; troll dolls scrambled about the hill, playing ball, rolling in the grass, or just running hand-in-hand, joyously laughing. Short and stubby, troll dolls were only five inches tall with wide ears and toothy grins, bright, energetic eyes, and thick, neon-colored tufts of hair which rose over their heads as if combed straight up, doubling their height or more. Not one doll was wearing a stitch of clothes.

"They're so precious and innocent," Princess Gracely

said.

"Stupid ...," Muskay began a scathing retort, but Great Aunt Virginia absently pressed the palm of her hand over his mouth. "Hilary, you know why we're here, don't you?"

I smiled and boldly I led the way up the hillside.

"I played with these," Mom said, staring at the amazingly happy dolls.

"Our family is part Scandinavian," Mrs. Darby said. "In Norway and Sweden, troll dolls are sneaky and wicked and don't look innocent."

"Those older troll dolls live alone in the deepest forests," Great Aunt Virginia said. "Most dolls won't go near them. They're not really evil, but ..." she glanced at Muskay, "... Mischievousness can be taken too far."

"Only by those too simple to appreciate wry wit," Muskay said proudly.

Careful not to step on a troll, I stepped through the grasses and flowers, climbing my way toward the marble doors. As we drew near, the large crowd of troll dolls standing before the doors stepped back.

"Hello, Mr. Stoney," Great Aunt Virginia said, looking at a strange troll doll.

"Hello, Old Jumper," the troll said in a deep voice.

Great Aunt Virginia blushed slightly and her smile faded.

"He means 'Former Jumper'," Great Aunt Virginia whispered to us.

"Old Jumper, we can't go into Hall," Stoney said.

"We know, Mr. Stoney," Great Aunt Virginia said. "That's why we're here."

Mr. Stoney was slightly taller and much heavier than the other troll dolls, with a round stomach bulging out to half of his height. His tall hair was even thicker than the others, far less kempt, and shocking pink. Upon his right cheek was an ugly, jagged scar.

"Hilary, would you please ...?" Great Aunt Virginia asked.

With a heavy sigh, I stepped up beside the tiny stairs and opened both marble doors. Crouched inside the small hall, almost filling it, sat Falcon.

"I didn't know cowardice had to be practiced," Muskay sneered.

"I'm not cowardly, I'm cautious," Falcon said. "Now, if you would be so kind as to close those doors ...!"

"I don't think so," I said, and I reached inside and grabbed his arm.

Hiram helped me pull Falcon out of the Hall of the Troll Dolls. He grunted and resisted, but I whispered into his ear.

"I'll bet my jump rope could get you out of there ... although it might be ... less gentle."

Reluctantly, Falcon crawled out.

As soon as he emerged, many trolls ran inside, already laughing.

"Why do we have to get involved in every new threat to Arcadia ...?" Falcon demanded.

"That's what jumpers do." I said.

"Because we need you," Hiram said.

"We'll discuss the details later ... where certain ears can't hear," Great Aunt Virginia said. "Falcon, we need you to come with us."

"Where are we going?" Falcon demanded. "Look around you; half of the troll dolls are missing!"

"We'll all be missing if we don't find the 'new threat' soon," Hiram said. "The longer we wait, the fewer of us will remain."

"Let's depart," Great Aunt Virginia said.

"Thank you, Mr. Stoney," Princess Gracely said. "We won't be bothering you anymore."

"No fish," Stoney said slowly.

We paused, staring down at the large, fat troll with shocking pink hair.

"No fish ...?" Great Aunt Virginia asked.

"No food," Stoney said. "Creek is empty."

We glanced at the line of blue water flowing around the base of Troll Hill.

"I'm sure some fish will come soon," Hiram said.

"No fish for many days," Stoney said.

"That is strange," Muskay said. "What could empty a stream full of fish?"

"No fish," Stoney said again.

"We'll look into it, Mr. Stoney," Great Aunt Virginia said. "You wait, and we'll come back when we can."

With worried expressions, we thanked the trolls again and walked back down the hill.

"Could something have taken the fish ... or be eating them?" Mom asked.

"Maybe the water's polluted," Mrs. Darby said.

"We'll look into it later," Great Aunt Virginia said.

Always happy and playful, the troll dolls played in the grass, running from flower to flower, often holding hands. A boy and a girl troll ran past our feet, although only their exuberant faces showing any real difference. She had glittering green eye-shadow over her exaggerated eyelids and thick, ruby-red lips, while his boyish face mirrored her vacant, happy expression, and both their cheeks shined rosy-pink. The boy troll had brilliant bluebird-colored hair, the girl troll solar-bright yellow, both combed straight up in an explosion of shiny mane. They stopped and waved as we approached, and we waved back at them, but didn't stop to talk.

Mom and Mrs. Darby paused to look inside some of the many hand-dug doors we passed. Crude furniture, woven from sticks like a bird's nest, were carefully shaped into couches, chairs, and tables, filling the inside of each rough-hewn chamber, many with dolls sitting upon them. Each looked up and waved as faces filled their doorways and windows. Yet we were in a hurry and didn't examine the troll-homes for long.

"Falcon, are there really no fish in their creek?" Princess Gracely asked.

"I didn't investigate, but they've been complaining about it for the last five days," Falcon scowled.

"You've been hiding in Troll Hall for five days ...?" Muskay asked, his voice full of derision.

"Removing oneself from a dangerous situation is a sign of intelligence," Falcon said.

"That's not a sign I'd want anyone reading about me," Muskay said.

"Enough of that, Muskay," Great Aunt Virginia said. "Falcon, have you heard anything about what's happening?"

"Removing oneself from a dangerous ...," Falcon began again.

"Hiding places are hard on the ears," Muskay sniped.

"No more hiding," Great Aunt Virginia said. "We're headed to Bambole and we'll need all eyes looking for trouble."

"Bambole ...?" Falcon exclaimed. "But ... *Audrey's at Bambole ...!"*

"So is all the information," Hiram said.

"The ancient ones ... and the king and queen," Princess Gracely added.

Falcon stared disbelieving, and then he turned and started walking back up Troll Hill.

"Jump rope, jump rope, with Audrey make Falcon cope ...!" I said warningly.

Falcon spun and stared at me.

"Great Aunt Virginia never threatened friends with a jump rope!" Falcon argued.

He glared down at me, but I wouldn't be intimidated by a doll in any form.

"New jumper, new rules," I stared back at him.

"You'll lose either way," Muskay said. "If Audrey doesn't take you then you'll become one of those who simply vanish."

"The rag dolls, the marionettes, and Sparkle City all have missing dolls," Hiram said. "It's just a matter of time before we all vanish."

"Where are we vanishing to ...?" Falcon asked.

"We're trying to find that out ... before we learn the hard way," I said.

"Please, Falcon," Princess Gracely said. "We need your help."

"What can I do?" Falcon asked.

"You can stand watch ... while we do the work," Great Aunt Virginia said.

"What if we get caught?" Falcon asked.

"Then we'll find where the vanished dolls went ...," Muskay smiled.

Great Aunt Virginia gave me precise details, specifying where we needed to jump. She described a small but pretty garden, an overlook overseeing a hillside leading down to a wide lake. She warned me that I'd have to stop jumping as soon as we arrived. Muskay helped me compose a special chant for jumping there, as I couldn't think of any good rhymes.

"Magic rope! Magic rope!

> *Your brilliance envelope!*
> *Shine right! Shine bright!*
> *Take us now with all your might!*
> *Garden pretty, light and green,*
> *Over lands that can be seen,*
> *Your wide view we must dare,*
> *Take us! Take us!*
> *Take us there!"*

Gold and silver sparkles flowed from my blue cord. Their flashes soon expanded, forming a glowing circle several feet beyond its swings. Everyone stepped inside my sparkling circle, Hiram and Muskay holding tight onto Falcon, and the pressure of the magic built up. Finally, when it reached its zenith, the wide expanse around us changed to a tall yellow-tan wall. I stopped jumping at once.

Immediately I understood; everyone was pressed against the walls or leaning over the rail, trying not to get hit by my jump rope. Most were standing on flowers; this garden was too small for jumping with all of us packed so tightly.

"Very good, Hilary," Great Aunt Virginia said. "Muskay, check to see if our way is clear."

Muskay quietly slipped up some wide, even granite steps, sided by small, manicured bushes, and peeked out. Our little garden was hidden beside a large stucco building with yellow-tan walls and overlooked a wide, scenic valley, a peaceful blue lake filling the bottom of the picturesque setting. Beyond the lake stood tall evergreen trees, and all around the inside of our garden grew pink and white tulips, bright daffodils, and burgundy anemone. Normally I wasn't moved by scenes of natural beauty as much as by flashing lights, loud music, and celebrities on red carpets, but the serene grandeur of the little garden was silently impressive.

"All clear, but we'd better go in small groups," Muskay whispered from the top of the stairs.

"Muskay, take Charlotte and Hilary," Great Aunt Virginia said. "Hilary, keep your jump rope hidden, but be ready to start jumping at any second. Hiram, follow behind them with Madge and Princess Gracely. Falcon and I will come last."

I coiled my jump rope and tucked it under my arm as Mrs. Darby and I ascended the wide granite stair. Cautiously peering, I spied many magnificent buildings, most white and gleaming, a whole town of unmatched elegance. It looked as charming as the village of the rag dolls but sized for humans, with each building as imposing as a state capital.

One large building bore a metal sign shaped like a baby in diapers, and I guessed that the baby dolls were housed and cared for inside it. A meticulously-tended, wonderfully-landscaped park stretched out before us, shining with the colors of bright flowers amid stone walkways, shady trees, gazebos, and small park tables with benches. Around the park stood other wondrous buildings, and in the distance rose the most glorious structure of all, the castle, a real palace, more like a cathedral than a fortress, gleaming in the sunlight. Its sculpted turrets rose into towers, wide windows gleamed with scarlet curtains, and traces of gold glinted from its corners. No wall surrounded it; the tall doors to this castle lay open wide, and I yearned to enter there ... and to own a mansion just like it.

Dolls walked about in human form; some could saunter past you in the real world and never be noticed. Others were dressed in fancy clothes, too elaborate for daywear, or completely inappropriate. One teenage girl wore flannel pajamas, pink with yellow ducks, and one figure wore a fully-enclosed medieval suit of armor, but here in Arcadia, no one seemed bothered by their outlandish attire. Some looked completely out of place; a clown in full makeup walked beside a green woman with snakes for hair, and a young man sitting in the park wore only swimming trunks and a metal football helmet, was bulging with muscles, and had a mechanical right arm. All looked mostly human; I was no longer surprised by appearances in Arcadia, but an alarming number of guards also stood about, beside doorways or marching in pairs. Each wore a red uniform with a sword on their belt, and many carried tall halberds topped with metal spikes.

"Let's go," Muskay whispered. "Just walk casually."

He took our hands and together we stepped into view. I felt instantly vulnerable and longed to hold my jump rope in my hands, but I kept it coiled and hidden under my arm. With a flashing smile and eyes darting all about, Muskay turned us to walk upon the wide sidewalk, which was a mosaic of odd-shaped slate sections along the front of the yellow-tan building.

When we reached its main entrance, Muskay turned us to face the open front doors and we entered.

The decorations in the foyer were Victorian, but many styles and displays of older times shone from all over. I felt like I'd stepped into a museum. A giant golden statue of an Egyptian pharaoh stood foremost, surrounded by huge vases that looked Greek, as if from the Age of Hercules, all roped off from viewers. Roman shields that could only belong to legionaries covered one wall, and a suit of fancy armor that looked Japanese stood upon a pedestal. Flags of all sorts, all nations and centuries, hung from the ceiling. Yet, larger than anything, a huge hourglass rose against the back wall. As we neared it, I saw that our path led right into a door-shaped hole cut in its bottom glass. A thin line of sand was slowly trickling from the vast upper chamber, which was full of sand and falling onto a small mound that was only a foot tall. Into the lower chamber of the monstrous hourglass we stepped, walking upon level sand and skirting the small mound upon which the thin sprinkle was falling. The glass on the back side was also cut open and seemed to lead only to darkness. Yet, as Muskay didn't let go of our hands, we walked as he urged.

Mrs. Darby went first, and we entered a long black tunnel. I hesitated, disliking the dark. Yet Muskay pulled and I trailed him.

We emerged into a huge room lit by indirect golden lights, which seemed to be shining from behind endless rows of narrow stands, platforms set like stairs, or the seats in a theater. Hundreds of dolls stood upon these platforms, which rose to a ceiling hidden in darkness. These were extremely old dolls. Some were wooden and appeared to have been hand-carved. Others were stone, resembling flint arrowheads more than dolls. A few looked like metal, but those were old and corroded. Many reminded me of finger dolls, but most looked like tiny statues, their limbs permanently attached to their bodies. A few looked to have once been painted but most bore only the natural colors of their native substances.

These were the ancient ones, the oldest and wisest dolls in Arcadia, which in our world probably existed only in museums and private collections.

Before the ancient ones stood a single platform, like

where a conductor might stand before their orchestra. Unlike all the other square, perfectly straight shelves, this platform was circular. Upon it stood a doll that looked like a wide, squat, ornate bowling pin. The designs painted upon her were incredibly intricate and stylish, gleaming as if her gold-painted designs were made of the real precious metal. The styles of her decorations were obviously Russian, and I dimly recalled seeing dolls like her before. Her pretty face bore an aloof expression, serious and stern.

"Matryona, so good to see you again," Muskay said.

"Muskay, you sly trickster," Matryona smiled up at him. "We've been hoping to see you. We expected you to be here sooner."

"We came as soon as we could," Muskay said. "This is ..."

"Hilary, Audrey's friend, who helped rid us of Punch," Matryona said. "And this must be Charlotte Darby, Audrey's mother. Our welcome to you both."

"Thank you," I said.

"Charlotte, we understand how you must be feeling," Matryona said sympathetically. "No mother could bear well the kidnap of their child, nor be expected to tolerate it. I know; I'm a mother myself. Please remember where you are: Arcadia, not the world in which you were born. Situations here may seem dire and dangerous, but our magic is in the play, and the only victory here is the winning of the game. You can't fight for your daughter using the methods of your world, not without endangering her further. The best way to rescue her, the safest way, is to understand our rules, play wisely, and always strive to win the most-important game."

A general murmur followed this speech. Many heads of the ancient ones bobbed and nodded in agreement.

Mrs. Darby paused, then breathed a sigh that seemed to unburden her of an invisible weight.

"Thank you," Mrs. Darby said. "I'll try."

"Welcome especially to you, too, Hilary," Matryona said. "It's been many years since Arcadia had a second jumper and we're delighted you've rejoined us. We want you to think of Arcadia as your second home and know you'll always be welcome here, and, if you should ever need wisdom, the Hall of the Ancient Ones is open to you night and day."

"Thank you," I said again.

As I spoke, Hiram, Princess Gracely, and Mom entered behind us, and Mrs. Darby and Muskay stepped aside.

"Welcome back, Hiram and Princess Gracely," Matryona said. "Welcome also to you, Madge Martin, Hilary's mother. We're honored that you could join us."

Mom stared at the many old dolls; she seemed to be astounded.

"You're ... oh, my ... you really are ancient ones ...!" Mom seemed to be having trouble speaking. "Some of you ... must be ... more than antiques ... thousands of years old!"

"Many ancient ones are," Matryona said. "Some saw the first boats constructed, the first fields plowed, and watched the pyramids rise stone by stone."

Mom scanned the three walls of platforms, taking in all the ancient dolls, and then she suddenly bowed deeply.

"My respects to all ancient ones," Mom said, her voice tremulous. "I'd love to hear your stories someday!"

"You are welcome here anytime," Matryona assured her.

"Thank you!" Mom said.

Matryona nodded as deeply as her rounded shape allowed.

"You're a matryoska doll, aren't you?" Mrs. Darby asked Matryona.

"Yes," Matryona said. "We're also called babushka dolls, but I never liked that name. Matryona is a deviation of Matryoska, which means 'little matron'. Babushka means 'grandmother' or 'old woman', and what woman likes to be called 'old'?"

Great Aunt Virginia suddenly entered, her hand locked on Falcon's arm.

"Falcon, watch the door," Great Aunt Virginia said. "Matryona, so good to see you."

"Welcome, Queen of Jumpers," Matryona said.

"I need to speak to you all," Great Aunt Virginia said.

"At once," Matryona said.

Suddenly Matryona, the matryoska doll, turned around, and as she did, her top half flipped open, revealing a second, slightly smaller, yet nearly identical doll inside her. This doll had a man's face, and he jumped out and turned to face the ancient ones. As Matryona had, he opened by flipping back his top half, revealing another doll, another woman, inside him. She jumped out, and then she popped open, and inside her was a handsome boy. From inside him popped a young girl, and then she popped out another young boy. Doll after doll popped out, until the last, which looked like a baby, a figure of solid wood, bounced to stand on the end. Then all the dolls, except the wooden baby doll, simultaneously snapped their lids shut, returning to their original shape. Matryona remained in the center while the eight other matryoska dolls stood in a half-circle around her, all facing the ancient ones. As one, they began to chant.

> *"Hail the wisdom of the ages!*
> *Hail, great and thoughtful sages!*
> *A counsel of the ancients call*
> *Those who witnessed and know all!*
> *Hail to all, and pray attend*
> *Your thoughts to our needs now bend*
> *Hail! Greatest of the wise!*
> *May your wisdom open our eyes!"*

As if suddenly noticing we were there, many of the ancient ones lifted their heads and stared at us.

"I thank you for this time," Great Aunt Virginia said. "A new threat has arisen, greater than any I've ever faced."

"I will speak to this," came a slow, gravelly voice from a small onyx statue, three platforms from the bottom and halfway to the left. He was carved to look like he wore a feathered headdress with a face like a mask from a South Sea island, and he was no taller than a single finger. Many of the ancient ones exchanged glances, and then all looked at him.

"The voodoo doll has captured a jumper," the tiny onyx statue said. "I recall several times when voodoo dolls have invaded, and all were evil days. Whenever voodoo dolls have conquered, then many dolls were slain. To take down a voodoo doll, you must unwind the threads that hold them together; this shall forever free the captured dolls. For this reason, voodoo dolls hide in shadows, making tokens to enslave those whom they would control, until all awaken to do their bidding. While those tokens remain, nothing can break the hold of the voodoo doll. I have spoken."

"Do any concur?" the matryoska dolls asked in unison.

Another general murmur followed and many heads nodded.

"Do any disagree?" the matryoska dolls asked in unison.

A silence fell, and then another voice spoke up.

"I would address these guests," spoke a soft, aged, high-pitched voice from a small ivory doll, which was intricately carved and faded as if stained brown. She sat high upon the sixth platform, on the wall to the right, and looked to be Asian. Again, many of the ancient ones exchanged glances, and then all looked at her.

"In the past, four voodoo dolls have been driven from Arcadia when their lairs were discovered," the tiny ivory doll said. "The last sought to avoid this by hiding her lair upon a ship, which she moved to various locations in her attempt to evade discovery. Back then, those dolls who vanished were few ... and they were never seen again. Now, many dolls of Arcadia have vanished, and we must have them back. Beware the hidden powers of a voodoo doll. No good doll has ever laid a hand upon a voodoo doll, only driven them away. None have ever caught or destroyed a voodoo doll. I have spoken."

"Do any concur?" the matryoska dolls asked in unison, and again, a general murmur sounded, and many heads nodded.

"Do any disagree?" the matryoska dolls asked in unison, and none spoke up.

"I shall speak," another voice said, this one sounding like a child's voice from a tiny doll carved of wood, barely visible upon the highest shelf. "No voodoo doll has ever acted with such cleverness and planning as this. They targeted our best as if they knew us. Their methods are diabolically foolproof. Before they release a victim, they chain themselves up, and when the possession ends, then their victim is trapped ... while the voodoo doll goes free. A hundred dolls have recently vanished and a unique token for each must exist. Tokens take time to create, so they must have been working on this invasion for many months and crafted all the tokens they expected to need before they used even one. This implies the greatest threat of all: a smart enemy. Against a smart enemy only a smarter opposition can hope to prevail. These are my words and my message."

"Do any concur?" the matryoska dolls asked in unison, and then, "Do any disagree?"

The ancient ones replied to neither question.

"Let me be heard," another voice said, booming like a small bass drum from one of the larger ancient ones, a doll that looked like the broken tip of a stalagmite with a face and limbs scratched upon it, dead center before them. "This voodoo doll must have a lair nearby, but will have taken great pains to hide it. It may have used an existing structure, or dug a new cave, but to create a new token, it must dip that token into its bubbling cauldron, and that means it must make a fire. Where fire burns there's light and smoke. The first jumper the voodoo doll possessed was Virginia the Great. She must've made her token of Audrey only after she learned that Virginia was no longer the jumper. If she finds that another jumper has come, doubtless she'll make another token. Seek the light of her fire. Watch for the smoke of her fire. Find her fire and you'll have found her lair. Don't approach her individually; she'll possess you and turn you against your fellows. When you attack, all must attack. My speech is now concluded."

"Do any concur?" the matryoska dolls asked in

unison, and then, "Do any disagree?"

Again, no one replied, and no other ancient ones spoke up.

"Do any others wish to speak?" the matryoska dolls asked in unison, and then they turned to face us. "Do you have any questions that the ancient ones have not answered?"

I struggled to think of a good question but nothing came to mind.

"What does a voodoo doll look like?" Mrs. Darby asked.

"To this question, we can only speak of the voodoo dolls we have known," said a sharp, mouse-like squeaky voice, which came from a tiny doll that looked like it was attached atop a ceramic thimble. "The voodoo doll is made of twine and thread. A long length of twine is laid out in the shape of a body, two arms and two legs, each consisting of multiple loops of twine. Then the thread is applied, wrapping each part separately, the body, and then each limb, tightly looping them until each holds their shape. Then the head is set atop the body; a lollipop of bad taste, such that it is rejected by most. Often the candy head protects itself with a wide hat, and it clothes itself so other dolls can't guess its nature. All of the voodoo dolls driven from Arcadia have shared this construction, although each has disguised themselves differently. The voodoo doll that has possessed Audrey may match this description ... or may not; don't rely upon any expectation, for the price will be great if you're wrong. This concludes my answer."

"Do any concur? Do any disagree?" the matryoska dolls asked in unison.

When no one else spoke, Great Aunt Virginia bowed low to all the ancient ones, and we followed her example.

"Great and wise ancient ones, we thank you for this audience," Great Aunt Virginia said. "We leave you now, grateful for the wisdom you've shared."

"Farewell," Matryona said, and suddenly the baby matryoska doll jumped up, and the next biggest opened to receive it, then closed, sealing it inside. Then that young girl matryoska doll jumped up and was accepted inside the boy beside her. Each of the dolls repeated this process until finally Matryona herself opened wide, and all of the matryoska dolls leaped to take their place inside her. With a snap, Matryona sealed them all inside her.

"Take great care, all of you," Matryona said.

"Farewell," Great Aunt Virginia said to Matryona. "We'll come back to see you as soon as we may."

With a nod of her head, Great Aunt Virginia led us back into the long, dark tunnel, and then out into the museum through the huge hourglass, past the thin, falling sprinkle of sand. No one else was there and we gathered around her.

"Well, that was informational," Mom said. "Good question, Charlotte."

"Yes, indeed," Great Aunt Virginia said. "Now we know everything we can and need to gather allies. Hilary, the big building across the way is the castle, the Royal Palace, and that's where we need to go. We can't be seen entering there, so we'll need to jump us."

I pulled out my jump rope and stood ready.

"We need to arrive inside the tallest tower," Princess Gracely said. "How we'll do that I don't know. The top of the tower is even smaller than the garden overlook."

"Hilary will have to choke up on her jump rope," Great Aunt Virginia said. "We'll have to crowd close and still it will be tight."

"Perhaps Hilary should peek out the door and look at the tower," Hiram said. "Ten feet off, in any direction, might land us with no floor beneath our feet."

Nodding, I stepped to the open door and looked out. A woman walked past, holding a large stuffed animal in her arms, with two guards following her. I hesitated, but the guards seemed intent upon her and didn't notice me. I glanced up. Between the branches of the trees in the park I spied the tallest tower in the palace, the destination I had to hit. With a clear view of my target, I returned to the others and wrapped my cord three times around my palms. I was slightly worried but I began jumping, and then realized I didn't have a chant. The others crowded as tightly as they could around my flipping rope and still there wasn't enough room. I kept jumping, trying to invent a rhyme, to think of anything out of which I could make a new chant, but nothing came to mind.

Suddenly Muskay jumped inside my flipping rope, his hands on my shoulders, almost pressed against my back. He jumped in unison with me, ducking under my rope, and began to chant.

> *"To the tiny tower top*
> *Put us inside*
> *Straight we climb*
> *Straight we fly*
> *Our fortunes to bind*
> *To the tiny tower top*
> *That we know*
> *Inside the tiny tower top*
> *We must go."*

I joined in Muskay's chant and we bounced with ease, although we had to single-jump, for my shortened rope flipped faster than usual. The strain of jumping seemed less wearing, as if Muskay was sharing my magical burden. The others squeezed even closer, wincing for fear of being hit by my rope, when the gold and silver sparkles began, and then we jumped in earnest.

Chapter 10

Facing Our Foe

Curved walls appeared tight around us, pushed us closer, and someone fouled my jump rope. I pulled it in and stopped jumping at once. The round room was cramped, and out the windows we could see a long ways, overtop trees, down onto other buildings, and far off to distant towns.

"They're not here," Muskay said, looking around.

"Who?" Mom asked.

"The king and queen," Hiram said.

"Since they're not here, maybe we should leave ...?" Falcon asked.

"Maybe they went downstairs," Princess Gracely ignored Falcon.

"Let's find them," Great Aunt Virginia said.

"Falcon is standing on the trapdoor," Hiram said.

Pretending surprise, Falcon stepped aside, and Hiram seized the iron ring set into the floor and pulled. The trapdoor opened, revealing a narrow passage, leading to a stairs.

"I'll lead," Muskay said. "Please, try to be quiet."

Muskay led and we followed. The steps were narrow and winding but not dark; every level in the tower hosted a small place to stand and several windows, so we looked out in all directions as we descended its circular route. Inside, the tower was built of exposed wooden braces, which we used for handrails, and at every landing we squeezed through another trapdoor. We weren't silent; Muskay and Princess Gracely could walk silently, and I was the best of the rest of us, but the loud steps of our shoes on the stair announced our coming to anyone nearby.

After our fifth landing, a deep voice cried out in a hoarse whisper.

"Muskay!"

"Thank the doll-makers!" a woman's voice said.

We descended into a large, windowless room, the first dark place we'd seen in the palace. Under the high ceiling, our stair circled twice before we reached the floor, and when we did, several of us bit back screams.

Chained by short links affixed to the floor, with stout cuffs around their ankles, a tall man and a beautiful woman stood trapped before us. Matching cuffs on their wrists held their arms above their heads, pulled by long chains running up to vanish into small holes in the high ceiling.

"Your Majesties!" Muskay ran up, and he reached for their cuffs.

"Quiet!" the man said. "There're guards outside that door, and they check on us regularly!"

"We'll get you out," Princess Gracely said.

"Without the key, you'd need a jumper," the woman said.

"We have a jumper," Great Aunt Virginia said, and she laid her arm on my shoulder. "This is Hilary, who helped Audrey fight Punch."

I stepped forward, and in the light coming through the trapdoor I saw the man and woman clearly. Despite the shadows, both had bright red hair, almost orange, and matching large freckles. Their clothes were very rich and well-mended, but of a rather plain, country style. A bright bow tie was fastened around his spotless white collar, and his shirt bore small red and white checks. His pants were blue and rather short, ending just below his knees, and his socks bore horizontal red and white stripes. He wore stout, well-polished black shoes. The Queen wore a plain blue dress with polka dots, and overtop she wore a white apron bearing tiny embroidered red hearts, and her red and white striped socks and black shoes matched his.

"Raggedy Anne and Andy!" Mom and Mrs. Darby exclaimed.

"King Andy and Queen Anne," Princess Gracely corrected them. "Your Majesties, these are the mothers of both jumpers, who came with Hilary and Great Aunt Virginia to help us."

"We are honored to meet you," Queen Anne said.

Great Aunt Virginia pushed forward and she and Muskay examined the cuffs.

"Hilary, we need to get these off," Great Aunt Virginia said.

"They'll see the gold and silver sparkles under the door!" King Andy nodded to the door.

"I can fix that," Mom said. "Charlotte ...?"

Both were still wearing light jackets. They took them off, walked over to the door, and quietly laid them at its base, blocking the light coming underneath from the next room.

"What about the slapping of the jump rope?" Queen Anne asked.

"Plan both chants before you begin." Great Aunt Virginia said to me. "After we free them, we'll need to escape right away."

"To where ...?" I asked.

"Anywhere," Great Aunt Virginia said.

"No one ever found us at the Factory," Princess Gracely said.

"Yes, but if the guards hear Hilary say 'Factory', then they'll know where we're hiding," Muskay said.

"I can do it ... without saying the name," I said. "I ... just need a few moments."

"Not too long, please," Queen Anne pleaded. "We've been locked in here for days."

"Have you seen the voodoo doll?" Hiram asked them as I walked away.

"No, but Audrey comes here often, not as herself," King Andy said. "There's another set of chains over there, attached to that wall. The voodoo doll imprisons Audrey with us when she needs to possess someone else."

"You must free her, too," Queen Anne said. "That poor little girl!"

I tried to ignore their conversation, matching up words for my chants. I needed both to be simple and repetitive so I didn't forget them, but not too short or the strain would be greater. I silently wished I was as good as Audrey and Muskay at rhyming. Also, I'd already jumped everyone twice, and each bounce was a tremendous strain. Now I'd be jumping with two more.

Finally I lifted my jump rope.

"I'm ready," I said, and everyone gathered around

me.

> *"Locks break, open wide,*
> *Chains be free!*
> *Fasteners divide!*
> *End restraints, make peace,*
> *Bindings cease, friends release,*
> *Unclick, unlock,*
> *Let us see, let us see,*
> *Locks, now open!*
> *Obey me!"*

On my third recitation the cuffs began to shake as if resisting me. The strain was intense, but I kept jumping, yet I had to jump lightly or I'd be heard. On my fifth chorus, all eight locks clicked, and the chains on their ankles fell away. However, as the cuffs on their wrists burst open, suddenly the cuffs shot upwards, pulled by their long chains, which rapidly vanished into the holes in the ceiling from which they'd emerged, and into which they noisily retracted.

"Uh, oh!" Hiram said.

"I knew this was a mistake," Falcon said.

CRASH!!!

The banging clatter above us was deafening, worse than any sound we could make. The chains binding their hands must've been upholding a great weight, and once they were released, the weight crashed down, a sneaky signal that the prisoners had been released.

Voices rose from outside the door; we weren't the only one who'd heard the alarm.

"Get us out of here!" Muskay shouted.

As I lifted my jump rope the door burst open. Seven guards in red uniforms ran inside. All had tall halberds, small axes mounted on long poles, each topped with a slim, pointed spike. As one, they aimed their halberds at us and charged.

King Andy and Queen Anne jumped forward. The guards ran at them, but they dodged with amazing speed, then spun and jumped in opposite directions. The guards turned their weapons to face them and charged again, but King Andy and Queen Anne avoided their best attacks. They jumped with the speed of the flying glamour dolls, possessed the flexibility of the rag dolls, demonstrated the coordination and dexterity of Muskay, and the poise and fluidity of Princess Gracely. Together, they evaded every halberd-led attack of the guards, but they couldn't keep it up forever.

I started to jump rope and made up a new chant on the spot.

> *"Guards sleep!*
> *Sleep deep!*
> *Eyes close!*
> *To sleep goes!*
> *Into dreamland!*
> *Sleepy seem!*
> *Fall deep!*
> *Go to sleep!"*

I jumped hard, throwing in lots of tricks, using all my might; Front Kicks, a Front Back Cross, and a Wounded Duck. As in my fight against Punch, failure wasn't an option, no matter the strain. After my second recitation, the guards hesitated and several yawned. The others attacked poorly, and when King Andy and Queen Anne dodged them, four guards ran the points of their halberds straight into a wall, and then they fell down. The others just slowly collapsed. By the time I was halfway through my fourth recitation, the last of the guards dropped and began to snore.

"Hilary, get us out of here!" Great Aunt Virginia

hissed.

Without stopping and restarting I changed my chant.

"Take us back! Take us back!
Jump us now on the right track!
To where Hiram goes to bed
To where Gracely rests her head
To where Muskay sleeps at night!
To where they hide without a light!
To their secret place, I say!
Jump us right!
Jump away!"

I jumped hard, adding a Side Straddle, but I'd only finished reciting it once when, through the door, came the last person I expected to see:

Audrey!

Audrey ran inside, her eyes alight with wicked glee, her jump rope in her hand. She was wearing a black dress I'd never seen before, with lace and sequins, like a glamour doll's funeral dress sized for humans, and atop her head rested a gold crown.

"I've got you!" Audrey cried. "Now you're all mine ...!"

Suddenly Audrey glanced at me, saw the jump rope in my hand, and startled.

"Who are you ...?!?" Audrey shouted, aghast.

My jump rope was already flipping, so I turned to face her, Speed Rope jumping as I'd done against Punch.

"Drive back!
Drive back!
Drive a-way!
Blast hard!
Blast back!
Blast today!"

The familiar yellow beam streamed from my jump rope, struck Audrey, and knocked her backwards. She screamed as she fell, rolling head over heels, and Mrs. Darby screamed as well. Audrey slid back against the doorway and grabbed its edges to keep from being blown through it. I kept up my chant, focusing; *I was a better jumper!*

Audrey suddenly swung her jump rope like a sword, sliced through my beam, and blasted it back. I was struck and knocked backwards; my beam failed and Audrey jumped up. She separated her handles, one into each hand, and began to jump rope.

"Destroy her!
Kill her!
End her life!
Fire and lightning!
Cause her strife!"

Audrey's chant startled me; *Arcadia was a game!* Being that serious should cast her out, but Audrey's sparkling green cord kept flipping, her chant repeating from her drawn-back lips.

Suddenly flames and bolts of lightning burst from Audrey's jump rope and raced toward me. I flinched, but her magic struck the sparkles of my flipping blue cord and were knocked aside. The others screamed and ran away, leaving me to face Audrey alone.

I changed my chant and added a Cross Cross and an Irish Fling.

"Wind and water!
Blast away!
Hit Audrey!
Make my day!"

A strong breeze blasted Audrey, blowing back her hair, and heavy rain began to fall just over her crowned head, drenching her face. Yet Audrey resisted my gale and shouted into the wind and downpour, adding a Behind the Back Cross and a Leg-Over Cross.

"Darkness black,
Take her back,
Shroud her eyes,
Conceal her lies!"

A cloud encased me, momentarily reminding me of the terrifying shadow puppets. My vision grew dark ... until I couldn't see a thing. Yet I'd fought darkness before and already knew the chant.

"Bright light,
Shine bright!
Bring the day!
Ban the night!"

Almost instantly I could see again. I grinned; I'd used that spell to fight my way to Judy's cell door where I pulled off the heavy paddle that locked her inside. Shadow puppets couldn't bear bright lights and had fled before me, but Audrey wasn't a shadow.

Audrey snarled at me, her face twisted with a fury only seen on a child's face during their worst tantrums. With a cry of rage, she skipped forward and charged at me with her flipping gold and silver sparkling green cord. I skipped toward her, my blue cord equally sparkling. We ran into each other with a force like hitting a wall, and both of us fell, our jump ropes collapsed. Slack, our sparkles vanished.

Audrey squeezed both of her handles in one hand, then swung her jump rope at me. I dodged aside, and where her cord struck the floor a great *boom!* shook the room and cracks appeared in the stone beneath it. I joined my handles and met her next swing with one of my own; our cords met like steel swords and clashed so violently the force of our blows drove us apart. Yet Audrey ran at me and swung again, and I slashed hard, barely catching her blade before it struck me.

As each *clash!* drove us backwards, Audrey ran forward to continue her attack. I met each of her blows, but worry crossed my mind. I'd been angry with Audrey, but if I struck her now then I'd only be hurting Audrey, not the voodoo doll possessing her. Yet the voodoo doll had no reservations about hurting me and attacked with renewed vehemence. I struggled to counter her blows, but I knew that eventually she'd hit me ... unless I hit her first.

"Great Aunt Virginia!" I cried between attacks. "What do I do?"

"Audrey!" Mrs. Darby screamed, resisting as Mom and Hiram held her, keeping her from charging her daughter. "Stop that! Obey me!"

"Don't hurt Audrey!" Great Aunt Virginia shouted. "We've got to escape!"

"I can't fight and jump us away!" I shouted.

"We can give you time!" King Andy shouted. "A few minutes to flee ...!"

"No!" Great Aunt Virginia shouted. "We came to free you ...!"

"You need Hilary more!" Queen Anne shouted. "There's no other way ...!"

Both King Andy and Queen Anne jumped at Audrey. With no choice, she paused her attack against me to swing at them, but their dexterity dodged her jump rope with ease. They surrounded her, and every time one of them had to dodge Audrey's attacks, the other tried to reach her from behind, stretching out an arm to try and snatch the jump rope from her hand. I had to stop my attacks for fear of hitting them. Yet they faced the same predicament I'd confronted; neither could harm the voodoo doll by attacking Audrey, and both were reluctant to hurt her. As skillfully as they dodged eventually they'd fail.

"Hilary, jump us out of here!" Muskay shouted.

Reluctantly I began jumping, already regretting leaving King Andy and Queen Anne behind.

> *"Take us back! Take us back!*
> *Jump us on the right track!*
> *To where Hiram goes to bed*
> *To where Gracely rests her head*
> *To where Muskay sleeps at night!*
> *To where they hide without light!*
> *To their secret place, I say!*
> *Jump us right!*
> *Jump away!"*

While King Andy and Queen Anne darted in and out against Audrey, who was screaming at them in outrage, the others gathered around my flipping blue cord. Mrs. Darby had to be restrained by Mom, Hiram, Muskay, and Princess Gracely; she was still trying to pull free and reach her daughter. I chanted and jumped fast, and saw several near misses, where Audrey's swinging cord caught and tore against King Andy's red and white checked shirt, and against Queen Anne's skirt and apron, which already bore several rents, making them look like their original 'raggedy' names. I focused on my chant, hoping our rapid escape would allow them to flee. However, as everything around us started to fade, I saw Audrey charge down King Andy, and he fell beneath her jump rope.

Darkness encased me save for the gold and silver sparkles of my flipping cord. At first I was afraid; I'd aimed for the Factory but I didn't recognize anything.

"We're back!" Hiram said.

"Poor King Andy ...!" Princess Gracely said.

"He sacrificed himself for us, and Queen Anne sacrificed herself so we could save everyone else," Great Aunt Virginia said.

"We almost sacrificed ourselves ...!" Falcon complained.

"Now the voodoo doll knows about us ... and Hilary," Mom said.

"Where are we?" I asked, still jumping, my sparkles illuminating everyone.

"In the basement ... of the Factory," Princess Gracely said. "Here, I've got a candle."

The strain was weakening me. I didn't want to stop jumping until something else, besides my sparkles, was lighting the darkness, but I couldn't ... I stumbled and almost fell. My sparkles faded and the darkness closed in. I staggered, unable to see anything, and tried not to panic, and then someone pulled one end of my jump rope from my hand. I almost cried out, but Princess Gracely's candle suddenly lit, illuminating Great Aunt Virginia holding the handle of my jump rope over it.

"There, that's better," Princess Gracely said.

"Muskay, get some more candles," Great Aunt Virginia said.

Mrs. Darby was sobbing, still being held by Mom and Hiram.

"My baby ...! My baby ...!" she moaned.

"Don't worry, we'll free Audrey," Mom said.

"But she ... *that wasn't my Audrey!"* Mrs. Darby sobbed.

"No, that was the voodoo doll," Hiram said. "But don't worry; Audrey must be fine ... or she wouldn't be possessing her."

"We'll rescue her soon," Great Aunt Virginia said. "Remember, Arcadia is a game. In every game, sometimes you win, and sometimes you lose. However, when the game never ends, you can lose one day ... and win the next. Audrey is still in the game and so are we ... and I, for one, intend to win soon."

"We all do," Mom assured Mrs. Darby.

"Hilary, are you all right?" Princess Gracely asked, and everybody looked at me.

"I ... I'm fine," I panted.

"You're perspiring ... and short of breath," Great Aunt Virginia said. "You're tired ..."

"No, I'm not ...!" I began.

"You fought well and hard ... against another jumper ... which is something I've never had to do," Great Aunt Virginia said. "You've been transporting the lot of us all day. I know how draining that is. We're done for the day. Hilary needs to eat and rest ..."

"I ...!" I began to argue.

"It's not polite to contradict your elders," Great Aunt Virginia said. "If I say something wrong then I'd appreciate your correction, but you appear to be tired, and you must be hungry by now, aren't you?"

I frowned.

"Yes," I admitted.

"We'll go back home," Great Aunt Virginia said. "Muskay, Hiram, and Princess Gracely need rest, too. We'll play better if we all start fresh tomorrow."

"We have all we need here ... except untroubled rest," Muskay said.

"It's time we return," Great Aunt Virginia said.

"Yes, let's go ... for now," Mom said, looking right at me.

I knew better than to argue with Mom, so we gathered close together, took hands, and soon the familiar wave passed over us. I felt the tingling, gripped tightly to Mom and Mrs. Darby, closed my eyes wearily, and when I opened them again we were back in Great Aunt Virginia's apartment.

Chapter 11

Winning Thrice

"Aunt Virginia," Mrs. Darby began as we appeared in the real world, "Mrs. Matryona, the matryoska doll who speaks for the ancient ones ...

"Mrs. Matryona does not speak for the ancient ones," Great Aunt Virginia said. "The ancient ones are our wisest, smart enough to know that arguments are the bane of intelligent conversation. Mrs. Matryona works as the orchestrator of the ancient ones, who prevents their lofty discussions from becoming arguments and allows each their full chance to speak uninterrupted by any other. Her experience as a mother makes her perfect for the job."

"Yes," Mrs. Darby said. "She said the best way to rescue Audrey, the safest way, was *'to understand our rules, play wisely, and always strive to win the most-important game.'* What are the rules, and which game is most-important?"

"The rules are the same in every game," Great Aunt

Virginia said. "You play with the pieces provided. In baseball, the pitcher doesn't sneak in a cannon to shoot the ball at the batter. If he did, the game would be ruined, because no bat could survive the impact, even if you could manage a hit. The pitcher would be kicked out of the game. In Arcadia, if you ruin the game, you get kicked out ... as Hilary did when she wanted to use Arcadia to bring riches in our world. You can't use Arcadia here, any more than you could bring a gun to Arcadia and win by shooting a doll; that's not how the game is played."

"I carry a gun in my purse," Mom said.

"But you didn't try to use it in the game," Great Aunt Virginia said. "If you had, you'd have been kicked out."

"Which is the 'most-important game'?" Mrs. Darby asked.

"Like life, here in our world, more than one game is being played in Arcadia," Great Aunt Virginia said. "Each doll is playing numerous games; competitions to pass the time, goals to accomplish remarkable things, even the quest to fall in love and have a wonderful life. Each game has a valued prize to be won: attention and admiration, the respect of the other dolls, to increase one's abilities, to rise in one's social status, or to find true love ... all these are goals we share with dolls.

"However, in some ways, dolls are smarter than humans. They know that to keep Arcadia a wonderful, friendly place, no one can win all the time. Losing isn't always a failure; sometimes losing is simply the joy of letting someone else win, of allowing others to experience the momentary successes you know. The key to happiness is to recognize all of the games around you, and not only know which games are most-important to you, but to understand which games are most-important to those whom you care about.

"Rescuing Audrey, which can only be done by banishing the voodoo doll, is our most- important game, and that game we must win. Lesser games, such as who will choose and manage the next performance of the marionettes, is another game, about which several dolls probably care deeply. Hilary has the jump rope and could force her choice of entertainments, if she wanted to, but that's not a game she needs to win. By not always needing to win, by allowing others to have some victories of their own, dolls live in a happier world than we do."

"The magic of play," Mom said.

"...t the evil of greed," Mrs. Darby said.

"...ely," Great Aunt Virginia said. "Now, Hilary, yo... a difficult day and you've performed your d... a jumper magnificently. Tomorrow may be just a... so your goal for tonight must be to get plenty of ...rt now, and I'll begin dinner."

...help," Mom said.

...here anything I can do?" Mrs. Darby asked.

"Indeed there is," Great Aunt Virginia said. "This morning you proved to yourselves that tea isn't needed to enter Arcadia, but I think it's much nicer to sweeten our journeys with some fresh, steaming tea ... and we don't pour tea into dusty cups."

"I'll wash," Mom said.

"I'll dry," Mrs. Darby said.

With shared smiles, Great Aunt Virginia vanished into the kitchen. Mom and Mrs. Darby began collecting the dishes of the magic tea set, even the serving dishes that we never used, and carried them to the sink.

I went back to my room, where I found my dolls carefully arranged on my bed, two piles forming eyes and the long, stuffed snake making a wide smile. I smiled back at them, then picked them all up and hugged them tightly.

However, playing with inanimate dolls no longer fascinated me. I set them against my pillow, straightened the ones that fell over, then went back into the hallway. A quick glance showed me only a few doors in the hallway, but I was careful not to count them; it would only spoil the game. I walked back into Great Aunt Virginia's living room, looking around at all the old stuff, fearful of touching most of it. I knew Great Aunt Virginia wouldn't mind but some of her antiques looked delicate and I didn't want to accidentally break one. Of course, she could probably fix it as she'd once repaired Audrey's jump rope ... but that wasn't part of the game.

I wondered what television shows I was missing and wished I'd brought my computer. Dolls and Arcadia were fun, but I missed my grown-up toys. Yet this felt perplexing; after Audrey and I had stopped speaking, I'd hated my TV and computer, angry that I couldn't play with dolls anymore. If I could have only one ... no matter which I chose, I'd always miss the ones I didn't have.

My eyes roved over the books, some of which had titles I didn't understand. A Midsummer Night's Dream stood out, as did Little Woman, Sense and Sensibility, and Jane Eyre. Some books I knew because they'd been made into animated movies, like Tarzan of the Apes, Treasure Island, and The Jungle Book. All looked much thicker than I expected, especially The Jungle Book.

With nothing else to do, I plucked it from the shelf and thumbed through it. I knew the story of Mowgli, the boy raised by wolves, and his adventures with Baloo and Bagheera, but there were also stories of a mongoose named Rikki-Tikki-Tavi, a white seal named Kotick, and an elephant named Toomai. Curious, I sat and started reading ... and was startled when Mom came in to invite me to dinner. She smiled when she saw me reading.

"I found her reading a book," Mom said proudly as we sat at the dinner table.

"Hilary wins the prize," Mrs. Darby said with a smile.

"What prize?" I asked.

"Our respects," Great Aunt Virginia said. "The respects of three adults ... for the game you won ... even if you didn't realize you were playing a game."

"I wasn't playing a game; I was reading," I argued, and all of the adults laughed.

"Reading a book is winning thrice," Great Aunt Virginia said. "You win the experiences of the characters, learn the lessons they learned, which become deeper understandings which will help you in later life, and you earned the respects of three adults."

"Four adults, when I tell your father," Mom said.

After a delicious dinner I returned to the living room, paused to compliment the counterparts of Hiram, Muskay, and Princess Gracely as they sat before the newly-washed magic tea set, and then I returned to my book. Several hours passed in adventurous splendor, in jungles and seas all around the globe. When I started yawning Mom sent me to bed. I went as ordered and had the most delightful dreams.

The next morning, after we were all washed, dressed, and breakfasted, Mom set the metal teapot upon the gas stove, lit a match, and ignited the burner. Mrs. Darby selected herbs for our tea and I ground them in the pestle, stirring them firmly with the mortar. Although I knew it wasn't needed, I blew gently upon the powdered herbs before I cast them into the steaming ceramic teapot. Soon Great Aunt Virginia, wearing an oven mitt, took the boiling teapot and invited us to join her in her living room, which she again called her 'parlor'. We sat as before, and I no longer held any reservations about sitting at the table with Hiram, Muskay, and Princess Gracey. I got the distinct impression, just a feeling, that both Mom and Mrs. Darby wished they were small enough to sit with the dolls.

We had a lovely conversation about Arcadia in the old days, when dolls frequently travelled to visit the cities of other dolls, and even paper dolls could be seen wandering outside. We included Hiram, Muskay, and Princess Gracely in our conversation, laughed at their imagined comments, and complimented them often. When the tea cooled enough to drink, I felt we were already halfway into Arcadia, and the tingling sensation and dizziness quickly overwhelmed us.

Chapter 12

Mr. Magee and Judy

We arrived at a huge oak dining table, set with the exact same magic tea set we'd been using in Great Aunt Virginia's apartment, only larger, with full-sized dishes appropriate for adults. Each, I noticed, bore the same pink and blue floral pattern as the smaller tea set. Muskay, Hiram, and Princess Gracely were sitting in the same places their doll-counterparts had been sitting in, with Falcon beside Hiram, and to my surprise, as we appeared, they were laughing and complementing Great Aunt Virginia on a wry comment, which I knew she hadn't said. Yet I said nothing; they were playing the same game in Arcadia we played in the real world, and doubtless their help assisted our journey.

This tea party was illuminated by six lit candles, set in silver stands, circling a low vase of colorful flowers. We were in a room I'd never seen before, but I recognized the walls and ceiling as the basement of the Factory.

"Welcome back," Hiram said.

"Always a pleasure to see you again," Princess Gracely said.

"Virginia, the joy of your return equals the sadness of your absence," Muskay said.

Great Aunt Virginia blushed deeply, but to my astonishment, she extended her hand to Muskay, whom she was sitting beside, and he took her hand and kissed it. My eyes, Mom's, and Mrs. Darby's all widened to see this familiarity between prim, proper Great Aunt Virginia and the mischievous Muskay, yet Hiram and Falcon pretended not to notice, and Princess Gracely smiled.

"Enough nonsense; we've much to do," Great Aunt Virginia said.

"Upon what grave risk shall we be endangering our lives today?" Falcon asked.

"Today we visit The Palace," Great Aunt Virginia said. "We told the flying glamour dolls to report their findings to Mr. Magee and they've had more than enough time to scour the countryside."

"And after that ...?" Falcon asked.

"That depends on what we learn from the glamour dolls," Great Aunt Virginia said. "The key to finding the voodoo doll is to locate her lair; that's our main priority."

"Can't we finish our tea?" Falcon asked.

"Not at the speed at which you pretend to drink," Muskay said to Falcon.

"We leave in ten minutes," Great Aunt Virginia said. "If we have to invade her lair today then a little more rest will only help us."

"Palace! Palace!
We come to thee!

Your glorious grandeur
We must see!
Stage and curtain!
Lights shine certain!
Take us now
To Judy!
We must see her
And Mr. Magee!"

I'd been warned about The Palace. It wasn't
gleaming white with a high, crenellated stone wall, or had
tall towers streaming long red banners. The Palace was a
grimy little shack, an old, two-story theater with a big sign
encircled by gold-colored light bulbs, and some of them
glowed brighter, looking newer than the rest. I
suspected that the rag dolls and the hand puppets had
labored long to clean and repair it, yet the sign overhead
was still faded red paint with 'The Palace' written in
large, swirling letters. Most of it still looked grimy and
run-down, shaded by overgrown trees, but the long
branches that Audrey had said lain upon its sunken roof
had been cut and removed. Behind clean, uncracked
glass panes, ornately-framed posters covered the front of
its freshly-painted walls, advertising live performances
with very antique-styled drawings of jugglers, arm-in-arm
dancing girls in knee-length skirts, and smiling men in
tuxedos with top hats and canes. The marquee above
the unlit ticket-taker's booth read 'The Amazing Arnold
and Mr. Magee', and under it, in smaller letters, it read
'Ventriloquist Extraordinaire'.

"Come," Great Aunt Virginia said. "Let's waste no
time."

Great Aunt Virginia rapped on the old timbers of the
wooden door with her ebony cane. The aged door
creaked open and she pushed inside. The Palace was lit

by tiny flames from small oil lamps burning in polished wall-sconces, which gave the air a humid, greasy smell. We entered a wide room where brass fountains behind a bar must've once dispensed popular drinks, and a big, bright mirror, reflecting our images, stood behind the bar. The rest of the walls were covered in faded, blood-colored, felt-striped wallpaper, which had peeled in many places, upon which was hung more framed posters of actors who probably never lived to see the twenty-first century.

Great Aunt Virginia led the way through the swinging wooden doors into the main chamber of the old-fashioned theater. Red-cushioned wooden seats sat in long rows. The aisle led past two dozen rows of chairs to a wide stage which was brightly-lit by more tiny oil lamps placed evenly around the front edge of the stage behind little brass shields, which prevented their lights from shining upon the hundreds of empty chairs. Beyond the footlights, the stage was bare save for a single empty wooden chair in its center. Dark red curtains hung on both sides of the stage while a bright gold curtain hung behind it.

"I should wait here," Falcon said, but both Hiram and Muskay grabbed one of his arms.

The Palace was eerily silent yet screamed of delighted crowds and loud applause.

Great Aunt Virginia led us down the aisle and through a narrow doorway beside the stage into the darkness of the very back. Old doors, some with five-pointed stars painted on them, lined a hallway lit only by the reflected lights from the stage, which came down a tiny open doorway leading up a small flight of five steps. I peeked out at the empty stage as we passed the bright doorway; never had I seen a stage from this angle. Then we passed onward.

"Welcome," breathed a soft voice from the shadows. "Here; this way."

"He loves being dramatic," Muskay sighed.

"We know where you are, Mr. Magee," Princess Gracely said. "We're not afraid anymore."

We followed the voice up another short stairs and found ourselves on the backstage behind the golden curtain, which had many tiny holes we couldn't see from its front, each streaming a thin ray of light through the otherwise dark chamber. We passed many ropes that were tied to wooden fixtures, each rope running straight up until it vanished in shadow; I could make out no ceiling and suspected it was very high. Many wooden crates were stacked behind the ropes, and then I saw a tall lamppost, but only the front half; a prop once used to decorate the stage. A great wooden heart stood behind it, surrounded by what looked like a grand doily, but it was only red-and-white-painted wicker bent into curling, decorative shapes. The backstage was littered with old props, and we threaded between them until we came to a great gold-painted throne, which was mostly hidden in shadow. Upon the throne sat the largest doll I'd seen in Arcadia, save for Punch and Judy, and as I watched, its ivory eyes opened.

"Welcome, my honored friends," the ventriloquist's dummy said, leaning forward so a single spot of light streaming through the holey curtain illuminated his face. He was made of masterfully-carved wood with moving eyes, with a mouth and ears that flapped on hinges, and his eyebrows raised and tilted from side to side. He wore a dusty black tuxedo made to fit him, and he had shockingly orange hair that was slicked back as if greased. He lifted a hand and waved us forward, and I noticed a stiff wire hanging from his wrist, such as a puppeteer might use to mimic life in his wooden dummy. This dummy, however, was very alive, deep and mysterious; no dummy at all.

"Shame on you, Mr. Magee, for hiding in the dark," Princess Gracely said. "We're your friends ...!"

"I won't trust anyone until the voodoo doll is vanquished," Mr. Magee said.

"Mr. Magee, it's always an honor to visit you, even backstage," Great Aunt Virginia said. "I'd like to introduce you to the jumper that helped my Great Niece Audrey defeat Punch; this is our good friend: Hilary."

Mr. Magee swiveled his wooden head, and his ivory eyes, with their painted black pupils, rocked back and forth and finally settled on me.

"Good Friend Hilary, welcome back to Arcadia ... and welcome to The Palace."

"Thank you," I said.

"And these are the mothers of both jumpers, Charlotte and Madge," Princess Gracely waved to both of them.

"A privilege to meet you at last," Mom said.

"Audrey speaks of you often," Mrs. Darby said. "When the current crisis is resolved, I hope I can see one of your performances."

"Once the voodoo doll is gone the crowds should return," Mr. Magee said. "Our audiences have been somewhat thin of late."

"Have the flying glamour dolls been here?" Hiram asked.

"Yes, but I promised to summon Judy before I told you the news," Mr. Magee said, and he lifted a little wooden hammer and struck it against a small bell beside his throne. The bell rang out, and then silence fell, but only for the moment.

With a *bang!* that startled all of us, a trapdoor by our feet flew open and a huge figure burst upwards, towering over all of us. Judy was a giant doll, so large that I'd forgotten how formidable she looked, and she still held a resemblance to her lost husband, Punch. Popping up as if on a giant spring, like the world's largest Jack-in-the-Box, she rose almost eight feet tall, with a huge head like a papier-mâché Mardi Gras mask. A giant puppet, a marionette without strings, Judy wore a scarlet dress, but her expression was smiling, not furious at her husband, as she'd been when I'd first seen her. To my relief, she wasn't carrying her massive wooden paddle, such as might be used to row a canoe, with which she and Punch had constantly fought ... when not making up with ardent kisses.

Mom, Mrs. Darby, Princess Gracely, and Falcon all screamed as she'd popped up out of the trapdoor, but she quickly calmed everyone.

"Peace, my friends, peace!" Judy said. "I didn't mean to frighten, but after all my centuries no doll can refuse their true nature. Greetings especially to my ally in combat, my friend and jumper Hilary the Brave, who drove back the shadow puppets, rescued me from my prison, and who holds my trust forever. Welcome also to Madge and Charlotte; Audrey has spoken sweetly of each of you, and it's my pleasure to greet you."

Mom and Mrs. Darby both seemed too startled to speak, staring up at a doll bigger than any adult.

"They asked about the glamour dolls," Mr. Magee said.

"We're sorry to report bad news," Judy said.

"Bad news ...?" Great Aunt Virginia asked. "Were the glamour dolls attacked ...?"

"Were they possessed?" Princess Gracely asked, worry filling her voice.

"Neither attacked nor possessed," Mr. Magee said. "They found nothing. No new buildings, no old buildings being used, no smoke rising from a cave or chimney, no sign at all."

"They reported that they searched everywhere, even flying into the shadowy branches of the swamp and the Aging Forest," Judy said.

"The voodoo doll has well-hidden her lair this time," Mr. Magee said.

"They searched the villages, the cities ...?" Muskay asked. "What about wagons? Any new carts ...?"

"No new vehicles at all," Mr. Magee said. "I even had them look for hot air balloons in and above the clouds. They searched thoroughly."

"Can it be invisible?" Mrs. Darby asked.

"That wouldn't be playing the game fairly," Great Aunt Virginia said.

"We had them search at night, too," Judy said. "In the daylight, the smoke of her fire would be visible. At night, the light of her fire would be seen."

"Camouflage," Mom said. "Making something look like something else."

"She must be doing that," Hiram said.

"How can we find a disguised lair?" Princess Gracely asked.

We all stared at each other; no one spoke.

"She's clever, but she can't have thought of everything," Muskay said. "The clues we need are out there ... we just have to find them."

"But will we find them before all the dolls vanish ... including us?" Princess Gracely asked.

Great Aunt Virginia frowned, then bowed her head

and walked away, into the shadows. I couldn't blame her; she'd ordered all of us here ... and would feel terribly guilty if anything happened to Audrey ...

We stood in silence, not saying anything. Finally Great Aunt Virginia glanced around, then she turned back to face us. She stared at us long and intently.

"Let's summarize everything that we know," Great Aunt Virginia said. "Perhaps we missed something."

I found it hard to believe that we'd missed anything, but I couldn't refuse Great Aunt Virginia.

"Well, we know the voodoo doll is here somewhere," Muskay said. "In every attack by a voodoo doll, they had to travel inside Arcadia, so we assume they can't possess people from too far away."

"The only way we've ever defeated a voodoo doll has been to track down and destroy their lair," Hiram said.

"A lot of dolls are missing," Princess Gracely said. "We don't know where they are or why they were taken."

"The voodoo doll has plans we haven't discovered," Mom said. "Learning her plan could be as valuable as finding her lair."

"She has Audrey ... and we must free her!" Mrs. Darby said.

"The ancient ones said nothing can break the hold of the voodoo doll as long as she has the tokens that enslave those she controls," Falcon said.

"When did you visit the ancient ones?" Great Aunt Virginia asked.

We all hesitated, exchanging worried glances.

"Ummmm ... Great Aunt Virginia, have you seen this?" I asked.

With my hands at my sides, I rotated my wrists, as if I were flipping my jump rope. Muskay, Mom, and Mrs.

Darby caught on at once. Muskay stuck each of his thumbs into one of his ears and waved his hands. Mom curled both of her forefingers and hooked them, and Mrs. Darby interlocked her fingers and turned her palms down, facing the ground. Falcon, Mr. Magee, and Judy looked confused, but Princess Gracely and Hiram recognized our signs. Princess Gracely held up one thin finger, then kissed it, and Hiram clapped his hands twice.

We all stopped and looked at Great Aunt Virginia, wondering why she hadn't touched her forehead.

"This isn't Great Aunt Virginia," I said, looking right at her. "Hello ... voodoo doll!"

Great Aunt Virginia looked appalled, but then a wicked grin stretched her lips and a maniacal gleam lit her eyes.

"You must be Hilary," Great Aunt Virginia said, but speaking with a deep, slow, drawling voice. "I thought you were banished."

"Not as banished as you're going to be," I said to her.

"What can you do to me?" Great Aunt Virginia chuckled evilly, glaring at me. "Hurt ... or kill ... this former jumper? You couldn't beat me when I was Audrey, and King Andy and Queen Anne won't ever be saving you again."

"Release my daughter!" Mrs. Darby shouted.

"Audrey is mine!" the voodoo doll sneered. "All in Arcadia will soon be mine, including every doll!" Great Aunt Virginia's face turned to me. "Jumper, if you have any sense, leave now ... before I claim you, too. Leave Arcadia forever ... and save yourself ... or else!"

"You should leave!" Mom said to the voodoo doll. "Think, if you're as smart as you seem to think you are. The ancient ones remember every time a voodoo doll has attacked Arcadia, and each time they failed. You'll fail, just like they did. Your only hope is to abandon your plan, destroy your tokens, and flee ... before you end up like the other voodoo dolls."

"I've conquered other lands," the voodoo doll's voice spoke from Great Aunt Virginia's lips. "I've tried to capture Arcadia twice before, and each time I've learned from my mistakes. Now my plan is foolproof. You'll all soon bow down before me, your undoubted voodoo queen ...!"

"We'll thwart you and pull your threads apart," I promised.

"How ... now that I have your oldest jumper?" the voodoo doll asked. "Say good-bye ... I'm leaving."

"You're not going anywhere ... not with Great Aunt Virginia's body," I warned.

"How can you stop me?" the voodoo doll laughed, a slow, wicked laughter. "You can't hurt your beloved old jumper, but I can ... and I will, if you try to stop me."

"I've got the jump rope," I warned.

"I could cut myself ... or jump off a cliff and leave Virginia to suffer the landing ...!" the voodoo doll laughed.

"I'll ...!" I began.

"Hilary, let her go," Mom said. "We can't risk hurting Great Aunt Virginia."

"But ...!" I argued.

"No time is good for threats," Mom said. "Don't worry; this game isn't over."

"You'll never stop my victory," the voodoo doll said. "Your only hope is to quit this game! Return to the jumper-world ... and never come again!"

"Evil people always make mistakes," Mom warned the voodoo doll. "You will, too. You're not as smart as you think you are."

"I'm smarter," the voodoo doll said. "I'm centuries old, and I've learned lessons jumpers don't live long enough to discover. By the time you're as smart as I am, you'll be long dead."

We glared at the voodoo doll hiding inside Great Aunt Virginia's body.

"You won't keep her," Muskay growled, glaring at her.

"If you humans have any brains at all, then this is good-bye, for we'll never meet again," the voodoo doll said. "If you ever see this body again then you'll be seeing your own doom. The rest of you, just wait; I'll take possession of each of you soon enough!"

With a maniacal laugh, Great Aunt Virginia turned and walked away, down the back stage's short stair and up the narrow hallway. I wanted to chase after her, to stop her, but even with my jump rope ... *what could I do?*

"We've lost," Princess Gracely said, an emptiness to her voice that I'd never heard before. "How can we win without Great Aunt Virginia?"

"We're not going to win," Falcon said.

No one else answered. We all listened as the voodoo doll walked the length of the theater, entered the foyer - we heard the swinging doors - and then the front door clicked closed.

Great Aunt Virginia was gone ... and we'd just told the voodoo doll everything we knew.

Chapter 13

A Terrible Loss

We stood in shock. Great Aunt Virginia had been possessed by the voodoo doll, gotten us to reveal all our secrets, and run off into the night. I could've bound her with my jump rope, if I'd thought of it, but to what good? The voodoo doll had control of her mind and body, and I couldn't do anything to break their connection without finding the voodoo doll.

"We can't just stand here," Hiram said. "We have to do something!"

"We have to see the hand puppets," Muskay said.

"Why?" Falcon asked. "What good are they?"

"The first possession happened to a hand puppet," Muskay said. "If we understood why then we might have a clue."

"We should visit everyone," Princess Gracely said. "If there are any clues to be found ..."

"Then we'll find them," I promised, and I raised my jump rope.

"If there's anything we can do, The Palace is at your service," Mr. Magee said.

"You and Judy stay here ... and guard The Palace," I said. "We can't leave any dwelling unoccupied or the voodoo doll may hide in it."

A hand fell upon my shoulder. I looked up into the face of Mrs. Darby.

"You're a worthy jumper," Mrs. Darby said.

Mom smiled brightly, but I couldn't.

"I've been waiting months to get back here, and I'm not going to let any voodoo doll spoil my return ... or hurt Audrey!" I said.

Mr. Magee and Judy applauded this little speech, but I waved them off.

"There's work to be done," I said. "Thanks for your help."

"Stay in touch," Judy said. "Call upon us if we can aid in any way!"

With brief flurries of gratitude swapping both ways, we departed. Falcon suggested he should remain behind, but we took him outside and Hiram held him while Muskay composed a chant and I began jumping.

> *"To the hand puppet's workshop*
> *Let us fly!*
> *To the shop of Boss Fist*
> *We must try!*
> *Puppets with hands inside*
> *To your workshop we must hie!*
> *Where hammers pound and axes chop!*
> *Where saws saw and bevels drop!*
> *Take us now! Don't be shy!*
> *To your workshop we must fly!"*

We arrived at the workshop of the hand puppets, which was the biggest building I'd seen in Arcadia before visiting Bambole. It was a wooden structure, long and tall, solid and sturdy, and had only small, high windows far overhead. Yet, strangely, all was silent. The last time I'd been here the noise was deafening; hammering, the grinding-scrapes of saws and files, and many loud bangs and clatters of chisels and axes.

Now ... not a sound.

Through a wide door we entered. The workshop of the hand puppets was mostly a carpentry shop, yet it had a large forge against the far wall where molten metal was usually being poured into small clay molds. A large steam whistle hung on a pipe, affixed to the wall by the door. Many wooden devices stood unfinished, including a wooden carriage that could only be driven by the residents of Bambole, doll-sized beds and tables, and a new set of office shelves that looked like those used by the paper dolls. The workshop reeked of sawdust and paint fumes, but not one hand puppet was there, working or not.

"Where is everyone?" Princess Gracely asked.

"Hiding ... if they've got any sense," Falcon said.

"I've never seen this workshop empty of hand puppets," Muskay said.

"We'd better investigate further," Hiram said.

"If we look for trouble we're likely to find it!" Falcon argued.

"If we don't look for trouble, eventually trouble will find us," I said.

Muskay led us back outside and around the corner of the building, where I saw the distant city of the hand puppets topping the hill adjacent to this. Some of its buildings looked like miniature skyscrapers and others were as ornate as cathedrals.

We walked down the long hill and up the gentle slope

to the top of the next hill. The city of the hand puppets wasn't as far away as it looked ... because the small buildings were such perfect replications. The skyscrapers of the hand puppets were only eight feet tall, but of such perfect design that they could've been models built by architects. Most of their buildings were only two or three feet tall, but each had the same exacting, meticulous details in doors, windows, and signs over businesses. Paved streets divided the little buildings, lined by eight-inch concrete sidewalks, and small traffic lights hung over the intersections. Toy cars buzzed past on their one freeway, which led to the next hilltop, where stood a residential section of little houses surrounding a miniature shopping mall. Many hand puppets were walking around the modern city, each hurrying about their business, some with briefcases, others wearing tool belts, and many carrying tiny shopping bags.

Mom and Mrs. Darby stopped and stared, amazed by the tiny metropolis, but we kept walking.

Unlike the rag dolls, the hand puppets didn't seem afraid of us; many stopped to watch as we approached.

"Halt!" cried a hand puppet in a blue uniform with a badge on his chest. "No Bigs allowed in this city without a permit."

"Officer, this is Hilary, the new jumper," Princess Gracely said. "We're investigating the missing dolls ..."

"We've got every inspector on those cases," the officer said.

"We were just at the Factory," Muskay said. "Where are the workers ...?"

"Laid off," the officer said. "One day, Boss Fist just walked in and laid off all the workers ... shut the place down!"

"That's terrible!" Princess Gracely said.

"Where's Boss Fist?" Muskay asked.

"Gone," the officer said. "Vanished ... right after he put all the laborers out of work ..."

"Possessed," Hiram concluded.

"Possessed ...?" the officer asked.

"There's a voodoo doll in Arcadia," Muskay said.

"Voodoo ...?" the officer scoffed, but a woman that looked like a sock puppet, with banana-yellow hair and a pink dress, stepped forward.

"Is there really a voodoo doll ...?" she asked.

"Yes, and the ancient ones say it's not the first time," I said. "We need information ..."

"What kind of information?" the officer asked.

"Rumors said that a hand puppet started acting strangely over a month ago," Muskay said. "Disobeying orders, starting his own project ..."

"It's true," said the sock puppet. "My husband worked the milling machine, and that worker went crazy and wouldn't let anyone stop him."

"What was he making?" Hiram asked.

"A barrel," the sock puppet said. "A tall, thin barrel, half as tall as this jumper, and as wide as her waist. He wouldn't say why or let anyone help him. Boss First argued with him and he threated to hammer him flat."

"Where's this barrel?" Hiram asked.

"Gone," the sock puppet said. "He wheeled it out one evening, after everyone else was asleep, and the theft happened that very night."

"Theft ...?" Hiram asked.

"Somebody stole a bellows from the forge!" the sock puppet said. "The mad puppet later denied it, and denied even building the keg ..."

"We locked him up for his own good," the officer

said. "Poor chap is still out of his head."

"Can we talk to him?" Princess Gracely asked.

"Nope, he's gone ... one of the vanished dolls," the officer said.

"Probably the first vanished doll," Hiram said.

"Possibly ... that was certainly the start of it," the officer said.

"How many puppets are missing?" I asked.

"We can't keep track ... they disappear too fast," the officer said.

"Half of my friends and family have vanished ... without a trace," the sock puppet said.

"Listen to me, both of you," I said. "This is a formal request from a jumper: tell your superiors ... and everyone else ... we have proof that a voodoo doll has returned to Arcadia."

"*Proof* ...?" the officer looked doubtful.

"We talked to the voodoo doll inside The Palace," Hiram said. "She's captured Audrey the Great and Virginia the Grand."

All the puppets looked horrified by this news.

"We're trying to find her lair," I said. "No buildings should be left unattended ... especially not your workshop. Guard it night and day. Any strange events or suspicions should be reported; send all messages to The Palace, to Judy or Mr. Magee."

"I'll carry your message to the captain on duty," the officer promised. "Don't expect him to take your claim of voodoo seriously ..."

"I'll tell everyone!" the sock puppet said emphatically, and all the other puppets nodded vigorously.

We stepped back and the hand puppets turned away, hurrying off to spread our news. We looked at each other questioningly.

"A barrel ...?" Mom asked. "What would the voodoo doll want with a barrel ...?"

"And a bellows ...?" Mrs. Darby asked. "Why would anyone want ...?"

"A barrel can hold liquid ... and a bellows can pump the liquid," Hiram said.

"What liquid?" Princess Gracely asked.

"Who knows?" Hiram asked.

"It could be anything, but other than water, there's only one place anyone can go to order special liquids," Muskay said.

"The paper dolls!" Princess Gracely said.

"Yes, our next stop is ... the office of the paper dolls," I said, and I turned to Muskay. "I've never been there, so I may need your help ..."

"We'll get there together," Muskay promised.

Muskay and I spent a while working on a chant, and when we finished I pulled out my jump rope.

"Cave of the paper dolls
We fly to you!
Gateway to your office
We go through!
Where the paper folds flat
That's where we must be at!
Where countless stacks of paper lie
To paper dolls, we must fly!"

We arrived at the base of a great stone cliff between its rock wall and a row of thick hedges that seemed to have been planted just to shield this spot from view. A dark cave opened in the high rock wall, its mouth ten feet tall. Directly over the mouth of the cave was a huge, wooden-framed window built right into the rock-face of the cliff, which Audrey had told me provided light to the paper dolls through a series of mirrors lining a narrow vent. Just inside the cave the light quickly vanished.

"This way," Hiram said, motioning us into the cave.

"Let's hurry," Princess Gracely said.

"I hope you can see in the dark," Muskay said to me.

"Ignore him," Falcon said. "This is the safest residence in Arcadia."

"Then why hide in the cramped hall of the trolls?" Muskay asked.

"Because trolls don't try to put me to work," Falcon sneered, sounding disgusted.

Never before had I been in a real cave. I'd always considered them fanciful oddities that only people in fairy stories visited, and I cautiously brushed my fingers against its rough stone walls just to prove it was real. The air of the cave was unexpectedly cold, even near its mouth.

Not far inside, just out of the daylight, a pink-painted wooden wall blocked our path from floor to ceiling. Many huge flowers were painted on the wall, no two the same, and three white doors stood in the wall. The biggest door reached almost to the ceiling and was twice as wide as Hiram. The second appeared to be a normal door, and the last was so small only tiny dolls could use it. On each door, reverently painted in silver and gold, was a fancy pair of scissors.

Falcon opened the middle-sized door and Princess Gracely rushed us through as if every second that the door remained open was dangerous.

Inside the door stood a vast office building ... if one outer wall was removed and each floor was only one foot high. Tiny desks sat in rows in each room, little stairs slanted between the floors, and every back wall seemed to be a huge filing cabinet with dozens of tiny drawers on every floor. It was oddly dark for an office; the only light came from the ceiling, where an odd assortment of mirrors were arranged all over, reflecting the sunlight from the window above the mouth of the cave into every corner of the many offices. On each level, small figures were working, a lot of them very busily, some hurrying about, but hard to see in the dim light.

A small woman with blonde hair and a deep frown approached us. She held out her arms as if she could block our path. This woman was made of paper, just a picture of a woman, a flat, two-dimensional paper doll, so realistically-drawn that she could've been a photograph.

"This is an authorized-only area!" the paper doll shouted.

"We apologize, Madame Paprus," Princess Gracely curtsied to the tiny paper doll. "We're here on important business ..."

"You've come at a terrible time!" Madame Paprus said. "We have no ...!"

"This is Hilary, the new jumper," Hiram gestured to me.

"Hilary?" Madame Paprus asked. "Where's Audrey?"

"Audrey is with Great Aunt Virginia," Princess Gracely said. "Both have been captured ..."

"By the voodoo doll," Madame Paprus finished.

"How do you know that?" Hiram asked.

"Paper dolls aren't helpless or foolish," Madame Paprus said. "Most of us who've been taken have returned."

"How ...?" everyone asked.

"The voodoo doll locked us in a cabinet under paperweights," Madame Paprus said. "Well, there's no plan so great that it can't be toppled by too much paperwork. We folded ourselves, slipped out through the gaps, and came back here."

"Back from where ...?" Mrs. Darby asked.

Madame Paprus looked up, suspicious.

"Forgive us," Princess Gracely said. "Madame Paprus, this is Charlotte and Madge, the mothers of Audrey and Hilary."

"Welcome to the Official Offices of Arcadia," Madame Paprus said to both. "To answer your question, the captured paper dolls were imprisoned in Bambole, in the locked cabinet of the hotel."

"Were there any other dolls there?" Muskay asked.

"We never saw any other dolls," Madame Paprus said. "However, we kept our ears unfolded, and several stayed to discover whatever they could after the others fled. When they got back here, they reported that the other vanished dolls were sent ... to the graveyard."

"Graveyard ...!" I exclaimed.

"Where ...?" Mom demanded.

"Nowhere," Mrs. Darby answered. "Audrey has explored everywhere and she's never reported any graveyard."

"There is no graveyard," Muskay said. "At least ... there never was before."

"This is terrible!" Princess Gracely said.

"No, it's impossible," I said.

"What ...?" several asked.

"Arcadia is a game," I said. "The voodoo doll may have designated someplace to be a 'graveyard', but it can't be ... what a graveyard is in our world. No one could be killed; that's not how games are played."

"You're right," Muskay said. "Every death in Arcadia has been an accident; no doll has ever willingly killed another doll."

"But ... what purpose could the voodoo doll have for a graveyard, except ...?" Princess Gracely asked.

"It's another clue," Mom said. "Madame Paprus, the hand puppets reported that a doll under the control of the voodoo doll built a large wooden keg ... and stole a bellows to fill it. Have any unusual orders for liquids come in the last few months?"

"I'll have my people check right away," Madame Paprus said, and she turned to face her busy workers. "Formy! Formy, come down here!"

From the top shelf of the offices came a reply, and a fairy stepped to the edge. She was a paper doll, like the others, but she had long, rolled-up wings that she uncurled and flapped, and then she jumped off. She didn't really fall, but drifted down like any slip of paper, her flapping wings giving her some control over her movement. As she reached the floor, she bent her paper legs down to stand upon, and once settled, her wings curled behind her.

"Yes, Madame Paprus?" Formy asked.

"I need all purchase orders for any liquids for the last two months," Madame Paprus said. "Let me know at once if you find any unusual orders. We need them right away."

"Yes, Madame Paprus," Formy said, and she ran back to the offices, to the lowest level, where she went from paper doll to paper doll, demanding to see their recent orders.

"We do have another clue," Madame Paprus said. "This was the strangest order I'd ever gotten, and it came almost three months ago."

She led us closer to the offices and we stared amazed. Some dolls were rummaging through stuffed filing cabinets, pulling out sheets of paper no bigger than a business card and thinner than a receipt. Once their arms were full, these papers were carried and divided onto many of the desks. At the desks sat other paper dolls, reading, sorting, and filling out the tiny forms on the papers, and then piling them atop tall stacks ... making them even bigger. Other paper dolls collected the stacks, and carried them to various stuffed filing cabinets, carefully inserting each slip into a different place. Lights flashed in one office where a sign over the door read 'Copy Room". In another office, on the third floor, blank slips of paper were being stamped by a rubber stamp, which printed upon each form tiny lettering with spaces for names, addresses, ID numbers, and other boxes too small to read. Then each stamped form was carried to a tiny clothes line, where it was hung up to dry. The clothes line was on a set of pulleys, and one doll was turning it, moving the freshly inked forms through a window into another room, where another doll took them down, then rushed them to a desk where a different paper doll started to fill them out.

"What's all the paper for?" I whispered to Muskay.

"No one knows," Muskay whispered back to me. "It's the biggest mystery in Arcadia."

I tried not to giggle and he winked at me.

"Here it is," Madame Paprus said, and she pointed to a large, rolled up scroll laying on a wide table. Cautiously, Princess Gracely reached down and picked it up, and as she started to unroll it, Falcon retreated to the rear, closer to the doors, but Hiram grabbed and held him.

"What is it?" I asked, looking at the paper.

"I don't know," Princess Gracely said.

"It's a map ...," Mom said. "... a topographic map of

Arcadia."

"It's very old," Madame Paprus said. "The hand puppets made it ages ago, when they were planning the first of the doll cities. When the request for it came, I sent a copy to insure we didn't lose the original."

"Who ordered it?" Princess Gracely asked.

"Raggedy Anne," Madame Paprus said. "If it were anyone but the Queen of Arcadia I would've refused."

"Queen Anne was possessed," Muskay said.

"We know that now," Madame Paprus said. "Doubtlessly the voodoo doll wanted the map to plan the location of her new lair."

"But ... we had the glamour dolls search all of Arcadia," Princess Gracely said. "They searched for new buildings, ships, even balloons ...!"

"Are there any other caves marked on the map?" Mrs. Darby asked.

"I don't see any," Mom said, scanning the map. "This cave is marked, but it says 'location of the new paper doll project'."

"This cave was constructed, not natural," Madame Paprus said. "Real caves are damp, and damp and paper don't coexist well."

"This map is another clue, but we don't know what it means," Princess Gracely said.

"Is anything on there marked 'graveyard'?" I asked.

Mom scanned the scroll carefully, then shook her head.

Suddenly Formy came to the edge of the forth level, holding a stack of papers.

"Madame Paprus!" Formy called down. "I have the receipts! We have orders of perfume for the glamour dolls, seven cloth dyes of different colors for the rag dolls, and turpentine, oak stain, and furniture polish for the hand puppets, all in the usual amounts."

"That's expected," Madame Paprus said. "Anything else?"

"Several waxes and fresh paints for the marionettes, and boot-blacking and tin polish for the tin soldiers, signed by General Walnut," Formy said.

"Thank you, Formy," Madame Paprus said. "Well, there's nothing suspicious there. We fill those orders every month, especially tin polish."

"It makes no sense," Muskay said. "She had a wooden keg custom-built for her. Kegs hold liquid. What else could she want a keg for?"

"This voodoo doll is especially troublesome," Madame Paprus said. "The last one almost destroyed Arcadia, and would have, if we hadn't found her boat."

"This is the same voodoo doll," I said. "We spoke to her ... when she captured Great Aunt Virginia."

"I'd like to speak to her," Madame Paprus snarled. "I've got a shredder with her name on it."

"We can't kill ... and she can't kill," Princess Gracely said. "That alone gives us hope for the missing dolls."

"When you do catch her, I hope you file her away permanently ... in a locked drawer," Madame Paprus said.

"We'll do our best," I promised.

"I think we're done here," Muskay said. "Madame Paprus, could you make us a copy of this map? It might be important."

"Just slide it into the copy room," Madame Paprus said, and as Mom re-curled the scroll and slid it through the marked door, Madame Paprus shouted. "Rush order!"

"Rush order!" many paper dolls repeated her shout, and others repeated it after them.

"If there's anything else we can do, just ask," Madame Paprus said as lights flashed in the copy room.

"We will," Princess Gracely promised. "Thank you, Madame Paprus."

"You must get rid of this voodoo doll," Madame Paprus said. "We're days behind schedule, working overtime, and work's piling up."

"We'll do our best," I promised.

When our copy of the map arrived, carried by six paper dolls, four printed, colored, and looking antique, and two drawn in crayons of many colors, Mom took and examined the map, nodded, and we started to leave. We shouted our thanks as we walked to the huge wall with three doors, each of a different size. However, Madame Paprus was already shouting orders behind us, and the paper dolls were running to fetch more forms, so we couldn't be certain they heard us.

Falcon opened the middle door and we all marched out in silence.

When we reached the wall of bushes, I lifted my jump rope, but Hiram stepped back, away from us.

"Not coming ...?" Princess Gracely asked Hiram.

"Is that an option ...?" Falcon asked.

"Where are we going?" Hiram asked.

We stopped and looked at each other, puzzled by his question.

Hiram grinned and stared at us through thinned eyes.

"Oh, I'm coming, all right," Hiram said. "I'll be coming ... soon ... for all of you."

We all paled. With a quick glance at Hiram, Muskay stuck each of his thumbs into his ears and waved his hands. Mom curled both of her forefingers and hooked them, and Mrs. Darby interlocked her fingers and turned her palms down, facing the ground. Princess

Gracely held up one thin finger, then kissed it. With my hands at my sides, I rotated my wrists as if I were flipping my jump rope.

"What's with the gestures?" Falcon asked.

"You'll need to invent one, and we'll all need to change ours ... now that the voodoo doll has seen them twice," I said, looking at Hiram.

"You're not as stupid as you look, jumper ... or should I say ... Hilary?" Hiram spoke with the voodoo doll's deep, slow, drawling voice.

"Stealing my friends won't help!" I snarled.

"We'll see how you feel when I've made a token of you," the voodoo doll spoke through Hiram. "Where are you going now? The rag dolls ...? Theater City ...?"

"Come with us, if you can," I said.

"Oh, no ... I've got other dolls to steal," the voodoo doll said. "Poor jumper ... soon you'll have no more dolls to protect ... or parents ...!"

"I'll find you ...!" I promised her.

"No," the voodoo doll said, grinning with Hiram's face. "I'll ... find you."

With a deep, wicked laugh, Hiram turned and walked away, between the hills, toward the woods.

"Can't we stop him?" Mrs. Darby asked. "Shackle him ... or trap him ... for his own good?"

"What good would that do?" Muskay said. "You heard her in The Palace: *'If you ever see this body again then you'll be seeing your own doom'.*"

"What does it mean?" Princess Gracely asked.

"It means that the chance exists we'll soon see those dolls who disappeared," Muskay said. "She's taking them for a reason, a purpose, which only she knows."

"So they're safe," I said. "She's not harming them ... not if she needs them."

"Yes," Muskay said. "But if we prevent her from taking someone, then we'll be putting them at risk, because she'll have no other purpose for them. We'd be making them ... expendable."

"She can't kill," Princess Gracely said. "No doll has ever ...!"

"True, but that doesn't mean no doll ever will ...," I said.

"We should leave Arcadia," Falcon said. "Now ... before we're taken ...!"

"I'm not going anywhere," I said. "She's made this personal; it's her or me!"

"No, it isn't," Mom said. "Hilary, remember what Great Aunt Virginia said. This is a game. If you make it serious then you'll be banished again, and that's exactly what the voodoo doll wants."

"That's a good idea," Mrs. Darby said. "She'll never expect that."

"What ...?" I asked.

Mrs. Darby looked at Hiram's disappearing form.

"I think we should talk somewhere else," Mrs. Darby said. "Where the voodoo doll can't possibly hear."

"Talk about what ...?" Falcon asked.

"A trap," Mrs. Darby said. "The next time the voodoo doll appears, it's time that we give her exactly what she wants."

"But ... the voodoo doll only appears when she's taking one of us," Falcon argued.

"Precisely," Mrs. Darby said. "Which is why we need to have everything ready."

"Where do we go?" I asked.

"Jump us back to the workshop of the hand puppets," Mrs. Darby said. "It's time we did a little stealing of our own."

I felt unusually tired, but then, since coming to Arcadia this morning, we'd visited Mr. Magee and Judy, the hand puppets, and the paper dolls. I forced myself to focus, feeling my mind drift from exhaustion, but managed to get us back to the workshop of the hand puppets in one piece. However, we didn't stay for long.

No one was there yet, despite that we'd told the officer someone needed to be guarding it, but it made our theft easy. Mrs. Darby and Mom told us to wait and they hurried inside. Soon they returned, clutching a small hammer, some wire-cutters, and an old tin can. Once returned, they had me jump rope all of us back to the Factory.

I was sweating and gasping before the sparkles of my blue cord surrounded all of us and carried us to the Factory. When I finally stopped it was abruptly; I almost tripped on my own cord. Jumping rope was wonderful exercise, but combined with the drain of magic, jumping quickly took its toll.

We arrived upstairs and I staggered to a wall and leaned against it.

Mom and Mrs. Darby smiled.

"Here's the plan," Mrs. Darby said. "We took this can of thin, broad-headed nails, which are used more for decoration than functionality. With the clippers, we can make the nails really short, shorter than thumbtacks, and nail them to the bottoms of our shoes."

"That's the bait for our trap," Mom said. "We need to know where the vanished dolls have gone. Fortunately, there're few paved roads in Arcadia. With these nails in the bottoms of our shoes, we'll leave easy-to-follow tracks wherever we go. Whichever one of us the voodoo doll takes, she won't know about the special nails, and when she runs off, in one of our bodies, then the others will be able to follow her ... to her lair."

"Where we'll have her trapped!" Princess Gracely exclaimed. "Brilliant!"

"Those dolls that she takes, and the humans, may not be going to her lair," Muskay said. "They could be going to her 'graveyard'."

"That's true," I said. "However, we need to find both. Even if we capture the voodoo doll inside her lair, we'll still need to find and rescue the vanished dolls."

"Either way, it'll give us information we don't have," Muskay said. "We also need to change our signs so the voodoo doll can't trick us."

Work was slow; the clippers had to cut the nails diagonally, so they had a sharp point, and we had to hammer them into the soles of everyone's shoes so that they didn't poke through and stab our feet. We carefully nailed them around the outside edges of our soles, where we could, even for those of us wearing sneakers. When we finished, Falcon and Muskay went outside, walked about in the grass, and came back reporting that a blind doll could follow the tracks they left.

Next, we changed our signs, mostly swapping them around. I took Great Aunt Virginia's sign and lifted one finger, then touched it to my forehead. Mom took Princess Gracely's and held up one thin finger, then lifted it to her lips and kissed it. Mrs. Darby took Hiram's and clapped her hands twice. Princess Gracely took Mom's and curled both of her forefingers and hooked them. Muskay took my signal, and twirled both of his hands at his sides as if he was flipping a jump rope.

"What can I do?" Falcon asked.

"You can take mine," Muskay said, and he stuck each of his thumbs into his ears and waved his hands.

"I'm not doing that!" Falcon said.

"Then we'll assume you're possessed," Muskay grinned at him.

Falcon frowned but didn't argue.

"What do we do now?" Princess Gracely asked.

"We go home," Mom said. "Hilary is tired and we need her rested when we confront the voodoo doll."

"Also, if the voodoo doll wants to take one of us, she'll probably go for Hilary," Mrs. Darby said. "If she rests here then she'll be vulnerable. I doubt if the voodoo doll's magic can reach our world; if the voodoo doll tries while we're there, then she'll fail."

"While we're gone, you're vulnerable, but not at great risk," Mom said to Princess Gracely, Muskay, and Falcon. "If the voodoo doll is focusing on Hilary, then she'll be making a token of her, not one of the rest of us."

"And ... if one of you is taken tonight, then you'll leave a trail, and we can follow you tomorrow," Mrs. Darby said. "Still, take every precaution and use your secret signs often."

"Ummm, Hilary, how do we get home?" Mom asked.

I looped my jump rope around the back of my neck and held out each of my hands.

"Just like Dorothy did," I half-smiled. "Take hands and think *'there's no place like home'.*"

Chapter 14

Great Aunt Virginia's Apartment

Mom, Mrs. Darby, and I appeared in Great Aunt Virginia's living room.

"We're here!" Mrs. Darby announced.

"When Audrey took Hilary to battle Punch, we sat here and watched them vanish," Mom said. "I wonder how our bodies transfer from ...?"

"Probably not a good idea to examine that too closely," I said.

"She's right," Mrs. Darby said. "We don't want to banish ourselves."

"I don't think Hilary was ever banished," Mom said. "Arcadia is a game. Hilary was told that she was banished and she believed it. Her belief, not magic, prevented her from returning."

"That explains us," Mrs. Darby said. "We didn't believe in Arcadia, not really, even after we saw our daughters vanish. Adults don't believe in such things ... so to most of us, make-believe lands are closed."

"That makes sense," Mom said. "Only after several months, after we'd accepted that Arcadia is real, could Great Aunt Virginia bring us ..."

"Enough!" I said. "If you examine Arcadia too closely you'll never get back there."

Mom and Mrs. Darby exchanged glances.

"I can't risk not going back for Audrey," Mrs. Darby said.

"We'll rescue everyone," Mom promised her. "It's a game ... and all games eventually end."

"We need to end with a win," I said. "Let's review; we've got a rumor of a 'graveyard', a mysterious barrel and a bellows, but no liquids, and we're running out of friends."

"We also have the map," Mom said. "I left it with Princess Gracely ... I wish I'd brought it."

"What good is the map?" Mrs. Darby asked. "We can see how tall the hills are ..."

"Maybe she wants to build something ...?" I suggested. "Maybe she needs a good site ..."

"What she may build is not as important as what she might have already built," Mom said. "Yet the map showed us nothing, just the rivers and creeks, the forests, elevations ... and the locations of the doll cities ... except for Sparkle City, but the glamour dolls weren't around when the map was drawn."

"We know where all of that is," Mrs. Darby said. "Maybe ... maybe it isn't for building ... maybe it's for using ..."

"Using ...?" Mom asked.

"A road," Mrs. Darby said. "Topographic maps are used to make roads."

"Why would she want a road?" I asked.

"Maybe she wants to drive something in," Mrs. Darby

said. "A car ... or a bulldozer."

"That doesn't sound very doll-ish," Mom said.

"She can't be bringing something like that, a modern device, from this world to Arcadia," I said. "The magic is in the play. No games I know use a bulldozer ..."

"She must've needed the map for a reason," Mrs. Darby said. "Come, let's see what Great Aunt Virginia has for dinner."

"Do you think she'd mind?" Mom asked.

"I'm sure she'd insist," Mrs. Darby said.

We went into the kitchen. However, her refrigerator was mostly empty. We opened a pantry and found baskets of uncracked wheat, unshucked peas, and bags of what Mom called 'farm food'.

"I'm not used to cooking like this," Mrs. Darby said.

"How about pizza?" Mom asked, and she pulled out her cell phone.

While we waited for the delivery, I puttered around the house. Mom and Mrs. Darby kept discussing the barrel, the bellows, and the map ... as if a sudden revelation would solve everything. That's adults every time. Day in and out, they talk ... until they start to believe that thinking and talking can solve every puzzle. However, Arcadia wasn't a puzzle, it was a game. Games require playing, doing as much as thinking. What we needed, more than anything, was to be doing something.

When the pizza-delivery driver arrived, Mom and I went downstairs, paid, and took the elevator back up. I was in the middle of my second slice when an idea struck me.

"Mrs. Darby, where haven't we been?" I asked.

Mrs. Darby swallowed before answering.

"Excuse me?" she asked.

"We've been to the rag dolls, Sparkle City, the

covered cart-stages of the marionettes, Troll Hill ...," I ticked them off.

"The Palace, to see Mr. Magee and Judy, Bambole, well, the Hall of the Ancient Ones and the highest tower ...," Mom added.

"The workshop and the city of the hand puppets," Mrs. Darby said.

"And the office of the paper dolls," I said.

"And the Factory," Mom added.

"Exactly," I said. "And ... at every place, we've found clues. Games have to be fair, and that might mean there are more clues out there ... at places where we haven't looked."

"We haven't been to the fort of the tin soldiers," Mrs. Darby said. "Or the Aging Forest, or Waterfall Bay ..."

"What's WaterFall Bay?" I asked.

"It's just a place," Mrs. Darby said. "Audrey said that it's a pond where a small stream pours over a cliff into a pool. The dolls call it a waterfall although it's only five feet high. No dolls live there, only a flock of rubber ducks. Audrey said it was pretty, but not impressive."

"Nothing has pointed us there ... or to the Aging Forest," Mom said. "Surely the flying glamour dolls checked both."

"Sometimes there are caves behind waterfalls ... at least, in the movies," I said.

"It wasn't on the map, but anything could be possible," Mom said.

"We should start with the fort of the tin soldiers," Mrs. Darby said. "General Walnut has probably vanished, but if there're any clues there then someone should be able to tell us."

"I agree," I said.

"What makes you think there are still clues to be

found?" Mom asked.

"If there's no way to win then it's not a game," I replied.

"We have to win," Mrs. Darby said, "and that means we should get plenty of rest."

I didn't need either mother to tell me they meant me ... so I said good night and went to get my travel toothbrush from out of my suitcase.

As I entered my bedroom I found all my stuffed animals in the center of my bed, shaped like a heart, and outlined by the snake. I smiled at them, and before I got ready for bed, again I picked them all up and hugged them tightly.

The next morning, as I walked out into the living room dressed, but with my hair still damp after my bath, I found Mom standing in the living room staring at Mrs. Darby. To our amazement, Mrs. Darby was standing in the kitchen scooping hot pancakes off a cast-iron griddle and flipping them onto plates. The kitchen table was set for three and a big glass pitcher of orange juice was sitting amid our waiting glasses ... next to bowls of cut grapefruit.

"Where did all this come from?" Mom asked. "Did you go shopping?"

"It was in the refrigerator," Mrs. Darby smiled. "Even the freshly-made batter."

"Last night the refrigerator was empty!" Mom said.

"We feared it would be empty," Mrs. Darby said. "I think this apartment, and everything in it, has a lot in common with Arcadia."

Once again, Mom and Mrs. Darby repeated the same conversation they'd been repeating when I went to bed. I shook my head. Adults are like the offices of the paper dolls, full of pointless hurrying and endless details, yet seldom accomplishing anything despite their firmest efforts.

Breakfast was delicious, and afterwards I helped Mom wash and dry the dishes while Mrs. Darby took her turn in the bathroom. Great Aunt Virginia's apartment was the most wonderful place! I'd always wondered why she lived here when she could obviously be rich and live anywhere. I wondered if I'd rather live here, surrounded by magic, than indulge in a fabulous estate without a single charming feature or doll that welcomed me every night. I also wondered: if I wished for it really hard would a hair dryer appear in the bathroom?

When Mrs. Darby emerged, dressed and ready, we started to make the tea. We chose the herbs together and Mom filled the teapot and lit the stove while I ground the spices.

I sat in my chair at the table although there was plenty of room on the couch. We'd never traveled to Arcadia without Great Aunt Virginia, and Mom and Mrs. Darby seemed to be thinking the same thing; we gushed compliments on each other and upon the dolls of Princess Gracely, Muskay, and Hiram, although his counterpart had been taken. We even slipped in a few compliments about the other dolls in the room, atop the bookshelves and peeking out from the corners as if spying upon us. Mom and Mrs. Darby even complimented the antique furniture and everything in the apartment. Sipping our tea, we were having such a good time I was startled when the tingling sensations began; I never had this much fun with adults and almost didn't want to leave.

Chapter 15

Invasion of the Fort

Arcadia bloomed around us. Around the big table in the basement, illuminated by candles, sat Muskay, Princess Gracely, and Falcon, but only empty seats remained where Hiram and Great Aunt Virginia had sat. Their absence struck me terribly.

"Today we go to the wooden fort of the tin soldiers," I announced. "There must still be clues to be had, and that's the only remaining doll village."

Muskay, Princess Gracely, and Falcon exchanged glances.

"What ...?" I asked. "Are there more ...?"

"Many," Muskay said.

"The Vale of the Gnomes lies on the north edge of Arcadia," Princess Gracely said. "The Mountain of the Green Soldiers lies to the west."

"The Unicorn Fields aren't far outside of Arcadia," Falcon said. "The mountain beside them is where the singing birds live ... with the Tiki men."

"The craziest lands lie to the south, just outside Arcadia," Muskay said. "Those lunatic mouse and rabbit dolls are always getting into trouble."

"Arcadia is only one of many kingdoms," Princess Gracely explained. "Yet we don't need to worry about them. This is our home, and we must look to ourselves to save it."

"The fort's a good idea," Muskay said. "Anything that's affected all of Arcadia will affect them, too."

"We leave when you're ready," I said.

We arose as one and ascended the stairs to the main room, where I could jump easier. Then, suddenly, a terrible heaviness fell upon me. I staggered, feeling as if I was being squeezed from every direction, and a deep, feminine laugh whispered in my ears. Muskay grabbed to support me but I pulled away.

"*No!*" I shouted, gritting my teeth against the pain. "*It's the voodoo doll! She's trying to possess me ...!*"

Forcing myself to stand, I whipped out my jump rope and began a Double-bounce, struggling against the horrible black claws I could feel pressing into my skin. My chest ached so deeply I almost doubled over, but I had to keep jumping, fighting against her control. My heart felt as if someone had stabbed a long, sharp pin right into my chest. Its pressure almost overcame me.

Yet, as the first sparkles of my jump rope began, the pain lessened. I pushed myself harder. I did several jump rope tricks, Skier, X-to-Straddle, and Heel Exchange, and my sparkles brightened. Finally I heard shouts; Mom and Mrs. Darby, and even Muskay and Princess Gracely, were cheering me ... yells of encouragement. As their faces become a blur behind the sphere of sparkles encasing me, the pain vanished entirely, and I jumped harder and faster, expanding my circle until they were all inside my glittering ball.

> *"Fort of the tin soldiers!*
> *Here we come!*
> *Arcadia's in trouble!*
> *Which must be undone!*
> *We can't stay!*
> *Must go today!*
> *Fort of the tin soldiers*
> *Is where we play!"*

The basement of the Factory faded away.

We appeared in a wide clearing, near its edge, under the branches of tall trees. All of them grabbed me before I fell, and I struggled to stand on shaking knees.

"I'm all right," I assured them. "She didn't take me."

"We need you to prove that," Muskay said.

Understanding, I lifted one finger, then touched it to my forehead. This seemed to content them.

"The magic of the voodoo doll couldn't take you while you were inside the jump rope's sparkles," Falcon said. "That might work in our favor."

"It explains why none of the possessed people would let Audrey transport them," Mom said.

"Yes, because when the sparkles began, she'd lose control over her victim," Mrs. Darby said.

"It was close," I said. "I could feel her overcoming me. If I hadn't had the jump rope ...!"

"If any of us feel her attacking us then we need to let you know," Falcon said.

"You'd have to jump inside the rope as it starts," Muskay said. "Princess Gracely and I can do that, but the rest of you would have trouble, and Hilary can't jump rope indefinitely."

"I'll do what I can," I said.

"Hilary, Madge, and I can fade back to our world, if we have to," Mom said.

"Only if we can sense it," Mrs. Darby said. "Great Aunt Virginia and Hiram didn't report strange feelings before they were possessed."

"Maybe only jumpers feel it," Princess Gracely said.

"Or ... maybe only those holding jump ropes," Muskay said.

"Great Aunt Virginia will tell us when we rescue her," I said. "For now, where are we?"

Everyone looked around. Behind us, the forest seemed calm and welcoming, and I wasn't surprised to see a small, stuffed green turtle lift up its cloth head to glance at us. To our other side was a wide clearing of many low hills, and upon one stood a miniature compound, wide for its size, with a thin, two-foot-high crenellated stone wall that enclosed a vast courtyard complete with long rows of tiny barracks and other buildings. The stone palisade surrounded at least a square quarter-mile and was filled with many, perhaps five hundred tin soldiers, all standing atop the wall, their rifles pointed outside the wall, with even more sticking out at the gates and atop their signal towers. In the distance stood a huge corral filled with tiny rocking and hobby horses, and all were saddled and ready to ride.

Centermost stood a white southern mansion, over four feet tall, and this one looked like it had been modeled from the movie 'Gone with the Wind'. It was painted colonial white with dark green shutters, had a roof with a low slope, and tall, white pillars rose from a rectangular porch as wide as the front of the building. Near the top of it, above the pillars, stood a wide, empty balcony.

"What do we do?" Princess Gracely asked. "If we step out there, will they shoot us?"

"Probably; military minds are obedient, not observant," Muskay said.

"Perhaps we should retreat," Falcon suggested.

"Let me try," I said, and I held my jump rope ready and motioned them, especially Mom and Mrs. Darby, to duck down low behind me, in case their guns were more dangerous than the cork-loaded blunderbusses with which they'd fought against Punch's glamour army.

"Help!" I shouted suddenly. *"Help! Help!"*

"What're you doing?" Mom asked.

"Soldiers aren't trained to shoot people asking for help," I whispered over my shoulder.

"Help!" I shouted again, and Mom, Mrs. Darby, Muskay, and Princess Gracely began shouting with me. *"Help! Help!"*

A hundred guns aimed in our direction but not one fired. We spied some movement, and then the gate opened and a small squad of six tin soldiers came riding out on miniature stick ponies. They raced toward us, pistols or swords in their hands, bouncing on their stick ponies. As they came closer I rose up and waved at them.

"Help us, please!" I shouted.

They rode close and reined in before us.

"What do you need?" one of the tin soldiers demanded.

"To see General Walnut ... or whoever is in charge now," I said.

"General Walnut is there, but he's one of the few," the tin soldier said. "Who may I report is asking ...?"

"I'm Hilary, friend of ...," I began, but the word caught in my throat. Audrey, I was going to say, but we still hadn't spoken in friendship. "I'm a friend of Great Aunt Virginia the Bold. I helped her and Audrey fight against Punch."

To prove my point I held up my jump rope. The tin soldiers exchanged glances.

"Please help us!" Princess Gracely said. "We're in trouble, trying to fight a great evil ...!"

"We've suffered losses," Muskay said.

"Half of our soldiers have deserted," the tin soldier said.

"We don't think so," I said. "Gone, definitely, but not of their own will."

"Kidnapped ...?" the tin soldier asked.

"As a jumper, she needs to make a full report to General Walnut," Princess Gracely said.

"We'll send back a rider," the tin soldier said. "Then we'll escort you inside."

On his stick pony, one tin soldier rode swiftly back, and then the others escorted us. Falcon tried to stay behind but Mom and Mrs. Darby seized him and he reluctantly followed.

Both gates opened wide as we approached, and some tin soldiers stepped closer to look at us. I walked past them carefully, as did Muskay, but Princess Gracely's wide, flowing skirt knocked many of them backwards, out of her path. The others followed, past tall flagpoles that didn't reach our waists, looking down upon manned signal towers raised above everything but the white mansion.

To our dismay, a tin soldier came out of the mansion and stood looking up at us from the front steps.

"General Walnut sends his pardon to the newest jumper, but his military duties preclude his presence at this time," the tin soldier shouted, as if reciting a rehearsed speech.

"That's crazy ...!" Muskay said.

"You go back inside and tell General Walnut that we require an immediate audience ...!" Princess Gracely said.

"And if he doesn't come out, tell him that we're coming inside ... all of us ... no matter what it does to his office!" I said.

The tin soldier paled, then saluted, crisply about-faced and marched back inside. We glanced at each other, then looked around at the hundreds of tin soldiers standing ready on the wall, their muskets raised and firmly plugged with tiny corks, with which they'd pummel their attackers.

A small door on the top balcony opened slowly and a white feather appeared. Around the corner peeked a wooden eye.

"Nice to see you, General Walnut," Princess Gracely said, her voice lacking its usual lightheartedness.

"General Walnut, do you remember me?" I asked.

"Walnut?" the voice answered. "Who's that?"

"Well, I guess I'll just have to tear the roof off this house and find him!" I said harshly.

The eye and feather withdrew, and we heard hard woods gently banging together. Then, reluctantly, General Walnut appeared, stepping out onto the balcony with two other nutcracker dolls. Each was garishly-uniformed, with comically bushy beards, mustaches, and eyebrows of fake fur.

"Improper protocol!" General Walnut cried, his wide wooden mouth flapping as if on a hinge. "Disgraceful! Treasonous!"

"Please, forgive us, General Walnut, but we're in desperate need," Princess Gracely said.

"Irregular! Against regulations!" General Walnut said, and both of the other nutcrackers bobbed their heads in agreement.

"There are five of your brethren missing," I said. "Where are they?"

"Civilian demands of military matters?" General Walnut said. "Unthinkable! Inexcusable!"

"Fine," Muskay said. "We know where your missing brethren are. We know where the missing tin soldiers, marionettes, glamour dolls, rag dolls, and hand puppets are ..."

"As well as those missing from Bambole, including Great Aunt Virginia ... and Audrey the Grand," Princess Gracely said.

"We know who's taken them, and they'll soon take you, too," I said.

"Oh, stop this!" Falcon said. "We're all in trouble, and this pointless arguing is wasting time ... time that should be spent fleeing Arcadia!"

"No one's fleeing," I said. "General, a voodoo doll has taken all the missing dolls, and we've heard about a 'graveyard' ..."

"If we don't stop her soon then we'll all be taken," Muskay said.

"Our time is running out," Princess Gracely said.

"Impossible!" General Walnut said. "Absurd!"

"We didn't come here to convince you," I said. "I really don't care if you believe me or not, but we need information ... and you're going to give it to us!"

"Belligerence!" General Walnut said. "Insubordination!"

I reached down, seized General Walnut around his chest, and lifted him up to my face, almost touching my nose.

"Help!" General Walnut cried.

"Hilary, be careful!" Princess Gracely shouted. "We can't afford for you to be banished again!"

"Put him down!" Muskay urged, fear in his voice. "Hilary, this is why dolls don't live in Bambole anymore ... it's impolite to treat them like playthings!"

"Hilary ...!" Mom said in her deepest voice.

I glared, angry, but their words penetrated deep. I couldn't afford to lose Arcadia again ... and I was losing it ... and my temper ... one friend at a time.

"Hilary, please ...!" Princess Gracely said.

I sighed heavily and set General Walnut back onto the balcony.

"I'm sorry," I said. "I know ... Arcadia is a game, but I'm losing friends, and it feels real."

"It's real to us," Muskay said. "But we know our limits."

"That sounds like something Hiram would say ... but he's gone," I said.

"I'll say it for him," Muskay said.

I nodded.

"General Walnut, the new jumper makes a formal petition," Mrs. Darby said, stepping forward. "The Jumper of Arcadia requires you to provide her with all information of current activities on this base ... for the last three months ... especially those which were unexpected or can't be explained."

"Dishonorable!" General Walnut snapped, and then he bowed his head. "Unfortunately, it is a proper request." General Walnut glared up at Hilary, then turned and spoke to Mrs. Darby. "Who are you, and by what authority do you make this request?"

"I'm Charlotte, and jumper Audrey the Grand is my daughter," Mrs. Darby said. "This is Madge, and this jumper, Hilary the Great, is her daughter.

"Civilians ...?" General Walnut gasped.

"Mothers," Mrs. Darby said. "As our daughters are minors, we have absolute legal rule over them, and even the military must acknowledge our required consent for our daughters to say or do anything."

"Well, that isn't a military matter," General Walnut said. "Mothers always outrank daughters ...!"

"And, as mothers, we make formal request through our daughters, both Audrey and Hilary, the two jumpers of Arcadia," Mrs. Darby said. "We're also intimate friends, and I'm a blood relative, of Great Aunt Virginia, whom you've reported to for decades. In the name of all three jumpers, I request an immediate report on all relevant activities of the tin soldiers ... for the last three months."

General Walnut looked perplexed, and then he turned to the other two nutcracker dolls. They all began whispering, their wooden heads so close together that they knocked and clacked loudly. None of them seemed to be listening to the others, so they kept whispering louder until we could clearly hear the worry in their voices.

Finally they broke apart and General Walnut turned back to Mrs. Darby.

"Very well, but our report isn't good," General Walnut said. "Over half of our army is missing, Absent WithOut Leave. Soldiers of every rank are gone, both officers and privates. We've done all we could, but we can't stem the losses."

"What else?" Mrs. Darby asked.

"All military operations have been canceled," General Walnut said, and he looked ashamed. "Every soldier is on Red Alert and has been for a month."

"What started it?" I asked. "When did it all begin?"

"Everything went wrong when those six horses were stolen," General Walnut said, addressing Mrs. Darby as if she'd asked.

"What six horses...?" Mrs. Darby asked.

"The seahorses," General Walnut said. "Six of our finest stick ponies ... our best at fording rivers, you know ...in their pen at sunset ... and gone before sunrise."

"No!" Mom shouted.

We all startled ... and turned to stare at her. Mom was staring at us, her eyes bulging.

"The voodoo doll ...!" Mom screamed. *"I ... hear her!"*

"Jump!" Princess Gracely screamed.

"We can't jump here!" Muskay said, and he grabbed Mom's arm, pulling at her. *"Help me get her into the open!"*

We all grabbed Mom, and she struggled, as if fighting herself more than us, but we pulled hard at her, half-dragging her away from the white mansion. She screamed, thrashed, and writhed as if in pain, and I let go, pulled out my jump rope, and instantly started jumping.

"Hurry ...!" Mrs. Darby urged me, clinging onto Mom.

My jump rope flipped fast; I jumped as I'd never jumped before. *I couldn't lose Mom! I couldn't ...!*

The sparkles quickly began, and I threw in my best tricks, Double Cross, Leg-Over, and several others, until my sphere sparkled and started to expand.

A hand reached out ... Mom's hand ... and caught my jump rope in mid-swing. I stumbled ... and my sparkles faded.

Mom stopped thrashing and looked down at me with

a wicked grin.

"Give it to me, Hilary," she said. "Give me this jump rope, daughter ... right now!"

I hesitated.

"No," I said.

"Give me the jump rope, you stupid, ungrateful whelp!" Mom screamed at me. "As your mother, I order you ...!"

Everyone froze, staring with disbelief.

"You're not my mother," I said slowly.

I lifted one finger, then touched it to my forehead. Mrs. Darby clapped her hands twice. Princess Gracely curled both of her forefingers and hooked them. Muskay twirled both of his hands at his sides, and Falcon, reluctantly, stuck each of his thumbs into his ears and waved his hands.

Mom glared at all of us, then shook her head.

"This body belongs to your mother," the voodoo doll said from Mom's mouth, her deep voice and accent sounding nothing like Mom. "Give me that jump rope ... or I'll hurt your mother!"

"You can't," I said. "I was so angry with General Walnut I almost pulled his head off, but I didn't ... because I can't. Arcadia wouldn't allow it, not even from a jumper. You're a doll ... even more bound to the rules of this land than I am."

"This land won't be Arcadia much longer," the voodoo doll said. "Soon it will be a new land ... my land!"

"Every would-be conqueror says that," I said. "History is littered with their failures."

"This time ... the failure will be yours," the voodoo doll said.

I stared at the face I knew so well ... yet which had

never looked so unfamiliar. Mom's face bore a furious, ugly expression I'd never seen before; an angry glare of hate.

"Surrender that jump rope and promise to take both mothers and yourself back to the jumper world, and promise never to return, and I'll let her go," the voodoo doll said.

"Mom would never forgive me," I said, "and I'd never forgive myself."

"You're a fool!" the voodoo doll scowled.

Without another world, Mom's body walked away, reached the wooden palisade and stepped over it, making a dozen tin soldiers jump out of her way. Without a backwards glance she walked away, across the clearing and into the woods.

I looked down; in the dirt of the courtyard, large footprints showed the clear imprints of the nails of the hand puppets we'd driven into all our shoes.

"Wait until she vanishes into the woods," I whispered. "Then we follow her."

The Heart of Play

Chapter 16

The Doll Graveyard

General Walnut looked as pale as a pine.

"That ... that's what happened to my other generals?" General Walnut asked.

"To them, and what will soon happen to all of us," Muskay said while I carefully watched Mom walk to the edge of the forest, noting the exact location where she entered it.

"Hilary, I'm sorry," Mrs. Darby said.

"General, we'll need everyone, the help of all the dolls," Princess Gracely said. "We're searching for the lair of the voodoo doll, but we dare not approach it with too few."

"Every resource I have is yours," General Walnut said. "All Arcadia must rise to face this!"

"Be ready at a moment's notice," Muskay said. "When our summons arrives we may not have much time. If we're slow, the voodoo doll will escape."

"She can't escape," I said. "Every time she escapes

she comes back stronger. We must put an end to her threat forever."

"Capital!" General Walnut exclaimed. "Commendable! Admirable!"

We followed Mom's tracks to the exact spot where she'd vanished between the trees. The marks of the nails on her shoes left clear scars upon the ground. Apparently the voodoo doll didn't know where to find the trails, as Mom stumbled long through the brush before she found one. The dirt of the trail was harder, but some dried, fallen leaves lay crushed upon it, marked with the patterns of her nails. We followed her deep into the woods.

More and more stuffed animals appeared as we walked, peeking out from behind bushes, watching us with wary eyes. Yet we spied them easily; their neon pink, blue, and yellow fake furs stood out against the natural colors of bark and leaves. Princess Gracely waved to several, but as if afraid they turned away and dashed off.

Soon we reached an area thick with stuffed animals, too many to hide well. We heard them rustling ahead of us, hurrying to get under cover before we passed by them. Above us, birds flew, both real and stuffed, and their chirpings filled our ears.

Suddenly Muskay pounced into a thicket and a loud squeal followed. Muskay rose from the bushes holding a stuffed sheep, which looked terrified, squirming and screaming complaints.

"Muskay, why ...?" Princess Gracely asked.

"That's what I want to know," Muskay said. "Why are they hiding from us?"

Abruptly, a great thrashing of leaves and snapping of

branches arose, and then a real, tall unicorn, white with a golden horn, approached us from one side, and a tall, horned stag came from the other side. Two live monkeys and a huge gorilla dropped from the trees, and other animals rose from the forest fauna, mostly stuffed animals, but also real rabbits, kittens, puppies, a wildcat, a snake, and what looked like a water buffalo suddenly converged on us. The water buffalo snorted angrily and the unicorn lowered its deadly horn.

"I'm not with them!" Falcon cried, pressing back against a tree trunk.

"Wait! Wait!" I cried. "What do you want?"

"Let our friend go!" came a call from above us.

In a bright flash of scarlet and orange feathers, a stuffed parrot winged down from above and settled in the sharp antlers of the stag.

"Release the sheep ... or suffer the consequences!" the parrot shouted.

"Muskay, put it down gently," Mrs. Darby said.

"I wasn't going to hurt it," Muskay said as he put the frightened sheep down. "Just got tired of being stared at ....!"

"We're not here to hurt anyone!" Princess Gracely said.

"Half of us have vanished, especially the birds," the parrot said. "I'm one of the few, so we take extreme caution when someone looks like they're going to make off with one of our own."

"The voodoo doll's former lair, her boat in the swamp, was spotted by the birds, so she probably holds a grievance against them," Mrs. Darby said.

"What's a voodoo doll?" the parrot asked.

"The doom of Arcadia," Falcon answered.

"Not if we have anything to do about it," I said firmly.

"The voodoo doll is a terrible threat whom we're trying to defeat," Princess Gracely said. "We're chasing her latest victim; she just passed through this forest."

"We saw her," the parrot said. "Was that our enemy?"

"No, but she was possessed by our enemy," I said. "We're trailing her, trying to find where our enemy hides."

The stuffed and live animals exchanged glances.

"How can we help?" the parrot asked.

"Be ready for our summons," Muskay said. "When you see all the armies of Arcadia marching, that means we're surrounding our foe."

"Yes, we'll need everyone to aid in capturing her," I said. "She's a doll of string and thread with the head of a lollipop ... according to the ancient ones."

"They would know, if anyone does," the parrot said.

"We could use you, parrot," Mrs. Darby said. "You can help us follow her."

"Birds are now avoiding open sky," the parrot said. "Those who flew within view of both horizons were the first to vanish."

"Those she sees are taken first," Falcon translated.

"You must stay below the treetops," Muskay said. "We don't want you seen."

"We'd be very grateful," Princess Gracely said. "We need all the help we can get."

"Just fly through the branches and keep an eye out for the women who just passed," I said. "Remember to be quiet; we don't want her knowing that we're following her."

With flaps of bright wings, the parrot rose and flew off low between the branches. We took leave of the forest animals, slipped past them, and hurried down the forest trail.

We barely made it half a mile before the parrot returned to us.

"She reached the edge of the forest and ran out into the open," the parrot said. "She's not far from Troll Hill, but she's not headed there."

"What's beyond Troll Hill?" I asked.

"Bambole, but it's not the direct route," the parrot said.

"What will she run into, if she goes straight?" Muskay asked.

"Nothing," the parrot said. "That route leads nowhere but to the distant borders of Arcadia, skirting the swamp the whole way."

"The swamp?" Mrs. Darby asked. "That's where she hid her boat the last time!"

"Only those with wings or fins can traverse the swamp," the parrot said.

"Then we have her cornered," Muskay said.

"Or she'll lead us to some terrible trap," Falcon said.

We hurried on, easily seeing her tracks, and soon reached the end of the trees. There we spied our quarry, in the distance, running over the lightly-wooded hills behind Troll Hill. We waited, unwilling to be seen, and the parrot swooped down and landed on a branch beside us.

As she passed behind the hills, we emerged and hurried on her trail, quietly following. Unfortunately, the thick grasses padded her footsteps, leaving no trace upon the ground. We peeked over each hilltop, and when we couldn't see her, the parrot obliged us by flying up high enough to see her, and then flew down to point her direction.

Miles we traveled until we could see the towers of

Bambole in the distance to our left, above the tall trees of the forest that encircled it. To our right, we saw the thick, low trees of the swamp, from which a reek of mold and mustiness seeped. When we could, we ran, and when we finally topped the last rise, we stopped, stunned by the horror.

Below us, in a low field dotted with wide, craggy trees, lay a graveyard ... with hundreds of little mounds, and some not so little. Each was arranged in an orderly fashion, covering every inch of boggy grass, filling a large area. At the farthest end, a huge tree grew adjacent to the swamp, half upon the moist ground, and the other half growing out of the filthy waters of the swamp. Beside its gnarly trunk rested a black iron cauldron upon cold but blackened logs and ashes. A wide lid covered the cauldron.

As I watched, Mom lifted the lid and drew from its insides a long-handled ladle with a tiny, deep spoon on its end. Scooping up whatever broth had been brewed inside the cauldron, Mom lifted the ladle to her lips and drank deeply. Then she returned the ladle, replaced the lid, and walked to a space beside a large grave. She laid down upon the low, mossy grass beside it.

Alarm grew in my heart, and I rushed forward, calling for her. Her head lifted, and she looked at me, but she didn't rise. Suddenly the parrot flew past me, and I heard the others chasing me, calling my name, but I couldn't stop; *I needed my mother ...!*

The parrot landed beside her, and I ran up and fell to my knees on the muddy ground beside it.

"Mom ...!" I cried, and she slowly opened her eyes.

"Hilary ... my baby ...," Mom whispered weakly. "You ... must ... keep ... jumping ..."

"Mom!" I shouted, grabbing her arm and shaking

her.

Mom's eyes closed and she sighed heavily. As the others ran up behind me, her eyes fluttered open briefly, but she couldn't seem to speak, lost in a weary haze. At last she passed out ...

"What's wrong with her?" I demanded.

"She drank ... whatever's in that cauldron," Mrs. Darby said.

"Poison ...?" Falcon asked.

"I doubt it," Muskay said, and suddenly we all became aware of all the strange noises around us.

"What's that?" Princess Gracely asked, looking about.

"I know that sound," Mrs. Darby said. "It's ... snoring."

"Snoring ...?" Falcon asked.

One of the loudest noises was coming from the grave beside Mom. I stepped to it, looked at it carefully, and then realized what I was seeing. Cautiously I reached my hand towards it, touched the slimy mound with one finger, and pushed a swipe of it away. Where I'd disturbed the filth, where my finger had swiped the muck aside, I clearly saw ... human flesh.

"It's Hiram!" I exclaimed.

Quickly I used my fingers to wipe away as much of the slime and dirt as I could, exposing Hiram's face. He never awakened, but he snored even louder, and we poked and shook him. Muskay even slapped his face, but nothing we could do would awaken him.

"This must be ...!" Mrs. Darby knelt down next to the large grave on the other side of Hiram and wiped the dirt and slime from the shape hidden just under it. As she did, Princess Gracely bit back a startled scream; the aged face of Great Aunt Virginia lay underneath the thin layer of filth, sleeping much more silently than Hiram.

"They're ... lightly covered in dirt ... buried!" Falcon gasped.

"Yes, but they're alive," Muskay said.

"It must be whatever's in that cauldron," Princess Gracely said.

"We should dump it out, into the swamp," Mrs. Darby said. "Without it, the voodoo doll won't be able to make any more dolls vanish."

"I'll do it," Muskay said, and with determined steps, he walked straight to the cauldron, and not only tilted it over, but pushed the cauldron itself over the edge until it splashed loudly into the green, oily waters and sank out of view.

"That should damage the voodoo doll's plan," Princess Gracely said.

"Why can't I awaken her?" I asked.

"It could be magic ... or a drug," Mrs. Darby said.

"Perhaps the jump rope ...?" Princess Gracely suggested.

I pulled out the jump rope and began to jump at once.

> *"Awaken Mom!*
> *Awaken all!*
> *Open your eyes!*
> *Heed my call!*
> *Now is not the time to sleep!*
> *Now is not the time to weep!*
> *No more dreamland!*
> *Wake and stand!*
> *Arise! Arise!*
> *Open your eyes!"*

Gold and silver sparkles grew upon my cord, and the dark graves under the trees illuminated, but no movement showed. I kept jumping, doing lots of tricks to enhance my chant, but nothing helped. Hiram and the others kept snoring.

"Hilary, you can stop," Mrs. Darby finally said. "It's not working."

"It has to!" I said. "My magic ... my jump rope ...!"

"I suspect it would've worked, but don't forget ... the voodoo doll has a jump rope, too." Mrs. Darby said.

"Audrey ...?" Princess Gracely asked.

"It must be," Mrs. Darby said, and she reached out to a small grave and swiped a finger lightly over the filth of a small mound, revealing the closed eyes of a marionette. "Luckily, it doesn't look like any of them have been harmed. They're just asleep, and they must be safe here or the voodoo doll wouldn't have put them here."

"But ... we can't leave them here!" I said. "This is my Mom ...!"

"How are you going to carry her?" Mrs. Darby asked. "Look at all of them; they've been sprinkled with just enough slime to make them look buried, but none are truly dead."

"But ... why?" Princess Gracely asked. "Why would the voodoo doll do this to them?"

"When we find her, I'll ask her," I said. "Of course, if I get my hands on a lollipop, I might just get suddenly hungry ...!"

"Hilary, control your temper," Mrs. Darby said. "You can't get angry ... because we can't save anyone without you."

I exhaled deeply, frustrated, but trying to restrain myself.

"I know," I said to Mrs. Darby. "But ... what now? Do we uncover them all ... or do we leave them?"

"I think we should cover them back up ... and leave

them here," Mrs. Darby said. "This ... graveyard ...
seems to be like a safe zone, in a game, where you can't
be tagged. We know they're safe here, but if we try to
take them elsewhere, then we don't know what effect
that will have."

"I agree," Muskay said.

"So do I," Falcon insisted. "We should leave them ...
and save ourselves!"

"We're not abandoning anyone," Mrs. Darby said.
"We'll be back ... and rescue everyone."

"Let's cover them back up," Princess Gracely said.

"Either they'll awaken after we capture the voodoo
queen or we'll force her to tell us how to awaken them,"
Muskay said.

"How?" I asked.

"Either the jump rope will force her or we'll leave her
outside, without a hat, in the rain," Muskay said.
"Lollipops don't last long in the rain."

"We'll do no such thing," Mrs. Darby said. "The
fastest way for evil to win is to allow it to make good
people do evil things."

"I won't participate in such an act," Princess Gracely
said.

"Even I wouldn't do that," Falcon admitted.

"Muskay, imagination is a great gift but yours goes too
far," I said.

"Every creative genius has suffered that criticism,"
Muskay sniffed.

"Enough nonsense," Mrs. Darby said. "We have new
clues to consider ... and we shouldn't debate them
anywhere so open. Cover their faces back up, and
Hilary, you can jump us ... back to ... *you know-where.*"

Reluctantly, as he snored, I pushed the slime back
over Hiram's face, making sure not to plug his noisy

nostrils.

"What about Mom?" I asked.

"Someone has been coming out here to cover them up," Mrs. Darby said. "Chances are it's not the voodoo doll but another victim she's possessed. No doubt they'll come soon and care for Madge."

"But ... then they'll see the missing cauldron," Muskay said.

"True, but there's nothing we can do about it now," Mrs. Darby said.

"What can I do?" the parrot asked.

"We need to make everyone aware of what's happened," Mrs. Darby said. "You need to visit your friends in the woods, and all the other doll villages, and tell everyone what we've learned."

"I can do that," the parrot promised.

"Go now, before we leave," Mrs. Darby said. "I want to see you successfully escape."

With a nod, the parrot spread its colorful wings, flapped brightly, and flew off, low over the hills we'd crossed. He sailed over the grasses and vanished behind the slopes. I hoped I'd see him again ... but my hope was fading as my anger grew.

The Heart of Play

Chapter 17

Where Logic Fails

Staring about at all the slimy mounds in the graveyard, I lifted up the jump rope.

"Time for us to go ... where we should've gone in the first place," I said.

"Where?" Princess Gracely asked.

I didn't bother to answer her. I knew I was angry, letting my temper rise, but I was tired of this.

> *"Take us to the voodoo doll!*
> *Wherever she may hide!*
> *Take us to the voodoo doll!*
> *Let us be at her side!*
> *In her secret place*
> *Let us see her true face*
> *Find the enemy we know!*
> *Our worst and most-maddening foe!"*

The sparkles came slowly, but I kept jumping rope, and finally their twinkles swarmed over me. I kept jumping until my glowing sphere expanded, and everyone stepped inside. All had worried looks but I didn't care; I was furious ... and determined.

It was time to end this!

The strain was great, but finally the graveyard by the swamp faded away. We appeared beside a stream, upon a hillside of flowers, and many of the colorful blossoms were moving. Two familiar marble doors stood three feet tall atop a miniature stone stairs, buried into the side of a hill with countless tiny, dark, round, overgrown windows and doors tunneled into the ground.

"Troll Hill ...?" Muskay exclaimed. "We were just here!"

"Look around," Mrs. Darby said. "Maybe she's here ..."

"Maybe the trolls would know," Princess Gracely said, and she walked over and bent down to look at several troll dolls, visible mostly by their bright, tall tufts of hair. "Hello. Forgive me for interrupting your game. Have you seen any strange dolls around here?"

The troll dolls all looked surprised and every one of them shook their heads.

We wandered around the hill, looking into the many holes in the ground, all of which led to tiny troll houses. We kicked back the tall grasses, making sure that nothing was hiding underneath. Muskay jumped over the wide, fast-moving stream beside Troll Hill, careful not to fall into the white-water, and searched the far side. Falcon tried to search the Hall of the Trolls, and Princess Gracely and Mrs. Darby make him climb out of it.

We found nothing. She wasn't there.

"Take us back," Mrs. Darby said. "There's nothing we can do here."

We arrived at the Factory dispirited, fewer than we'd been when we'd left. I felt terrible; I'd come to rescue Audrey, and now I'd lost Mom, Great Aunt Virginia, and Hiram. I may be an expert jumper but I was a poor protector ... of the dolls or anyone else. In my hand I held my jump rope, and I was in Arcadia; I had the power to do almost anything. But Audrey had a jump rope, too, and where powers balanced, it all came down to the mind.

"Let's consider the clues again," I said.

"Why?" Falcon asked. "We've already ...!"

"Then we do it again!" I shouted.

"Hilary, lower your voice, or once your mother comes back I'll tell her about your outbursts," Mrs. Darby said. "We're all tired and frustrated. We mustn't let a bad situation make us behave poorly."

"That's true," Princess Gracely said. "Friendships can endure anything if both are patient and forgiving."

"And fed," Mrs. Darby said. "We have to return home for the night and start again in the morning."

"First, the clues ...!" I insisted.

"Well, we found the graveyard," Muskay said. "Madge was right; nobody was dead."

"We know where all the vanished dolls ended up ... and where we might be going," Falcon grumbled.

"We dumped her cauldron so we may not be going there soon," Mrs. Darby said.

"We know why the paper dolls were able to escape," Princess Gracely said. "Obviously the voodoo doll is careful not to harm her victims, and burying paper dolls under damp slime would quickly destroy them."

"That makes sense," Mrs. Darby said.

"We still have the tall, thin barrel and the stolen bellows," Muskay said. "We don't know why she wanted them."

"Or what liquid she'd be pumping into the barrel," Falcon said.

"Or ... she could be storing the liquid inside the barrel ... and using the bellows to pump it out," I said.

"Why would she do that?" Princess Gracely asked.

"No idea," I said. "I'm just trying to think of every possibility ..."

"Consider the possibility that we'll never figure it out ...," Falcon began.

"No more of that!" I shouted.

"Most of the generals have been taken from the wooden fort of the tin soldiers," Muskay said.

"And the six stick-ponies," Mrs. Darby said. "Why seahorses, I wonder ...?"

"Seahorses could pull a boat," Muskay said.

"The flying glamour dolls searched the creeks, the shores, and the swamp," Princess Gracely said. "No one has seen any boats."

"We still don't know why she wanted a topographic map." I said.

"We should visit Mr. Magee and Judy at The Palace tomorrow," Mrs. Darby said. "We've told everyone to send messages to them. Perhaps news has arrived that we don't know."

"Why don't we go tonight?" I asked.

"Because you're tired," Mrs. Darby said. "Audrey could come after us at any moment, and we can't afford for you to face her exhausted."

"I can't leave my Mom ...!" I shouted.

"What would your mother say if she were here now?" Mrs. Darby asked. "First, she'd tell you to stop shouting, and then she'd insist you act intelligently, not blunder around too tired to think clearly."

"All right!" I shouted, and then I lowered my voice. "All right ... just give a few moments .... I need to think."

More than a few moments passed. I stared at the darkening windows, at the closed door, and at the wall against which the glamour dolls, freed of their mesmerized hold, had hurled Punch. That battle had seemed so simple, so direct ... why did my first solo challenge in Arcadia, as the only jumper, have to be so difficult? Punch had his own body, so once we saw him, we could fight him. The voodoo doll was using our friends as her shields.

What were we going to do?
How could we fight her?
Where was her secret lair?

Muskay went downstairs and returned with a bottle of cider, and Princess Gracely scolded him for not bringing glasses for everyone. She went downstairs, returned with a tray of glasses, and started to pour for all five of us. I refused mine, too upset to drink, and Mrs. Darby announced it was time we returned for the evening, and then she went to look out the front door. Falcon tried to leave several times, but Muskay and Princess Gracely made him stay.

Mrs. Darby didn't return right away, and suddenly we heard a banging, as if someone were slapping their hand against the wooden floor. We ran into the outer room ... and Princess Gracely screamed.

On the floor, halfway across the hall, Mrs. Darby lay thrashing, clutching her throat with one hand and with her other slapping the floor to gain our attention. She looked frantic, eyes bulging, teeth gritted.

"The voodoo doll!" Muskay cried. *"She's taking Charlotte!"*

I pulled out my jump rope as we ran to her and

started jumping the last few steps. My blue cord sparkled at once and I pressed harder; *Mrs. Darby couldn't jump with me!* I had to expand it over her quickly, before ....!

Mrs. Darby quit thrashing, quit writhing, and a wide grin broke out on her face. I paled and felt like someone had kicked me in the stomach.

I was too late ...!

Inside the body of Mrs. Darby, the voodoo doll arose and looked around.

"Where is this place?" the voodoo doll asked, not bothering to use Mrs. Darby's voice. "This isn't Bambole ... oh, it must be the Factory. I heard how Punch was defeated here ... by his own wife, the fool jester. Too bad; if he'd won then I'd only have needed to possess him."

"You can't escape us forever," I said. "When we find you ...!"

"Stupid jumper, you've already lost," the voodoo doll said. "I am the new queen of Arcadia and I'll crush your resistance with ease."

"You haven't crushed us yet," Muskay snarled, stepping forward to stand beside me. "You never will ...!"

"Another dumb jester," the voodoo doll sneered at Muskay.

"You like insulting people," I said to the voodoo doll. "The worst insult of all would be ... to be you."

"I'm the best doll ever," the voodoo doll snarled.

"You're a coward!" I shouted. "You fight through others because you're too afraid to face me yourself!"

"I'm smarter than you are, too," the voodoo doll said. "I'm not going to let you goad me into taking unnecessary risks. I devised my plan of conquest very carefully, and I'm not going to deviate from it now.

Once I have all the dolls, then I'll be all-powerful, stronger even than two jumpers."

With a wicked laugh, Mrs. Darby rose, turned and walked toward the door.

I stood stunned, unknowing what to do. She was going to the graveyard ... or someplace worse. *I couldn't stop Mrs. Darby ... any more than I could stop Mom.*

Still laughing, the voodoo doll stepped outside and closed the door behind her, blocking our last view of Mrs. Darby.

She was gone.

I stood still, my teeth gritted.

"Stand back!" I snapped.

"What are you doing?" Princess Gracely asked.

"I'm going after Audrey," I said. "The voodoo doll is inside Mrs. Darby, and the ancient ones said she could only possess one body at a time. She might be headed to the graveyard, or Bambole, but it doesn't matter. It'll take her a while to get wherever she's going, and if I can get to Audrey now, while she's not possessed, then I may be able to free her."

"We'll come, too!" Muskay said.

"No, it might be a trap," I said. "She's sure to have planned for it. She somehow prevented us from jumping to her, and we bounced to Troll Hill instead. Wherever I arrive, I'll be tired. If I can't free Audrey then I'll fade ... and go back home. If that happens, I'll return in the morning, and we'll continue the fight."

"Hilary, this is dangerous," Princess Gracely warned. "Neither your mother nor Mrs. Darby would approve."

"They're gone, so that doesn't matter," I said.

> *"Audrey, Audrey. Jumper and friend*
> *To wherever you are my will bend*
> *Audrey, Audrey, to you I fly*

Audrey, Audrey, do or die!"

Disapproving expressions shined from the faces of Muskay, Princess Gracely, and Falcon as the sparkles of my jump rope grew denser, and slowly they faded away.

I appeared inside a room I recognized, the same dimly-lit room in which King Andy and Queen Anne had been imprisoned. Their chains were back, hanging empty, but Audrey was there, slumped onto the floor by the wall. I hurried to her and found her unconscious. To my dismay, her hands were shackled by heavy iron cuffs.

I felt terrible. We hadn't spoken in months, and the last time she'd tried to talk to me I'd threatened her and ordered her to leave me alone. Yet I never really imagined seeing her hurt, helpless, and I regretted everything I'd said.

"Audrey!" I hissed. "Audrey, wake up!"

I grabbed her arm and shook her. Her chains rattled loudly.

"Audrey!" I hissed again.

I shook her harder and lightly slapped her face. She never awoke, just like Mom in the graveyard, which was the worst happenstance; this meant the cauldron that Muskay had rolled into the swamp wasn't the voodoo doll's only supply of that evil brew.

"Audrey, please ...!" I implored. "I'm sorry ... sorry we ever argued, sorry that we fought! Audrey, please wake up!"

Audrey slept on.

I had only one hope. I lifted my jump rope and began jumping.

"Chains off! Hands free!
By my command, release Audrey!"

My chant was simple, too simple, yet I was desperate and too upset to invent anything more powerful. My gold and silver sparkles illuminated the whole room, and then I heard a sound.

"What's that slapping noise?" a deep voice shouted.

"Look! Light under the door!" another voice shouted.

"Unlock that door!"

"Where's the key?"

I jumped harder and faster, doing tricks, desperate to hurry. Once they came in I'd have to fight them, and I couldn't do that and free Audrey.

Audrey's shackles clicked open just as five guards burst inside.

"You're too late!" I shouted.

I stopped jumping, making my sparkles fade. As they lowered their weapons, I knelt down and grabbed Audrey.

"Home!" I whispered softly, willing us away with all of my heart. *"Mama, I want to go home!"*

As the guards charged us, the light suddenly dimmed and Arcadia faded away.

I opened my eyes. I was back in Great Aunt Virginia's apartment, kneeling on the hard red cushions of her couch. However, my arms were empty. I'd escaped from Arcadia, but I hadn't managed to bring Audrey with me.

Again, I'd failed.

Chapter 18

Alone with Regret

I climbed off Great Aunt Virginia's couch, careful not to upset the small table. I was furious but certain that, if I broke the magic tea set, then I'd never get back into Arcadia. Yet the silence of her apartment was unnerving.

In my bedroom, back in my parent's condo, it was never quiet. If you listened carefully you could always hear the footsteps in the apartment above us, the muted murmur of a television on too loud, or perhaps some music or a loud argument. Not a sound came from Great Aunt Virginia's apartment, not a pop or creak, not even the wind rattling the window panes. The other apartments might well have been empty, and even the sounds of cars failed to rise from the street outside.

The magic of Great Aunt Virginia's home was unnerving.

I'd always thought I'd love the absence of annoying distractions, yet this harmonious atmosphere was part of the magic of a woman who could cause roses to bloom, locked doors to open, and carry pitchers of iced tea around inside a carpet bag, traveling from one building to another, without spilling.

Great Aunt Virginia suddenly seemed unexpectedly intimidating.

It wasn't the magic ... or the quiet ... or the mystery. When alone, missing the companionship of people who you feared might soon be gone forever, the haunting silence denied you the distractions to draw you from your fears.

I hadn't awakened Audrey ... or brought her here. I'd lost Mom, and been unable to rescue her from the graveyard. I'd lost Mrs. Darby, and if anything happened to her then Audrey would never forgive me. *I'd failed at everything!*

I sat and stared at the stuffed dolls of Hiram, Muskay, and Princess Gracely. Slowly I pulled Hiram from his chair and hugged the plush teddy bear as if he were the Hiram I knew. *I'd failed Hiram!* Then I snatched up Muskay and Princess Gracely, who were both in Arcadia, at risk of being taken, and there was nothing I could do but hug them.

Unable to sit still, I arranged Muskay, Princess Gracely, and Hiram side-by-side on the couch, and then I stepped into the kitchen. I was hungry, but I didn't know if I could eat a bite. I opened the refrigerator and found little I recognized, but under a covering of tin foil I found a single slice of the pizza left over from last night. Yet Great Aunt Virginia didn't have a microwave and I'd never used a gas stove or oven. I pulled it out, set it on the table, and sat to eat it. No soda or bottled water were in her refrigerator, so I got a small glass from a cabinet and filled it with water from the sink. The cold pizza tasted like it always did, neither delicious nor exciting.

After eating, I washed my plate and glass and left them to dry in the rack; Great Aunt Virginia's wasn't the kind of place where you left dirty dishes in the sink.

I felt lonely. Our condo was much larger than Great Aunt Virginia's apartment but it seemed like a huge, empty museum. I walked along the bookshelves, looking at all the tiny dolls and statues that cluttered them, wondering if some small child had once cherished each, and if they were all in Arcadia ... or in some other realm of the magic land. I searched everywhere, peeking into each door. Great Aunt Virginia's bedroom looked as prim and proper as she did, her antique sled-framed bed looking newly polished and oiled. Mrs. Darby's guest room was larger than mine, with a four-poster bed of a wood so dark it was almost black. To my surprise, Mom's guest room was just as large, with a brightly-painted white canopy bed, clearly visible through translucent veil-curtains. Every bed was made, had thick pillows, and was laden with stuffed animals. I paused at my own bedroom door, then opened it and looked inside. Everything was the same as always, except my stuffed animals were spread out over my bed ... and their bodies spelled out the word 'Hope'. I rushed in and picked them all up, hugged them as one huge pile in my arms, and then carefully set them back, only this time, I left them spelling out the word 'Love'.

I was doing this all wrong. *Arcadia was a game that never ended, and as long as I kept playing eventually I'd win.* I had to keep thinking that. I couldn't allow sadness and despair to take me into a depression I couldn't fight my way out of ... in Arcadia ... or in Great Aunt Virginia's apartment.

I walked back into the living room. There were no

computers or televisions in Great Aunt Virginia's apartment, but that didn't mean there was nothing to do. I just had to provide the creativity I normally expected of my electronic toys. I looked at Hiram, Muskay, and Princess Gracely.

"So good to see you all together," I said. "That's how you should be. I wish I knew where Falcon was ... it'd be nice to have him here, too."

The first *'ping!'* startled me, and I jumped a little, but quickly I recognized Great Aunt Virginia's favorite music box, which had started all by itself. It tinkled a merry tune, the only noise in the apartment, and I forced myself to keep breathing normally. If a simple mechanical device had started on its own in our condo, or in school, or anywhere else, I'd have been frightened, but Great Aunt Virginia's apartment had always seemed to be a part of Arcadia. I just had to ... *but could I ...?*

"I'm still hungry ... and thirsty," I announced to all the dolls, and then I casually walked into the kitchen. I wasn't alone; I was surrounded by friends, most of whom I could play with in Arcadia, if not for the current crisis. I wasn't in danger here. I didn't need to surrender to fear; part of the worlds we live in, even the real world, was based on our attitudes, our outlooks, and our expectations.

With a smile, I opened the refrigerator, unsurprised to see it full. A huge salad filled a wooden bowl, lettuce and spinach leaves topped with cucumber, olives, carrot-shavings, croutons, strings of white and yellow cheese, and diced almonds. Beside it rested a tall, full pitcher of iced lemonade. On another shelf was a plate of fried chicken legs, a bowl of mashed potatoes, and what looked like coleslaw. Many dishes were covered in aluminum foil, and the vegetable bin that had been empty lay stuffed with large tomatoes, yellow squash, carrots with long greens sticking out of them, and unshucked corn.

Grinning ear-to-ear, I fetched a plate and took out two cold chicken legs and covered the rest of my plate with salad. I considered turning on the stove to heat the chicken but I didn't want to push my luck. I chose one of six matching glass jars in the refrigerator door, each hand labeled with the type of salad dressing in it. I chose 'sweet fennel seed', and it was delicious. The lemonade had slices of real lemon in it, and it was sweet, yet made my mouth pucker. The chicken was delicious, with a thin powdery crust and cooked to perfection. I feasted on the best cold supper I'd ever eaten, and I was delightfully full before I was done.

After I washed my dishes, I came back into the living room to find a book sitting in Princess Gracely's lap, The Jungle Book, which I'd stopped reading when Mom had sent me to bed. Hiram's teddy bear head was leaning on her right shoulder, Muskay on her left, with one bell of his tri-pointed jester's cap pressed against her ceramic cheek. I took the hint, and slid the book from them, and then arranged them back in their chairs around the table, facing me. Then I sat center on the red-cushioned couch and read to them of Mowgli and the Bandar-log, surprised that the monkey-people in the book weren't as nice as Disney had made them, and Ka the rock-python was much more sophisticated and powerful. I enjoyed how the book delved much deeper into the philosophies of survival, the complex 'Jungle Rules' of which the animated version shared only a few.

Soon I found myself yawning and I knew I had to be rested in the morning. Closing the book, I said goodnight to all the dolls, and kissed Princess Gracely,

Hiram, and Muskay on the tops of their heads before I went to brush my teeth.

On my bed, my stuffed animals lay arranged forming one word: 'Trust'.

Bad dreams tormented my rest. All I had left to help me was a handful of dolls. If I couldn't find a way to stop the voodoo doll today, then chances were the Arcadia I loved would be gone forever, along with Mom, Audrey, Mrs. Darby, and Great Aunt Virginia. I got up early, bathed and brushed my teeth, and went out to the living room. I wished Hiram, Princess Gracely, Muskay, and all the other dolls a good morning, and then stepped into the kitchen. I paused and filled my mind with good thoughts before I opened the refrigerator, and inside I found fresh milk, a bowl of cold grits, cooked sausages, and baked scones with many flavors of jams and butter.

After breakfast I had to try lighting the stove. As Mom had, I lit the match and held it next to the burners, then slowly turned on the gas. The fire suddenly ignited, and I blew out the match, set it on a plate, then filled the metal teapot with water and set it atop the little blue and orange flames. While it was heating, I chose and ground some herbs and spices in the pestle with the mortar, glad Great Aunt Virginia had taught me how to make tea. When the water started to boil turned off the stove and watched until every little flame died. Then I filled the ceramic teapot, blew upon my powdery tea, careful to follow every step of the process, and sprinkled my ground tea into the steaming pot.

Using an oven mitt, I carried the steaming teapot into the living room and set it on a hot pad between Hiram and Muskay. Then I sat on the red cushions of the couch, a little intimidated. I knew the process we always used to enter Arcadia but I'd never done this on my own. I was worried it wouldn't work.

I glanced at my doll friends, not knowing what to say. Petty compliments and pointless conversations didn't seem appropriate. I didn't know what to say. I wrapped my jump rope over my shoulders and sat fretting.

Could I get into Arcadia alone?

"Muskay, Hiram, Princess Gracely ... I need you," I said to the dolls. "I'm scared. I know Arcadia's a game, but I miss my Mom, Great Aunt Virginia, Mrs. Darby, and even Audrey. I've never felt this much responsibility ... and I'm worried I might fail. I don't know what to do. I can't find the voodoo doll, and I can't fight those she's possessing. No matter what I do, I'm wrong!"

No fake eyelash twitched. No plastic arm bent. No cloth smile widened. Hiram, Muskay, and Princess Gracely sat unmoving ... like all dolls in the real world. I felt foolish. Moments passed by, and I knew I should be making witty and flowery compliments ... but my fear was overwhelming my joy ... even my joy of visiting Arcadia.

The tea slowly steeped, and finally I stood up, poured four tiny cups, and sat back down.

"I know you can hear me," I said softly, almost a whisper, my glance switching back and forth to each of my doll-friends. "I need to go back, and I've never felt so reluctant. So much is expected of me, and if I can't ... do everything I must ...?"

I sipped my tea; it was too sweet; too much mint and cinnamon. I didn't like my choices of herbs ... or maybe my distaste for responsibility was seeping into everything. I wasn't fond of work, but I'd always known that my goals and ambitions were lofty, and competition for celebrity was fierce. Attaining even the slightest notoriety required immense effort ... meeting and conquering challenges that daunted most people. Yet I'd never realized how difficult, or how much fear, paved the roads to lofty ambitions. I couldn't stop; even if I could surrender my lifelong dreams, I couldn't abandon my Mom and friends, not to mention every doll of Arcadia.

I blew upon my tea to cool it and then drank deeply. I wanted to swallow as much as I could, since I had no idea how long I'd be in Arcadia this time ... or if I'd ever get to enter it again. Yet, as my cup slowly emptied, I felt no tingle.

"Please, I must go," I begged the dolls of Hiram, Muskay, and Princess Gracely. "I can't leave my Mom and friends under control of ... that treacherous, evil queen. I need them. I ... I love them."

The tingles rose and the dizziness returned. I closed my eyes, feeling the same vertigo I always felt, but I felt something else, something soft and comforting. I opened my blurry eyes, and there before me stood Hiram, Muskay, and Princess Gracely, in their doll-forms, standing before me, their arms held out. With tears in my eyes, I wrapped all three in my arms, hugging them tightly, feeling the love and warmth we shared.

I blinked wetly, and when I opened my eyes, my arms were empty ... and I was in Arcadia.

I was alone. I was in the main room of the Factory, staring at its empty stone floor, high, thin windows beaming in morning sunlight, and at its arched wooden ceiling crisscrossed with dark wooden rafters.

Where was everyone? Had they all been captured? Were they all possessed?

"Muskay ...?" I called, stepping backwards toward the door. "Princess Gracely ...? Falcon ...?"

I stepped back against the door, reached for the handle, and was about to flee outside when I heard a soft whisper.

"Hilary ...?"

Princess Gracely peeked around the corner. Her beautiful face was even paler, and never had I seen her more afraid.

"Princess Gracely!" I exclaimed, wondering why she was moving so slowly.

"We lost Muskay," Princess Gracely confessed. "She took him early this morning."

"Where's Falcon?" I asked.

"He's run off," Princess Gracely stepped out, looking cautiously around. "I told him to ... for all our sakes."

"Why?" I asked.

"The map we got from Madam Paprus," Princess Gracely said.

"The topographical map?" I asked.

"Muskay wanted it," Princess Gracely said. "He demanded it. He threatened to murder Falcon and I if we didn't give him the map ..."

"Why did he want it?" I asked.

"Muskay didn't want it; the voodoo doll did," Princess Gracely said.

"There must be something on it she needs ... or she doesn't want us to know about," I said. "Did she get it?"

"No," Princess Gracely said. "I managed to trap Muskay in a giant rhinestone, gave the map the Falcon, and told him to run off and take it far away."

"What happened to Muskay?" I asked.

"I couldn't keep him imprisoned," Princess Gracely said. "If the voodoo doll left him, trapped in my rhinestone, then I didn't know what would've happened. I gave Falcon enough time to get away, and then I released him. The voodoo doll called me many impolite names ..."

"She does like to insult people," I said.

"Finally she ran off ... Muskay's body ran off, ruled by her, I mean," Princess Gracely said. "I couldn't stop him ... her ..."

"We need to find Falcon," I said. "We need to make sure he's safe, and I want to see that map again."

Princess Gracely rushed to me and hugged me tightly.

"Hilary, I'm scared," Princess Gracely said. "I've never seen Arcadia so close to being lost forever."

"We can't let that happen," I said, and I pulled my jump rope off my shoulder.

It took me ten minutes to devise a chant even with Princess Gracely helping. Audrey and Muskay were best at making up rhymes, and we struggled without them. Creating decent chants took lots of concentration, and worry diffused my focus. I wanted a simple chant, but Princess Gracely confirmed that simple chants required harder jumping and would tire me out faster; the more complete our chant the easier my jumping would be. Finally we agreed on a chant.

"Falcon, Falcon, wherever you hide,
Falcon, Falcon, where you reside,
Across Arcadia let us look,
No delay our search will brook,
Take us, take us, into your view,
Falcon, Falcon, we jump to you!"

Princess Gracely stood outside my flipping rope as my sparkles began, and by my fourth recitation gold and silver flashes expanded. Princess Gracely carried herself so smoothly and gracefully I had no doubt she could jump inside my rope with me, but her wide, many-layered white dress, which I thought looked more like an elegant ball gown than a wedding dress, would foul my flipping cord. However, as my sparkling sphere expanded to include her, I felt the familiar strain and pushed harder.

The solid walls around us began to fade.

Blue sky appeared overhead and grasses grew at my feet. Princess Gracely and I were standing in a wide field surrounded by trees. I glanced in every direction; I'd never seen this part of Arcadia.

"I know this place," Princess Gracely said. "Muskay, Hiram, and I once hid in a trench over there, all night long. Great Aunt Virginia sent us here and set us to watch until she and Audrey could join us."

I knew this story; I glanced around, seeing the sole tree with the wide, dark shadow at its base.

"That's it, isn't it?" I asked. "That's the hollow tree where the rag dolls left their glittery fabrics for Punch, and you watched while the glamour dolls collected them ...?"

"Let's examine it," Princess Gracely smiled.

In the morning light we marched across the grassy field to the hollow tree. Its trunk was wide, its branches long and tall, and we circled it to look straight inside its opening.

Heavily shadowed, Falcon sat inside the narrow, dark gap, looking frightened. Yet, when he saw us, relief washed over his features.

"Here's the map," Falcon said, holding up the rolled paper. "Take it."

"Come out of there," Princess Gracely ordered.

"It's safe in here!" Falcon objected.

"We need you," Princess Gracely said.

"Do you really think the voodoo doll won't find you in there?" I asked.

Falcon's eyes widened and a shudder shook his frame. Princess Gracely and I exchanged exasperated looks. Together we reached inside and pulled Falcon out.

"You don't need me!" Falcon cried. "I did my part!"

"Our duty isn't done," Princess Gracely said. "Arcadia isn't free."

"Arcadia isn't safe!" Falcon insisted.

"Once we've done our duty, it will be," Princess Gracely said.

When Falcon was standing beside us under the wide limbs, I took the map from his hands and unrolled it, staring at it. It was very detailed; scarcely an inch wasn't covered with thin lines, listing numeric elevations, with the cities and villages of Arcadia clearly labeled. Each hill, forest, stream, and lake was marked, the waters shaded as if by pencil, with thin lines inside them. Little drawings were all over it, marking the inhabitants; a tiny marionette hanging by strings from a cross-brace by Theater City, a small likeness of Mr. Magee by The Palace, and a sketch of Mistress Flax beside the village of the rag dolls. Raggedy Anne and Andy, each with a tiny crown, was drawn beside Bambole, the largest city by far. Only empty space marked the locations of Sparkle City, the new home of the glamour dolls, and the Factory, neither of which had existed when the map was drawn. Many stuffed animals of diverse types were depicted in the deep woods, save for the Aging Forest and the swamp behind Bambole, which all dolls avoided.

Yet no clue was obvious as to why the voodoo doll had desperately wanted this map.

"Can you see anything?" I asked Princess Gracely and Falcon. "Why did Muskay want the map?"

Princess Gracely and Falcon looked over my

shoulders, scrutinizing the map.

"I see nothing unexpected," Princess Gracely said.

"I wonder who did this survey?" Falcon asked.

"These lands exist in your world, too," Princess Gracely said. "The elevations were probably copied from a map created there, with the cities of the dolls added."

"What are these?" Hilary asked, pointing at a circle of teepees in a forest to the south, below the wide lake. Beside them was drawn a strange doll I'd never seen.

"Anelodi," Princess Gracely said. "That's the Cherokee word meaning 'doll'. Anelodi was the village of the cornhusk dolls."

"Cornhusk dolls were made of the dried leaves of corn and favored by the children of American Indians," Falcon said. "Wonderful dolls, but the War of the Changebots rolled over their village and set it afire. Cornhusk dolls couldn't extinguish it, not without catching fire themselves, and so they left Arcadia to form a land of their own in secret, safe from the rest of us."

"That was many years ago," Princess Gracely said. "We miss them terribly, but respect their wish to live apart."

"They weren't the only ones to leave Arcadia," Falcon said. "Some of the ancient ones are paddle dolls. They had a village, too, with a great pyramid." Falcon pointed to an unmarked triangle on the map. "Paddle dolls came from ancient Egypt, but their city was destroyed long ago, when Great Aunt Annie was a child, before Great Aunt Virginia was born. Only a brick pyramid remains, and a thick forest has grown up around it."

"Not many paddle dolls remain," Princess Gracely said. "They're some of the oldest dolls to ever exist."

"What other kinds of dolls are there?" I asked.

"Oh, many kinds," Falcon said. "If you travel outside of Arcadia, you'll meet dolls you never imagined."

"Apple dolls never settled in Arcadia, but some have visited here," Princess Gracely said. "They have various kinds of bodies, from wooden to cloth, but their heads are made of dried apples, carved to show a face."

"Peg dolls dwell far away, in a place that you'd call the Netherlands," Falcon said. "Parian dolls are made of the purest white porcelain and mostly live in Germany."

"Where do voodoo dolls come from?" I asked.

"Their origin is as mysterious as they are," Princess Gracely said. "Many reports of them originate from regions you would call Haiti and Louisiana, yet there are older reports of them from Britain and other, more-distant lands."

"Voodoo dolls were made by wicked people ... for evil purposes," Falcon said, his voice fearful. "Such folk seldom leave records of their nefarious deeds."

"We must find the voodoo doll," I said. "Could she be at one of these ancient doll cities?"

"We could go to each and look, if you'd like, but there's little to see," Princess Gracely said. "The pyramid is a solid stack of bricks, about three feet tall, surrounded by deep forest. Anelodi is an empty glade; nothing of it survived the fire."

"Nevertheless, they're the only clues we haven't investigated," I said. "We can't discount them."

"We can't waste the time!" Falcon said. "Princess Gracely and I; how long before we're taken, too?"

"I'm open to ideas," I said.

"Here's an idea: flee ... while we can," Falcon said.

"We can't abandon our friends!" Princess Gracely scolded him.

"Then we'll join them ... in the graveyard," Falcon

warned. "How much help will we be then ...?"

"Let's try the pyramid first," I said. "Maybe it's not solid. Maybe there's a lair inside it."

I took out the jump rope, invented a chant, and prepared to bounce us there.

"To the farthest north we must go
Where paddle-dolls dwelt long ago
To forest deep, now empty
To the lost village, we must see
Pyramid! Pyramid! We jump to you!
Here we come to seek a clue!"

Journeying with only two others was less taxing than when I'd been carrying Great Aunt Virginia, Mom, Mrs. Darby, and all four doll-friends, yet it wasn't easy, probably because my chant had been too simple. We appeared in a tiny, overgrown glade with low tree branches reaching towards us, my jump rope slapping their leafless ends as my sparkles faded. Princess Gracely ducked, pulling the fine weave of her veil from the overhanging twigs of an ancient, craggy tree that looked mostly dead. Swiftly Falcon turned his head to each side, peering between the ancient trees as if unknown horrors might leap out at us from every shadow. I glanced around, seeing only dense forest which sloped downward to the southeast, where I spied a small lake I'd never seen before, not too far away. No stone pyramid lay in sight.

"I've only been here once ... when Great Aunt Virginia wanted to visit here," Princess Gracely said.

"I came out here to hide once, but there was no shelter, so I didn't stay long," Falcon said.

"Muskay remembers when paddle dolls lived here, but then, he's a very old doll," Princess Gracely said.

"Where's this pyramid?" I asked.

"It's this way ... I think," Falcon said, leading us away from the small lake. "This clearing is the closest we could jump to it, as the forest is so thick.

We trudged through the dense woods, often detouring around brambles, and it was obvious why we hadn't appeared beside the pyramid; there wasn't room to swing a jump rope between these trees.

Falcon got lost several times.

Finally we found it, growing in the shade of trees that probably hadn't even sprouted until after the city of paddle dolls was abandoned.

A dull, worn tan, the pyramid was made of shaped stone blocks and looked like a miniature version of the large pyramids in Egypt, of which I'd only seen pictures. Yet its base was littered with fallen leaves, thin branches, and moss was growing up its sides, threatening to hide it forever. I kicked back the fallen branches and used my fingers to scrape away the mold, which was dry, crumbled as I touched it, and made me sneeze.

"Bless you," Princess Gracely said.

"What're you doing?" Falcon asked.

"Looking for an opening," I said. "In our world, pyramids have rooms hidden inside them."

Finally I uncovered an opening, and I cleared all the moss away from it. I doubted if this was the lair of the voodoo doll; she wouldn't have kept its entrance cluttered, and this moss hadn't been disturbed for years. When it was cleared, I spied a small tunnel leading inside the pyramid. Princess Gracely removed a mirrored sequin from her dress and held it down so the light of the sun reflected into the tunnel. I laid down on the dirt and weeds and peered inside.

While the opening would've been too narrow for

Hiram's thick arm, I could've reached inside, but I was too smart to shove my hand into a dark place I hadn't inspected. Yet, upon looking, I saw only a large, empty chamber. Whatever the paddle dolls had stored in it they'd taken it away when their city fell.

"Nothing," I said. "It's empty."

"Well, at least we know the voodoo doll isn't here," Princess Gracely said.

"Every place we know of is a place where she isn't," Falcon said. "We need to know is where she is ... so we can avoid it!"

"She's got to be someplace," I said. "Let's try Anelodi."

Chapter 19

The Final Loss

When we arrived, Anelodi proved to be exactly as described. In a clearing rose a flattened mound, as if a great hill had been built, then cut off. Yet nothing stood atop the wide mound.

"There's a small ring of stones in the center ... buried in the grass," Falcon said. "That's all that's left of Anelodi."

"Did the cornhusk dolls dig this mound?" I asked.

"I believe so," Princess Gracely said. "According to Great Aunt Virginia, there are similar earthworks in your world ... much larger, of course."

We strode up onto the top of the mound, scanned the trees in every direction, and walked all the way around it. To the north of Anelodi stretched the wide, beautiful lake that had to be skirted if one was walking from Sparkle City to the village of the rag dolls. There were no visible doors or cave openings on the sides of the mound ... not that I'd expected it to have hidden tunnels, but I had to be sure. To all appearances, it was just a flat hill overgrown by tall grass.

While Princess Gracely walked on top, Falcon stretched out on the grass for a nap, and I kept searching the outside area, hoping to find something, but I was running out of excuses. When I returned to join them, I felt disheartened.

"Hilary, are you keeping us here on purpose?" Falcon asked, still laying on the grass. "Not that I mind ...!"

Princess Gracely flashed Falcon an angry look as if she were furious with him.

"There's nothing here," I said at last. "I'm not keeping us here ... but I don't know where to go next. We may have all the clues we're going to get."

"What clues?" Princess Gracely asked. "Perhaps we should reconsider them. We may have missed something."

"The clues haven't changed," Falcon said. "The vanished dolls went to the graveyard, but we don't know why. One of the hand puppets made a tall, thin barrel, and stole a bellows, and again, we don't know why. We don't know what type of liquid she could be storing in the barrel, but we assume the bellows must be pumping something into the barrel. General Walnut, at the wooden fort of the tin soldiers, reported the theft of six stick-ponies, specifically, seahorses."

"Assume ...," I said slowly. "You said ... we ... assume ..."

"Yes," Falcon said. "What else can we ...?"

"Assumptions may be false," I said. "The rest are facts. Anything that isn't a known fact is suspect."

"Suspect to what ...?" Flacon asked.

"Clues can be misleading," Princess Gracely said.

"Perhaps our facts are wrong as well."

"I think our facts are all proven," I said. "Let's consider our assumptions ... what if they're wrong?"

"How could they be wrong?" Falcon asked. "A barrel holds liquids. What else could a barrel be for?"

"Why must a barrel hold liquids?" I asked. "What else could a barrel hold?"

"A barrel could hold solids, I guess," Falcon said. "I mean, a barrel has a small opening, but if you wanted to, you could fill it with sand ... or a really fine dirt."

"That's true," I said. "But ... then, why would you use a barrel? Wouldn't a bucket work better?"

"I'd expect so," Falcon said. "There's a lot of things you could put inside a barrel, but you'd have to cut a bigger opening into it."

"Why make a barrel if you're going to cut it apart?" I asked.

"That I can't tell you," Falcon said. "Our other assumption is the bellows; we assume the voodoo doll is using it to pump some liquid into, or out of, the barrel."

"Bellows are used to pump air or water," I said. "Our only fact is that bellows can't pump solids, like sand or dirt."

"That's why we assumed it's a liquid," Falcon said. "Why would someone need to pump air into a barrel?"

"They wouldn't," I said, but then I hesitated. "Wait! There is a reason why you'd pump air into a barrel!"

"What?" Falcon asked.

"The only reason to pump air into a barrel ... is to pump a liquid out," I said.

"How would that work ...?" Falcon asked.

"Pressure," I explained. "If the barrel had two holes, and was full of liquid, and you pumped air into one of the holes, then the pressure would force the liquid out of the other hole."

"That makes sense," Falcon said. "But ... why?"

"I'm working on that," I said. "What other assumptions have we made?"

"None, really," Falcon said.

"What about the stick-ponies?" I asked. "General Walnut said they were seahorses ..."

"We assumed they'd be used to pull a boat," Falcon said. "However, the glamour dolls searched everywhere ... if there was a boat they'd have found it."

"How do we know they'd have found it?" I asked. "It could've been hidden ..."

"They searched everywhere ... in the sky, across the land, and upon the water ...," Falcon said.

Slowly a strange, unbelievable idea creeped into my mind. I held it a moment, wondering if I'd be considered mad ... if I suggested it.

"The glamour dolls searched ... upon the water," I said. "Did anyone think ... to look ... under the water?"

"Under ...?" Falcon asked. "What could be under the water?"

"A barrel," I said. "A barrel ... with the water pumped out of it!"

"It would float!" Falcon argued.

"It could be weighted," I countered. "Iron weights, or maybe just heavy rocks, could hold it down, even if all the water was pumped out."

Falcon looked at me as if I were crazy ... and Princess Gracely looked horrified.

"It would need a hole on the bottom ... like a doorway," I said. "Something big enough to let you put heavy rocks into its inside."

"But why ...?" Falcon asked. "Beside rocks, what could be inside it?"

"Anything," I said. "Anything small ... like a doll! That's it, Falcon! That's why we can't find her lair! It's underwater ... inside a barrel ... a submersible lair!"

"Then ... what are the seahorses for?" Falcon asked.

I hesitated, and then I held up the map and looked at it again.

"Here it is!" I cried. "We've been looking at it all the time! This map doesn't just show elevations, it shows depths! See, in all these shaded areas? See these thin lines? It clearly marks the depths of the lakes and streams ... where seahorses could pull it. That's why we couldn't find where the voodoo doll was hiding! The lair of the voodoo doll ... is inside a submarine!"

Suddenly the map was snatched from my hand. Princess Gracely yanked it away from me, glaring at me with an expression of fury.

"That can't be!" Princess Gracely hissed. "It's insanity!"

"No, it's science," I said. "You pump in air, and the air pressure inside the barrel forces the water out, and the weighted barrel rises. You pump air out, and water pressure outside the barrel forces some of the water, but not all of it, back inside, and the weighted barrel sinks. The stick-pony seahorses pull it. It all works!"

"The stream by Troll Hill!" Falcon said. "You chanted for us to go ... where the voodoo doll had her hidden lair ... and we appeared downhill of the Hall of the Trolls. Don't you see? Your chant worked! We appeared beside the stream ... but we didn't see her lair ... because it was underwater!"

"The white water," I said. "We couldn't see through it ...!"

"The missing fish ...!" Falcon said. "The trolls

complained that all the fish had left their stream ... they must've fled from the submarine!"

"Ridiculous," Princess Gracely said, and she turned and walked off across the top of the mound of Anelodi. We stared, confused, when suddenly Princess Gracely tripped and fell face-first onto the grass.

"Pincess Gracely!" I cried, and suddenly Falcon's hand seized me and held me back.

"As I said, there's a small ring of stones in the center ... buried in the grass," Falcon said. "In all the ages I've known Princess Gracely, I've never seen her trip ... not once ... not a single moment off-balance ...!"

We watched Princess Gracely stand back up, the map crushed in her grip. She looked down at her usually spotless white dress, now covered with grass and dirt, and glared at us with an expression that couldn't be our friend's trusting face.

"Voodoo doll!" I shouted.

"You're too late!" the voodoo doll's deep voice issued from Princess Gracely's usually calm face, now pink with rage.

"We know your secret!" I shouted at the voodoo doll.

"And I know all of yours!" the voodoo doll yelled. "You can't stop me ... there aren't enough dolls left in Arcadia to stop me. I've won! Your attempts to stop me have failed!"

"We'll find you ...!" I warned. "Give up now and we'll go easy on you ...!"

The voodoo doll laughed at us, a horrible, nasty laughter.

"I know what you know, puny fools," the voodoo doll said. "Gather your forces ... and march against me, if you dare! I've always known you might find my lair, and I've prepared for it. Now that I know you're coming, I can set other plans into action ... and thwart you again!"

I stared at the maniac, furious expression masking the beautiful face of calm, sweet Princess Gracely, and knew this was pointless. She'd been taken, the last person I could count on ... except Falcon, who was useless except for hiding whenever trouble came.

"Let her go," Falcon whispered. "We can't stop her now."

With a haughty sneer, Princess Gracely turned and stormed away ... taking our map with her. Helpless, we watched her go.

"We have the jump rope," Falcon whispered. "Bambole is an hour from here on foot ... we can get there before she does."

"What good is that?" I asked. "The voodoo doll is safely in her submarine."

"Then you can jump us to her," Falcon said. "We know she's hiding underwater ...!"

"I can't fight the voodoo doll and protect myself from her influence," I said. "What would you do ... if we jumped there ... and she enchanted me? If we do that ... then I'll need to protect myself ... and the burden of catching her would be yours ... and yours alone."

Falcon flushed scarlet and bowed his head.

"I know I'm not brave," Falcon said. "I never asked to be cowardly. I'm ashamed ... but what can I do?"

"Fight it," I said. "Brave people aren't immune to fear ... they just don't let it stop them."

"I can't," Falcon said. "I've tried to be brave ... many times. If we try ... and I fail again ... then Arcadia will be lost, and I'll be to blame."

"You can do this," I said to Falcon. "You're over five feet tall ...! You tower over every doll except Judy and Hiram ...! You're stronger, heavier ...!"

"Dolls are what we're made to be," Falcon said. "Didn't you wonder why Master Strand was taken, but General Walnut wasn't? Because the voodoo doll knew he was no real threat to her ... just like she knows I'm no threat ...!"

"Don't blame yourself," I said. "We need help, but the longer we take to find it the more time she'll have to move her submarine. Let's go to Sparkle City; we need the glamour dolls!"

Falcon didn't reply, just continued to blush and look away. I shook out my cord and stepped over it, then started to jump. Princess Gracely, possessed by the voodoo doll, was gone, vanished into the woods. We were short on time and I couldn't wait for Falcon to find his courage.

"To Sparkle City, take us there!
To Sparkle City, where we may share!
Wisdom and secrets with our friends!
To Sparkle City, there us send!"

Chapter 20

Rally the Troops

We arrived just outside of Sparkle City. It sounded like exactly the same music was playing, blasting out of their giant mirror-ball hall. As we appeared, ten glamour dolls hurried out from under us ... to avoid getting trampled or knocked over by my flipping cord. They ran outside my sparkling sphere, and then turned and glared at us as if we'd interrupted something important.

"We were talking ...!" one of them shouted.

"The time for talking is ended!" I shouted over the music. "We're raising all of Arcadia! We know where our enemy is, the one that's stolen all the missing dolls! We know where they are and we're marching to rescue them! We need everyone, anyone who can help!"

"But ... there's a party tonight ...!" one of the glamour dolls argued.

"There won't be any more parties!" I warned them. "Remember Punch, who took control of you ... and made him his slaves? If the voodoo doll takes you then you'll never dance or sing again ... you'll sleep in her graveyard, covered with slime, filthy and helpless for all eternity. We can stop her! We can free everyone, but we have to do it now!"

The glamour dolls glanced at each other, looking distressed.

"If we can defeat the voodoo doll, then we'll celebrate with the biggest party Arcadia has ever seen!" Falcon said enthusiastically. "The greatest party of all!"

The glamour dolls all cheered.

"Go tell your friends!" Falcon said. "Tell everyone! Get them all out here ... especially those with wings!"

"Hurry!" I urged. "We need to give special instructions to your fliers," I said. "The rest of you ... we need every doll! The future of Arcadia depends on you!"

The glamour dolls ran off, most into the mirrored sphere. Suddenly the music faltered and voices were raised in complaint, but we heard our message repeated, and soon over two hundred glamour dolls rushed out to stare up at us, and three glamour dolls with wings flew up to our eye-level.

"Where are the other fliers?" I asked.

"Vanished," the violet winged glamour doll said.

"They've been gone for days," the winged glamour doll wearing black said. "We're all that's left."

"We know where the voodoo doll is, and once we find her, we can release and return all your sisters that have vanished," I said.

"We know what to look for, but we need you to find her," Falcon said. "Find her, and come and tell us, and we'll capture her."

"Head to Troll Hill," I said. "That's the last place we knew where she was. Send all your walkers to Troll Hill;

we'll be there soon. You must bring us news of where she is."

"What do we look for?" the red flying glamour doll asked.

"She's underwater," I said. "Fly low over every lake and stream. You should be able to see it: a long, skinny wooden keg, floating under the surface, and it may have seahorses pulling it. Look in the stream flowing around Troll Hill first, and once you see her, fly up high and don't let her see you. Wait for us; we must approach her in large numbers ... or she'll possess us all."

The three winged glamour dolls, violet, black, and red, nodded, then flew off and vanished over the trees. All the other glamour dolls stood watching, eager to begin.

"We're headed to rally the other dolls," I said. "Hurry to Troll Hill and await us there. We've only got a brief window for victory!"

"If we lose, it'll be the end of all parties," Falcon said. "If we win, it'll mean the best party ever!"

The glamour dolls cheered, and with countless sparkles of colored glitter, they all turned and ran toward the west.

"Is that the direction of Troll Hill?" I asked Falcon.

"Close enough," Falcon said. "They'll figure it out when they reach the lake. We'd better get going."

"Where?" I asked.

"The Fort of the Tin Soldiers," Falcon said. "They're the farthest east from Troll Hill, which lies on the western side."

I took my time and composed a good chant, since I'd need all my strength when we faced the voodoo doll.

"Fort of the tin soldiers!
Here we come!

> *Arcadia's in trouble!*
> *Which must be undone!*
> *We can't stay!*
> *Must go today!*
> *With the tin soldiers*
> *Is where we play!"*

When my gold and silver sparkles faded we were inside the fort, right next to the white manor.

"General Walnut!" I cried. "We did it! We found her!"

All of the tin soldiers turned to face us, shocked expressions on their faces. One tin soldier, standing between the pillars atop the steps outside the white manor, stared up at us, then opened the front door and ran inside.

"Prepare to move out!" Falcon shouted to all the troops. *"We march to Troll Hill!"*

I looked up at Falcon and smiled.

"You sound pretty brave to me," I said to Falcon.

"Not much threat here," Falcon said, blushing slightly.

"I have faith in you," I said.

The balcony door opened and General Walnut attempted to peek out, but he was shoved through the door by the other two generals, who pushed to follow him, knocking their wooden heads together as they both tried to emerge through the door simultaneously.

"Nice to see you, General Walnut," Falcon grinned.

General Walnut looked worried.

"Ahem! Back again? Inexcusable!" General Walnut said. "Tish-tosh! We have military business ...!"

"Indeed you do," I agreed. "The glamour dolls are already enroute. We're visiting the other doll cities, rousing everyone. Our enemy was last seen at Troll Hill, and we're summoning every doll left to rise in defense of Arcadia. The war is beginning. Will the tin soldiers join us ... or will they hide behind the lines while other dolls fight?"

"Hide ...?" General Walnut exclaimed. "Dishonor! Disgrace! No tin soldier hides while their fellow dolls fight!"

"Then it's time to march!" I said. "Now, for Arcadia!"

"Your fort is the farthest dwelling from Troll Hill, so you may have to march the fastest," Falcon said. "We must hurry to the next village and inform them of the gathering."

"Capital! Excellent!" General Walnut cried. "*Soldiers, to arms! Leave no stragglers! Line up! Prepare to march!*"

Every tin soldier cheered. A rush began down the ladders from the wall, and they ran to form into orderly units.

"Time to go," Falcon said to me.

"Where ...?" I asked.

"The hand puppets," Falcon said.

I nodded and modified my chant from before.

> *"To the hand puppet's city*
> *Let us fly!*
> *To their city and shops*
> *We must try!*
> *Puppets with hands inside*
> *To your city we must hie!*
> *Where skyscrapers rise tall!*
> *Where hands hide inside all!*
> *Take us now! Don't be shy!*
> *To your city we must fly!"*

We arrived just outside the city, towering over the startled dolls at our feet. Away from our feet ran many different types of hand puppets, none of which looked the same.

"Hey, there, watch that jump rope!" shouted a hand puppet. "You almost hit me!"

To my surprise, this hand puppet was made of a brown-paper lunch bag with a face childishly drawn on the bottom of it in crayon, ending with its top lip. Its bottom lip was drawn on its flat side, just above its comical body, and as the bottom of the bag flapped open and closed, its mouth moved when it spoke, and inside the mouth, under the flap, a red tongue was drawn.

"Sorry," I said. "We're in a hurry."

"You're that new jumper!" shouted another hand puppet, this one masterfully made; a velvet child's face topped with fake fur hair, eyebrows that rose and lowered, and a mouth like Kermit the Frog, so perfect they could've been a regular on Sesame Street or The Muppet's Show.

"Yes, I'm Hilary," I said.

"Hilary the Grand," Falcon corrected me.

"Arcadia is rising to defend itself," I said to all of them. "Your friends and relatives that have vanished ... they've been stolen from you by the voodoo doll. She was recently at Troll Hill, and all of the dolls are meeting there to confront her. The flying glamour dolls will spot her and the tin soldiers are already on the march. We need the hand puppets to help capture the voodoo doll and free her captives!"

"We're with you!" the paper bag puppet cried. "Fists first!"

"Onward!" the child muppet cried. "Lend a hand!"

All the hand puppets cheered.

"Spread the word!" I said. "We need numbers to overwhelm her magical defenses! Bring everyone!"

At once, all the hand puppets ran back into their city, shouting for everyone to grip their weapons and march to war. I smiled, then glanced at Falcon.

"The rag dolls and the marionettes both inhabit the center of Arcadia and are equally distant, but rag dolls travel slower," Falcon said.

"Rag dolls first so they arrive together," I said.

> *"Magic rope! Magic rope!*
> *Your powers we evoke!*
> *Shine right! Shine bright!*
> *Let us now join in the fight!*
> *Let your magic powers flow!*
> *To the rag dolls we must go!*
> *This grave risk we must dare!*
> *To save the magic land we share!*
> *Take us! Take us! With great flair!*
> *Magic rope, take us there!"*

The charming miniature Victorian village of the rag dolls appeared, and we gazed at it appreciatively ... until we noticed the absence. Not one rag doll remained. No dolls walked on sidewalk or street, stood in a doorway, or peeked out a window.

"Where are they?" I asked.

"Maybe they've all vanished," Falcon suggested.

I inhaled a deep breath and then shouted loudly enough for the whole village to hear.

"Mistress Flax!" I cried. *"We need you! We found our enemy! Mistress Flax ...!"*

Almost a minute passed, and then a wee voice responded.

"Are ... are you the jumper?"

We looked down; peeking out of a half-opened window was a large young girl with a plastic face and a flapping jaw like the one on Mr. Magee. I recognized her; a Talking Tammy. I'd owned a doll just like her ... and wondered if the tape recorder inside her needed batteries.

"Yes, I'm ... Hilary the Grand," I said.

"Hilary the Grand, I'm afraid everyone's hiding." Talking Tammy said. "Mistress Flax vanished two days ago, in the night, and we've been terrified ever since."

"The time for fear is ... over," Falcon said, almost choking on his last word.

"Falcon's right," I said loudly, hoping all the hiding rag dolls could hear. "We know where the vanished dolls are ... and we know who took them! The voodoo doll was last seen at Troll Hill, and we're raising all the dolls against her. The glamour dolls are already almost there, and the tin soldiers and hand puppets are marching fast. We'll convene there, every doll that can, and then we'll defeat our enemy and restore everyone!"

"But ... what can we do?" Talking Tammy asked. "We're so scared ...!"

I started to speak, but Falcon waved me silent.

"Oh, we understand," Falcon said. "Don't worry. If the rag dolls are too afraid, then I'm sure the glamour dolls will rise to assume your duties. After all, they're newer, younger, and stronger ..."

"Glamour dolls?" Talking Tammy exploded. *"Those skinny, hard-legged bikini-wearers ... replace us ...? Never!"*

As she said this several voices cheered.

"That's what will happen ... if you stay home while the rest of Arcadia marches," I said.

Doors opened, and dozens of rag dolls emerged,

grim-faced and frowning.

"The rag dolls will stitch together, and we'll soon wrap this up!" a cloth doll with hair of blue yarn shouted, and every rag doll cheered.

"We've a few more allies to gather," I said.

"We'll meet you at Troll Hill!" Falcon said.

The rag dolls raised scissors, pinking shears, and seam-rippers, and cheered as one.

"To the marionettes," I said to Falcon.

> *"To the marionette's home*
> *Wide flat stages*
> *On the wooden-wheeled carts*
> *Used for ages*
> *Carry us, carry us*
> *To see their prancing*
> *Carry us, carry us*
> *To delighted dancing."*

The wooden carriages of Theater City appeared before us. A performance was going on, one stage brightly lit with tiny candles in the shielded footlights, with marionettes dancing in unison and singing merrily, while in the other carts hung marionettes from their strings, poised as if sitting on invisible chairs, watching the dancers, but with glum expressions. To our dismay, only a dozen marionettes sat in each cart, watching the show, and only six marionettes danced on their stage.

> *"Happy we are today!*
> *Happy! Happy! Hip-hooray!*
> *Singing all with one voice!*
> *Mari-on-ettes rejoice!*
> *We need no rest!*
> *We dance the best!*
> *We are all one!*

> *We are the fun!*
> *We dance and we sing*
> *With each rising sun!*
> *Always together, never apart!*
> *Deepest lies the marionette heart!"*

Sadly, no one seemed rejoiced. The dancing dolls were doing their best to enliven their viewers, to keep up their morale, but their glum moods seemed unbreachable.

When the song ended in a spectacular flourish of sparks and waving flags, and all the dancing dolls suddenly froze in a dramatic pause on exactly the final note of the music ... no one applauded or cheered. An utter silence followed.

Falcon nudged me and we both started clapping our hands.

"Excellent!" Falcon cried. *"Marvelous!"*

"Bravo!" I shouted. *"Wonderful!"*

The marionettes, both the dancers and the watchers, startled at our appearance.

"I know you!" one of the dancers shouted in a high-pitched woman's voice with a southern accent, and she pulled off her wide hat to reveal the smiling face of Miss Hangly.

"Miss Hangly," I bowed slightly. "A pleasure to see you again."

Miss Hangly shook her head.

"Another day ... and you wouldn't find me ... or anyone else," Miss Hangly said.

"Are you all that's left?" Falcon asked.

"Yep," Miss Hangly said, and some more marionettes came out onto the stage behind her, most carrying musical instruments in their arms. "We used to number in the hundreds, but now there's less than sixty of us.

Soon ..."

"Soon will never happen," I said. "We've found the voodoo doll and we've raised most of Arcadia. We're all headed to Troll Hill, and then we'll free all the marionettes she's taken."

The marionettes all cheered.

"We hoped our performance would raise everyone's spirits, but you've upstaged us rightly!" Miss Hangly said.

"Can we count on you?" Falcon asked.

"This curtain won't rise to find the marionettes off-stage!" Miss Hangly said.

The marionettes cheered again.

"Head to Troll Hill," Falcon said. "We've got one last stop to make, and then we'll meet you there!"

The marionettes gave one joyous shout, and then they grabbed their strings, pulled hard, and caught their cross-braces as they fell. Twirling them to bind their strings, they hung their cross-braces over their shoulders and jumped off their stages onto the ground, running as soon as they landed.

"Where are we going?" I asked. "Bambole?"

"No, Audrey is at Bambole, and we don't want to face her," Falcon said. "We need the strongest dolls in Arcadia: Mr. Magee and Judy!"

"To The Palace!" I said, and Falcon smiled.

"Palace! Palace!
We come to thee!
Your glorious grandeur
We must see!
Stage and curtain!
Lights shine certain!
Take us now
To Judy!
We must see her

And Mr. Magee!"

We appeared just outside the theater doors, under the marquee, and ran inside as soon as my sparkles stopped flashing. We dashed through the foyer, pushed through the swinging doors, and hurried down the sloped floor past the seats, careful not to trip on the uneven carpet. We burst through the door and practically leaped up the short stairs onto the back stage.

"Mr. Magee!" I called. *"Judy!"*

I couldn't see Mr. Magee in the dim light, but suddenly the trap door burst upwards. Even amid deep shadows the loud, unexpected entrance of Judy, the largest doll in Arcadia, exploding from beneath the floor with a huge *bang!* startled me. Falcon screamed and stumbled, and I grabbed his arm to save him from falling; his eyes were bulging and terror masked his face.

"It's Judy!" I assured him. "We're safe!"

"Are we ...?" asked a voice from the shadows.

"Mr. Magee ...!" Falcon cried, stepping back.

"We're all friends here," I said. "At least, I hope we are ..."

I stared at Judy and Mr. Magee. They glanced at each other, and Mr. Magee rolled his eyes, the pupils making opposite circles, and Judy raised her huge wooden paddle, which she carried in her hand, and then tapped it three times on the floor. Both looked satisfied.

"We're not possessed," Mr. Magee said. "Those are the signs we arranged between us, after seeing how well yours worked."

"Have you found the voodoo doll's lair?" Judy asked.

"Yes," I said.

"And ... no," Falcon said, his breaths airy from the gasps of fright from which he was still recovering.

"Her lair is inside a wooden submarine," I said. "She's been traveling all over Arcadia, hidden from our sight by sailing underwater."

"Last we knew, she was in the stream near Troll Hill," Falcon said. "We sent ... the flying glamour dolls ... to search."

"There're only three flying glamour dolls left," I said. "Most of the dolls of Arcadia are in her graveyard. The marionettes and rag dolls are mostly taken. We've sent everyone but the paper dolls there; the paper dolls already did their part."

"Why come here?" Mr. Magee asked.

"To ... to get you," Falcon said. "You're our biggest, wisest ..."

"I'll come," Judy said.

We all looked at Mr. Magee.

"I ... can't ...," Mr. Magee said. "I dare not go outside."

"Why not?" I asked.

Mr. Magee looked down and flapped his wooden ears.

"The ventriloquist who had me specially-made ... wasn't very successful," Mr. Magee said. "He paid my carpenter most of his promised price, all that he had, but he ... couldn't afford additional costs. He stitched my first outfit out of rags and pretended I was a hobo, but ... he couldn't afford paints. However, he had lots of makeup, and so he applied his theatrical makeup to my wooden face and hands. It looks fine ... but if I should ever get wet ...!"

"You needn't go near the water," I said.

"That's why I've never left The Palace, nor do I allow food or drinks on my stage," Mr. Magee said.

"The hand puppets have plenty of paints ...," Falcon

suggested.

"Look, we all have weaknesses," I said. "You're one of us ... we won't let anything happen to you."

"We won't make you come, but Hilary has to hurry," Falcon said. "All the dolls will be reaching Troll Hill soon and she needs to be there. I'll stay here and guard The Palace."

"You're coming," I said to Falcon.

"I've helped you summon the armies of Arcadia," Falcon said. "You've got them ... you don't need me now."

"Most of Arcadia is in the graveyard," I said. "We need everyone."

"Men ...!" Judy sneered. "Either they're like Punch ... too brave, willing to take any risk, or they're like these two ...!"

"We'll all go ... together," I said. "Arcadia needs every hope we have."

Slowly Mr. Magee rose from his gold-painted throne and stood before us.

"If Falcon goes then I will," Mr. Magee said. "We must all face our fears."

"Excellent," I said. "Let's go outside; I'll need a large sphere to carry Judy."

I led the way. Judy turned her massive wooden paddle sideways ... and urged Falcon and Mr. Magee to precede her. I stepped heavily; after all this jumping I was tired, and I had yet to face our foe. Yet our strategy was set. As we had against Punch, we'd moved all the pieces but we'd yet to win the game.

Now everything depended on me.

"Troll Hill! Troll Dolls!
Trouble to us calls!

Trouble here! Trouble there!
Magic take us everywhere!
Over valley! Over sea!
There now let us be!
Trouble now! Trouble still!
Take us now to Troll Hill!"

Troll Hill was buried under dolls; marionettes, glamour dolls, rag dolls, and of course, many bright-haired troll dolls, all of whom looked very surprised. In the distance, we saw the army of hand puppets marching toward us, and from the forest to the northeast we heard small feet stomping in unison and the tiny drums and trumpets of the tin soldiers. Behind each marched an even bigger army ... an army of stuffed animals, animals of every kind.

The three winged glamour dolls, violet, red, and black, flew down to us as soon as the sparkles faded.

"We found her!" the red glamour doll said.

"She's downstream, headed toward Durid Lake," the violet glamour doll said.

"Her ship moves quickly," the black glamour doll said. "We must hurry!"

"Lead us!" I said. "Show us the way!"

All three dolls nodded and winged off, just as General Walnut and the other two nutcracker dolls emerged from the woods, riding stick-ponies and leading eight long lines of tin soldiers.

"Our enemy is trying to escape!" I shouted to all the dolls, pointing south toward the flying glamour dolls. *"Hurry! We must catch her!"*

I stepped over my cord and began jumping rope. Judy and Mr. Magee stepped close, and Judy reached out to grab Falcon as he turned away. I ignored them, focusing on my chant, which had to be short as I didn't have time to compose a long one, so I threw in several jump rope tricks to ease my strain of jumping.

"To catch our foe
We must go!
Ahead of them
We must wend!
We must fly
We must try!
No escape can we allow!
Downstream we go – right now!"

We appeared beside a stream, deep and rushing, and behind us stretched a long lake, wide and mostly surrounded by trees. I glanced northward, and in the distance I saw the three flying glamour dolls, looking like fairies high up in the sky, and they were flying directly over the stream. They came slowly and we all knew why.

"Let's move up to meet them," Judy said.

We walked up the slight slope, away from the wide lake. If the voodoo doll reached the lake then she could dive to the bottom and we'd never see her ... or be able to reach her. However, we had our foe trapped; the submarine couldn't leave the water, our army was upstream, and we were downstream; *she had nowhere else to go.*

As we rapidly approached each other, the winged glamour dolls waved to us and pointed to the stream beneath them. We understood and waved back at them. In the distance, our army of dolls appeared, running downhill as fast as they could.

Just before we met, Judy jumped over the creek and stuck her huge wooden paddle deep into the water. We stopped, and soon saw it: a thin wooden keg, floating under the white water, with six green seahorses pulling it. Above it floated a straw, sticking up out of the water, such as might be seen growing out of any stream, but it was moving with the keg. Quickly it approached Judy's paddle, and as it neared, she swiped her paddle against it.

With a tall splash that made Mr. Magee jump backwards, Judy's paddle swept the wooden barrel and seahorses up out of the stream, flipping through the air, and it crashed down onto the grass before us.

We'd captured the voodoo doll's lair!

The flying glamour dolls swooped down.

"Wait!" I whispered. "We need everyone. Wait until all the dolls are here."

The submarine lay on its side, and clearly we could see a hole in its bottom, just big enough for most dolls to climb inside. The long straw, which concealed a thin metal tube, was still sticking out of its top, but now it lay bent and broken. The seahorses looked unharmed; they jumped up, still bound by thick threads to the barrel, wet, but seeming as at ease above the water as below.

Within five minutes all the other dolls arrived. I ordered them to form a wide circle around us; we'd caught the voodoo doll and I didn't want her escaping again. General Walnut ordered the tin soldiers to form the innermost circle of our ring and they pointed their guns at the submarine.

"Come out!" I cried at the submarine. "Come out, voodoo doll, and face justice for your crimes!"

A voice responded, but it was a man's voice, not the drawling tone of the voodoo doll.

"She's gone!" he shouted. "She knew you were coming and she left! Help me! I'm trapped in here!"

We glanced at each other, confused, but then I

looked at General Walnut and nodded. He gestured to his soldiers. Without hesitation, seven tin soldiers ran forward, pressed their backs against the bottom of the submarine, and slowly approached and peeked inside its hole.

"It's a U.S. Combat doll!" one of them shouted. "He's chained to the bellows ... inside the submarine!"

"Can you free him?" I asked.

The seven tin soldiers climbed inside the submarine with ease, as the hole was more than large enough for them. Then we heard several guns fire and feared the worst. However, one of the tin soldiers appeared at the opening and shouted to us.

"He's free! We're sending him out first!" the tin solder said.

The much-larger U.S. Combat doll slowly climbed out the hole, which was barely large enough for him to pass through, yet he made it with practiced ease. When he stood up, he was as tall as a glamour doll, several inches taller than the tin soldiers, well-muscled, and wearing a white sailor's uniform and hat.

"Thank you!" he said. "The voodoo doll captured me, brought me here, and forced me to operate and steer her submarine. I knew how powerful she was, and she threatened to do terrible things to the other dolls if I didn't do as she said."

"Where's the voodoo doll?" I asked.

"She said she had to go where she was most protected," the sailor doll said. "She appeared barely half an hour ago and ordered me to get back to the lake, then to sail west into the swamp, and to dock near her graveyard and wait for her."

"Most protected ...?" Judy asked. "Would that be her graveyard?"

"I don't think so," Mr. Magee said. "Her greatest protector is Audrey the Grand."

"Bambole," I said. "That's not far away. Let's all march there!"

"Wait!" the sailor doll said. "We can't leave her submarine! Most of her tokens are in it. Besides, if she gets it back into the water, she'll be able to escape to anywhere!"

"What should we do?" I asked.

The sailor doll sighed.

"Burn it," he said sadly. "This vessel is my only hope of getting back to my post, but she carries my token around her neck, and she'd just possess me again. Yet she only keeps a few tokens around her neck; hundreds of tokens are hanging inside her submarine. If we burn it, then she'll never be able to possess those dolls again." He looked up at us. "It's the only way to be sure."

I glanced at Falcon, Mr. Magee, Judy, General Walnut, and all the other dolls. Many heads nodded, and I knew we had no choice.

"We don't have time for another plan," I said. "Tin soldiers, get out, and back away from the submarine. Rag dolls, cut those threads and free the seahorses. I'll ignite it."

The outside of the submarine was wet, so I knelt before it, took one handle of my jump rope, and after all the tin soldiers had climbed out, and the seahorses were freed, I reached my handle inside, and as Great Aunt Virginia had done, I willed it to spark and flame. I added a simple chant to aid my hopes that it would work.

"Ignite, ignite,
Fire shine bright."

I tapped the wood inside it and a glow lit its dark

interior. Flames soon filled the inside of the submarine, and I pulled my jump rope safely back. As the smoke started to rise the dolls gave a cheer.

"I assume she keeps Audrey's token around her neck ...?" I asked.

The sailor doll nodded.

"We march to Bambole," I said. "We must catch our enemy!"

"Help me ... and be careful," Mr. Magee said, looking at the wild stream, and he reached up a hand to both Falcon and I. Understanding his fear, we grasped him tightly, walked to the edge of the stream, and jumped over, pulling him with us.

Most of the dolls walked to the edge of the stream but few could cross. Judy laid her paddle down across it, and it was wide enough to make a bridge the small dolls could walk across. The flying glamour dolls circled around the rising smoke pouring from the inside of the submarine, which was glowing from the fire within.

Suddenly a bright, white light shined from out of the hole in the bottom of the submarine. It beamed out, blinding, lasted for long moments, and then it slowly faded and vanished.

"That takes care of her tokens," I said. "She can't possess any doll she wants to anymore ... and Muskay dumped her cauldron at the graveyard into the swamp ... she must be running low on that elixir, too."

"She was furious about that," the sailor doll said. "She's weakened, but she still has Audrey, and she kept talking about her ultimate weapon ..."

"What kind of weapon ...?" Mr. Magee asked.

"She never told me," the sailor doll said. "She only said that, once she unleashed her ultimate weapon, she'd be the eternal Queen of Arcadia."

"We'd best wait," Falcon said. "Perhaps we should send a few tin soldiers forward first ... to reconnaissance any threats before we march blindly into ..."

"This is our winning moment," I said. "If we wait now she'll be able to escape ... or enact some other plan to thwart our victory. We have to win, and free Mom, Great Aunt Virginia, Audrey, and Mrs. Darby. Once we have them the voodoo doll will be alone and helpless."

"Go ahead," Judy said. "I'll join you as soon as all the dolls have crossed."

"May I join you?" the sailor doll asked. "I won't rest until I know the voodoo doll is captured and imprisoned."

I nodded to the sailor doll, glad to have him along. Then, with my left hand, I reached out and grabbed Falcon's arm before he could try to walk away. For the first time he didn't resist. I pulled him uphill, across the wide, grassy field. Mr. Magee marched beside us and the other dolls followed on our heels. I was pleased that the sailor doll followed; his knowledge of the voodoo doll might prove invaluable.

Unfortunately, we couldn't hurry; the short-legged dolls, even the glamour dolls, struggled to keep up with our strides, which we had to shorten. I dared not leave them behind. The voodoo doll had a token of me and I couldn't approach her alone, without backup, in case luck should go against us. If I were knocked unconscious, even for a moment, then she might possess me, and all the dolls of Arcadia couldn't match the full might of two jumpers.

Slowly we approached Bambole yet no challenge met us. This worried me. Our doll army could be seen from any tower or high window in the castle. Surely she knew we were coming. Had she powers we didn't know about? The voodoo doll was smarter than Punch, who'd boasted of his strengths and plans to anyone who'd listen. I had to take the greatest care ... I couldn't allow Arcadia to lose.

Chapter 21

The Unbeatable Army

We marched under the few trees, trailed by hundreds of dolls, wary of every step. We crossed the field, through the forest surrounding it, and finally walked between the many-towered castle of King Andy and Queen Anne and another building, which looked to be a huge, elegant manor, possibly where many of the inhabitants of Bambole resided ... perhaps even the homes of Muskay, Hiram, and Princess Gracely. The small dolls looked askance at the monstrous buildings, so much larger than their doll houses. Only Judy, who was taller than Falcon or I, marched fearlessly.

The city was empty. Not one horse-drawn carriage rolled upon the streets, not one resident walked the sidewalks, and not one face showed at any doorway or window.

"Stop!" I hissed, waving for everyone to stay behind me, and I lifted my jump rope. "This looks suspicious."

Judy and Mr. Magee halted at once, and Judy reached

out and grabbed Falcon, who'd started to walk backwards. Behind us, the dolls caught up and filled in a huge crowd.

I stepped forward cautiously, peering about. Nothing looked threatening ... except for the total absence of any sign of life, which screamed warnings inside my ears. I dropped my cord and stepped over it, ready to start jumping at the slightest sign of trouble.

Nothing attacked us. Slowly Mr. Magee led the dolls forward between the buildings, Judy pulling Falcon.

With a sudden rush, twenty guards, full-grown men as large as Hiram, charged out of the front doors of the castle, their bright red and gold uniforms flashing in the sunlight that glinted off their long, steel halberds. They ran out and faced me as a line. As one, they lowered their sharp steel points toward me.

"Jumper Hilary, you're under arrest!" one of them shouted. "Surrender your weapon ... and come quietly!"

I stepped back; I had the jump rope, but only a fool charges a line of steel spear-tips.

"Why ...?" I asked.

"Because King Andy commands it!" the same guard shouted.

"King Andy would never give such an order," I said. "The voodoo doll has a token of him ... she's making him say those things."

"Our orders are clear," the guard said. "We must take you into custody ... and drag you before Oyuncak and Bebekler, the thrones of Arcadia ... forcibly, if necessary."

I frowned at these guards. If I started jumping, they had only to run forward enough to let their halberds foul my flipping cord, and if they came any closer then their sharp points could stab right through me.

Slowly, carefully, I took one step to the side ... and then another.

"Stop!" the guard shouted.

"I'm just shifting ... with the wind," I said. "I hate having the wind blow on my face, don't you?"

I took another sidestep, slightly curving my path.

"Stop that!" the guard shouted.

"I'm not going anywhere," I said. "So, what exactly do you want me to do? Should I drop my jump rope here ... upon the grass?"

I took another sidestep.

"Stand still!" the guard shouted, and all the guards turned to keep their weapons facing me. "Yes, drop your jump rope upon the grass."

"But ... why do you want it on the grass?" I asked, taking another sidestep. "If I drop it, won't you just have to pick it up?"

"We'll get it, don't worry," the guard said.

"But ... if you want my jump rope ... why not just come here ... and let me give it to you?" I asked, and I took another wide sidestep.

"Stop moving!" the guard shouted, and again they turned their line to keep their sharp points oriented on me.

"I haven't tried to run away, have I?" I asked. "I haven't gone anywhere, have I?"

"Just stand still!" the guard shouted.

I took one last sidestep, and then halted, smiling at the guards. The doll armies of Arcadia were slowly creeping forward right behind them.

"Okay, I'll stop moving," I said, holding up my jump rope. "Is this a good place to drop my jump rope?"

"Yes, drop it right here!" the guard shouted.

"Not over there?" I asked, holding my jump rope out

to the side.

"I don't care!" the guard shouted. "Just drop it!"

"I guess I'd better drop it," I grinned. "After all, it's time someone got the drop on someone ... right now!"

With a mighty swing, Judy's paddle caught the backs of five guards and they crumpled to the ground. The other guards shouted, and suddenly little figures surged forward and swarmed around them. Tin soldiers fired their tiny guns, which struck the guards like rock salt; they cried out and fell back. Hand puppets jumped up and seized their halberds by their long poles, trying to wrest them away. The marionettes cast their long strings and looped their ankles, and the rag dolls jabbed at their feet, through their tall boots, with sharp sewing tools. Crying out, the guards all fell. The troll dolls swarmed atop them, jumping up and down as if they'd found a new toy to play upon. The sailor doll and glamour dolls joined the trolls, only they stomped more accurate targets, and where they had to, they bit fingers and forced the guards to drop their weapons. Mr. Magee seized one of the dropped halberds and turned it to face the guard who'd spoken, and Judy relieved the other guards of their weapons.

"Now tell me ... where's King Andy?" I demanded of their leader.

"I ... don't know!" the guard said. "In his tower, I suspect. He came out just long enough to command us to capture you ..."

"And then he went back into hiding?" I asked. "Where's Audrey?"

"She also closets herself in the king's tower," the guard said.

"Sure she does," I said. "When was the last time you saw King Andy and Audrey ... both ... at the same time?"

The guard looked confused, but I ignored him. I looked at the open gate of the castle.

"That's where our enemy hides," I said. "With Audrey; that's where the voodoo doll will feel most-protected."

"Are we going in there?" Mr. Magee asked.

"Right now," I said, and I stood back, lifted my jump rope, and started a double-bounce.

> *"Guards to sleep!*
> *Guards sleep deep!*
> *Shut eyes and mouths!*
> *Not a peep!"*

On my fourth recitation, a dreariness swelled over the guards and they all fell into snoring slumbers.

"Make the trolls stop jumping!" the sailor doll whispered to the glamour dolls. "We don't want them to wake up!"

At the urging of the glamour dolls, all the dolls jumped off the prone guards, the troll dolls looking like someone had just spoiled their fun. Falcon, I noticed, was standing back by an ornate park bench, looking hesitant. I jerked my head at him, and he shook his head, but then I nodded to the three flying glamour dolls, and they flew down behind him and blocked his retreat. He reluctantly came around the bench and marched forward, the winged glamour dolls carefully herding him.

"Follow me," I said, and I stepped toward the open doors of the castle.

The elated looks on the dolls, after their victory over the guards, faded. Our real challenge was yet to be faced.

With the dolls following, I stepped toward the main doors, which were open, yet the brightness of the sunlight outside cast the foyer in shadow. I considered using a light-spell to illuminate the front room, but I suspected that my real threat waited inside, and I didn't want to tire myself out. Yet I held my jump rope tightly, ready to start jumping at the slightest flash of silver or gold.

We stepped into the shadow inside the doors and slowly our eyes adjusted. The large foyer was a grand room with a vast crystal chandelier hanging overhead, ornate white tile mosaic floor, and doors and curtains worthy of Sleeping Beauty's castle. Grand staircases rose upon both the left and right-hand walls. Tall, imposing wooden doors faced us. There could be no doubt as to what lay beyond those tall doors.

"Stay by the walls," I whispered to the dolls on my heels. "Don't step under the chandelier." I glanced to see Falcon, Judy's hand clamped over his shoulder. "Falcon, go open those doors."

Falcon paled, but Judy pushed him forward, not letting go until they reached the forbidding doors. Then Judy released Falcon, stepped to the other side, and grasped the iron handle of her door. Swallowing hard, Falcon grabbed the iron handle of his door. Judy nodded, and simultaneously they opened the tall doors.

A massive throne room, bright, with a thirty-foot ceiling, shone through the open doors. I stepped forward, my jump rope ready.

Only two figures sat in the otherwise empty room. Upon Oyuncak and Bebekler, the massive royal thrones of Arcadia, awaited our enemies. The first, whom I knew well, was Audrey, her blue eyes staring at me, the handles of her jump rope in her hands. She wore black, and her pale skin shined between her dark dress and chocolate-brown hair, upon which rested a gold crown.

Propped up on the seat of the throne beside Audrey, beside a silver crown, lay a doll which looked as unmoving and lifeless as any doll from my world. She had a candy face on what looked like a licorice lollipop and wore a ragged dress of torn black veils over arms and legs of gray-green, badly-woven twine, fraying all over, bound with dark maroon threads. Upon her lollipop head lay a black veil-covered hat of woven dried straws, and around her neck hung many threads, each hanging a small figure, like a tiny ancient one; *the tokens with which she possessed both dolls and people.*

This was the enemy of Arcadia: the voodoo doll. She looked menacing, but I knew her body wasn't any threat to me ... her mind was possessing the body of Audrey, and Audrey was my biggest challenge.

Audrey rose from her throne, stared imperiously at all opposing her, and laughed a bitter, angry chuckle.

"You bring my next victims," Audrey's mouth moved yet the voice of the voodoo doll filled the hall. "I should thank you. It's such a waste, having to walk each of them to my graveyard."

"Release your victims, the people and dolls," I ordered Audrey.

"Now, Hilary, why would I do that?" the voodoo doll asked. "My plan is almost complete. Once you're defeated, that rabble at your feet will fall before me. If you would spare them utter torment, then lay down your jump rope, return to your jumper-world, and smash the magic tea set. You'll need it no longer; you won't want to visit my Arcadia."

"I'll never let you win," I said.

"You've no choice," the voodoo doll said. "I've taken everyone you could rely upon, and now I'm inside Audrey, your best friend. I can hurt you all I want, but

233

you can't harm me ... not without harming her."

"Audrey would want me to defeat you ... by any means ... to save Arcadia," I said.

"Brave ... but words aren't actions," the voodoo doll said. "It's easy to boast, but here I stand; what will you do? Break me? Kill me?"

"I'll ask you: *why ...?*" I sneered. "What good are victims laying in a graveyard? Why are you trapping the dolls ...?"

The voodoo doll laughed again.

"You'd like that, wouldn't you?" the voodoo doll asked. "This isn't a child's game like tag or jacks, where everyone knows how to win. This is chess, a real game, and I'm not a fool like Punch; I'm not going to reveal my strategy before I've won."

"You can't win," I said. "I'll checkmate you."

"You're already tired," the voodoo doll said. "You've had a busy day, jumping all over Arcadia, and just had to defeat my worthless guards."

"You knew I'd get past them," I said.

"I planned that you would," the voodoo doll said. "But not without using your jump rope, to tire you out before you faced me. You see? You can't defeat carefully-made plans."

I took a deep breath and tried to relax as best I could. I was tired, but I needed to continue the conversation; the longer I kept her talking the more time I'd have to recover.

"We freed your sailor ... and burned your submarine," I said. "All your tokens are gone."

"I'd already fed those victims my potion," the voodoo doll said. "I don't need their tokens anymore. Those subjects are mine ... forever."

"You will free them," I said.

"Why would I do that?" the voodoo doll asked.

"Because otherwise ... this will be the last game you ever play," I said. "You look like licorice ... and people eat lollipops!"

"You wouldn't dare!" the voodoo doll's voice grew angry. "You'd be banished!"

"Then we'd both lose," I said. "But ... the other dolls will win."

Audrey's blue eyes slid across the dolls behind me and an expression of pure hate masked her once-friendly face.

"Never ...!" the voodoo doll cried.

Audrey stepped forward, to the edge of her dais, and flipped her green jump rope over her head. I flipped my blue cord over my head an instant later. Almost immediately, gold and silver sparkles flashed upon her green cord, while my blue one sparkled slower and dimmer. I pressed myself, willing my rope to shine brighter; *I had to win this fight!*

> *"Destroy her!*
> *Kill her!*
> *End her life!*
> *Fire and lightning!*
> *Cause her strife!"*

I grinned; the voodoo doll wasn't as smart as she thought. She was using the same spell against me that she'd used before, so I knew what its result would be.

> *"Shield erect! Shield bedeck!*
> *Bounce away! Bounce today!*
> *By your shield you must protect!"*

Flames and bolts of lightning burst from Audrey's jump rope, exactly as before. Both raced toward me. I flinched, but her magic struck the sparkles of my flipping blue cord, and this time I deflected them right back at her. However, to my utter horror, the voodoo doll wasn't shielding herself, and while her gold and silver sparkles blocked most of her attack, part of her spell broke through ... and the scream that followed was Audrey's voice.

Audrey collapsed, twitching from the lightning and smoking from the fire, her clothes scorched and hair singed. I staggered ... and my jump rope fell slack.

"Audrey ...!" I cried, and I ran to her, across the throne room. She looked seriously hurt, blasted by her own spell ... and her injuries were my fault.

Slowly she stopped shaking, and then she looked up at me. To my surprise, a wicked grin stretched her innocent lips.

Audrey jumped up and swung her jump rope. Too slow to defend, I dodged her green cord and jumped back, then I swung my own. Our jump rope cords met like steel swords, sparkling and flashing, blue against green, and the force of the impact blasted both of us back. Driven apart, we paused to look at each other, and the impulse to charge forward and fight her to a standstill filled me, yet I couldn't; I might seriously hurt Audrey. I jumped backwards and started jumping rope.

"Spin around! Off the ground!
Swirl and twirl with every sound!
With each spin, by powers great!
Swirl! Twirl! Spin! Rotate!"

The voodoo doll flipped her jump rope, trying to block my spell, when suddenly she was struck. Suddenly she spun around, tripped over her own feet, and fouled her cord. I kept jumping, pressing my will, and the voodoo doll's voice cried out as she spun around again and again, hopelessly trying to regain her footing. She floated off the floor, spinning, twirling, a human tornado in Audrey's shape, and her scream filled the throne room.

I threw in some tricks, Skier, Front Back Cross, and Double Under, keeping her trapped in the air, swirling around faster and faster. I hoped she'd lose consciousness and drop her jump rope, but the strain of maintaining my spell pressed strongly. The voodoo doll was right; I'd been doing magic all day and was exhausted.

Finally I had to stop. Audrey slowly descended, still spinning, fell over, and skidded to a stop on the dais. At once she tried to stand, but she was so dizzy she could barely rise to her knees without toppling over.

I ran forward, onto the short stairs, grabbed her green cord, and tried to pull it from her. Audrey clung to her handles and struggled against me, falling onto one side but not letting go. As we fought for control, I considered hitting her with my jump rope, but I didn't know if that would kill her or not.

Audrey pulled hard, then rolled toward me, wrapping her cord around her, trapping her jump rope under the weight of her body. I tried to pull it out from underneath her, but suddenly she rolled again, to the edge of the short stairs, and kicked me with both her feet. I fell back, but I didn't release her cord, and then she rose and jumped at me.

I wasn't expecting a physical fight; Audrey slammed me flat beneath her, against the hard floor, and I bumped my head so hard that lights flashed before my eyes like magical sparkles of all colors. Audrey raised a fist, as if she were going to punch me, but I threw her off, rolling over and over to one side, getting away from her.

I jumped to my feet, but my head spun, aching, the little lights still flashing before my eyes. I felt exhausted.

Audrey also rose, shakily, still dizzy from the spinning
I'd given her. We faced each other, neither at our best,
but both determined to win.

I had to stop Audrey ... without hurting her. I wished
Princess Gracely were here; she could trap Audrey
inside a giant rhinestone, but I didn't have that power.

Falcon and Judy were waving at me; I glanced at them
and saw them both cover their eyes with their hands. I
knew what they wanted, except that I didn't know why.
Yet I had no better idea.

"Darkness black
Take her back
Shroud her eyes
Conceal her lies!"

I chanted hard as I jumped, and Audrey began
jumping, too. I recognized her chant.

"Bright light,
Shine bright!
Bring the day!
Ban the night!"

The voodoo doll chanted as hard as I did, matching
my speed. The throne room darkened, then grew bright
again, and kept flickering like someone was playing with
a light switch. I strove to jump as hard as I could, but my
darkness spell couldn't defeat her light spell.

Thinking hard, I suddenly changed my chant in mid-
jump.

"Steamy fog, thick and white,
Fill the air! Block the light!"

I speed-jumped as fast as I could, wishing that I'd
thought of a longer spell but having no time to make one
up. I focused on my chant, and as confusion masked
Audrey's face, a great white fog exploded inside the
throne room, filling it from wall to wall. Audrey's bright

light could easily be seen through the fog, but other than the light, all I could see was the gold and silver sparkles flying from my blue cord. Even the dolls, dais, thrones, walls, doors, and curtains became hidden from my view.

Then Audrey's voice cried her chant.

"Wind, I say! Wind today!
Windy wind, blow all away!"

Great gusts suddenly blew through the throne room. Her great white breeze tossed my dark hair about. The thick white fog quickly dissipated, and then it blasted upwards toward the ceiling ... and vanished.

As the fog cleared, the pounding crashes of huge feet filled the throne room. Judy was charging Audrey, and I screamed. Judy was huge ... and could crush Audrey for real ... and permanently. I started to shout but I was too late.

Audrey suddenly turned and swung her jump rope at Judy. The magic struck Judy hard and blasted her backwards, her huge body flying through the air. The other dolls scattered, screaming and running in all directions, ducking out of the way before she landed atop them.

"Hilary!" Falcon hissed, and I looked for him, but I couldn't see him. I glanced about and finally spied him; Falcon was standing upon the dais, half-hiding behind the thrones, and holding up his hand to show me something.

Pinched between Falcon's fingers was a short thread ... with a tiny voodoo token hanging from it.

"No!" the voodoo doll cried, and she raised the handles of her jump rope and started to flip it.

I charged her, not bothering to jump rope. Before her sparkles started, I hammered my shoulder into her back, with all my weight, knocking her onto her side. As

Audrey cried out I ran toward the dais. Falcon tossed the token to me, and I let go of one handle to catch it. I felt Audrey's token land in my hand and grinned.

"Don't ...!" the voodoo doll shouted to me. *"Hilary, wait ...!"*

I glanced to see Audrey upon her knees, her jump rope unready. I held up the token and looked at it; it looked like a tiny clay figure, wrapped with a thin scrap of red cloth, like a dress, bound around her with black thread, and with a grotesque face and brown hair painted upon it. I wouldn't have recognized this was Audrey, but a little green thread ran from one of its hands to the other; Audrey's jump rope.

"Think, before you do this!" the voodoo doll cried. "What do you want to do ... play with dolls forever? Live in Arcadia? Have nothing in your own world?"

I hesitated; *what was she talking about?*

"I can give you your dreams!" the voodoo doll said. "With the magic of your jump rope, and my powers, even the divisions between our worlds will fall away. Think of what you could achieve ... in your world ... with our mights combined ...!"

I lifted the handle of my jump rope but I didn't strike the token.

"Wealth!" the voodoo doll cried. "Fame! Power! You'd have no limits! We could rule forever, you and I! Surrender that token ... and I'll give you everything you ever wanted. We'll help each other ... and simultaneously rule our worlds! I'll be Queen of Arcadia ... and you'll be Queen of Jumperland!"

Images of my dreams passed before my eyes. I'd always wanted lots of money, screaming fans, fancy cars, and huge mansions. The voodoo doll was right ... with my powers and hers, working together, there was nothing we couldn't do.

I could have everything ... and be a queen in my own right ...!

Yet even dreams have costs. I'd have to abandon Audrey, Great Aunt Virginia, Mrs. Darby ... and my Mom.

The price was too high ...!

"The best fame comes from earning it," I said, and I tapped the tiny token with the handle of my jump rope.

"Enflame!"

The tiny token burst aflame, and a brilliant white light burst from it.

"Noooooo ...!" the voodoo doll screamed.

The white light beamed out and struck Audrey. She screamed and fell. When the beam ended, I threw down the token, onto the floor; it broke, but I wasn't satisfied. I stomped hard on it and crushed it into flaming dust.

Audrey lay screaming and writhing. I ran to her, fell to my knees beside her, and grabbed and held her tight. She was shaking and sobbing, but when she looked up, when our eyes met, she recognized me. I saw in her face the pained and frightened expression of the best friend I used to have.

"Hilary ...!" Audrey gasped.

"I've got you," I said, holding her. She seemed weak and weary, but herself again. "I crushed the voodoo doll's token! She can't possess you anymore!"

Audrey burst out sobbing and clung tightly to me.

"Yeee ... aaaahhhhh!" screamed a terrifying shriek, and we looked at the dais. From laying limply upon the throne, beside the silver crown, suddenly the voodoo doll herself jumped up and screamed at Falcon. He shrieked and jumped back, and as he cowered, the

voodoo doll leaped off the throne, landed on the dais, and ran toward the back wall.

"Get her!" Audrey hissed, and I jumped up and ran after the voodoo doll.

She ran quickly, one wide, frayed twine hand, made of five loops, holding her aged straw hat atop her bouncing lollipop head, streaming ragged black veils behind her. I hurried to catch her, but she ran toward a full-sized wooden door, and a moment before I reached her, she dropped onto her back and slid underneath it. She wasn't as thin as a paper doll but the gap under this door was wide enough to shove twine, veils, and a lollipop under ... she slipped underneath with ease.

I smashed into the door, then tried to push it open, but without success. I drew back my jump rope and swung at it with all my might; it struck and blasted me back ... but the door remained firmly closed, although a burned, blackened spot appeared upon its surface.

"It's locked!" I shouted. "I can't get through!"

Audrey was slowly rising. I ran back to help. She looked shaky and as exhausted as I felt.

"Don't worry ...," Audrey said, gasping. "We're two jumpers ... united against her."

"United," I said. "I like that."

Suddenly Audrey and I hugged tightly, and it was as if we'd never fought. We were friends again, and friendship could conquer everything.

"Let's get her," Audrey said.

"Together," I agreed.

We stumbled to Judy only to find her struggling to rise. The blast of the jump rope had blackened her gown with large scorch marks.

"I'm sorry, Judy," Audrey said. "I knew what she was doing ... but I couldn't stop her ...!"

"Not your fault," Judy said. "The rag dolls can make me a new dress and then all will be right. But first, we have a duty to finish ...!"

We helped Judy to rise, and as she stood, Mr. Magee came forward, pulling Falcon by one hand.

"Here's the hero!" Mr. Magee said.

The dolls all cheered Falcon, and he blushed scarlet.

"I'm so proud of you, Falcon," I said.

"We both are," Audrey added.

"All of you dolls are heroes," I said to them. "It's our honor to be your jumpers."

The glamour dolls, the trolls, the tin soldiers, the nutcrackers, the marionettes, the rag dolls, and the stuffed animals ... and the sailor doll ... cheered.

Nothing would open the locked back door. Finally, Audrey and I led the way back out the front door. The dolls followed us past the fallen guards, who were still sleeping, and around to the other side of the castle. The way was long, but when we reached its back the ground sloped downwards for a long way, yet we could see no trace of the voodoo doll. We pushed our way through the grass, heading for the only destination before the swamp stopped our progress; the graveyard.

"This isn't over," Audrey said to me. "The voodoo doll has some devious plan ... she's talked about it quite a lot. She never said exactly what it was, but she claimed to have an 'ultimate weapon' and that no power could stop her once her plans were ripe."

"I'm not afraid of her," I said. "She'll rue the day she came here ... and this time she won't escape to threaten Arcadia again."

We walked slowly, for the high grass was thick. Judy walked behind us, her wide feet flattening the grasses we pushed aside. Behind her, Mr. Magee and Falcon walked, stomping down whatever grasses remained. Behind them marched the nutcrackers and the tin solders, and behind them lay a flat trail that even an ancient one could travel.

We walked for half a mile before the slope flattened out, and there we saw the sad lumps of slime. Before us lay the graveyard, beyond which was the great, impassible swamp. Between us and the graveyard stood the small voodoo doll, veiled in black and staring defiantly at us.

"Now you're doomed!" the voodoo doll shouted. *"Now you'll regret ever coming to Arcadia!"*

I almost laughed. The voodoo doll stood alone, perhaps nine inches tall, and weaponless, while we had two jump ropes and several armies of dolls.

She was no threat ...!

Then the movement began. The still forms in the graveyard shifted. Hands covered in dirt and slime arose. Figures smeared in filth lifted, sitting up from their prone positions. Each looked horrible, coated in gook and gore, ghastly, yet moving and alive.

"Arise!" the voodoo doll commanded. *"I am your maker ... your queen! Arise, my army! Arise and defeat my foes!"*

As one, all the vanished dolls, all our friends that had been taken and forced to drink the evil voodoo doll's potion, rose and stood. Thousands were doll-sized, and under their slime-covered surfaces I could see Master Strand, Boss Fist, and Mistress Flax. Yet tallest among them stood our worst adversaries; King Andy, Queen Anne, Hiram, Muskay, Princess Gracely, Great Aunt Virginia, Mrs. Darby, and ... Mom.

"Zombie dolls ...!" Mr. Magee cried. *"A zombie army ...!"*

Staggering, with stilted movements, the zombie army came marching toward us, emerging from out of the shadows of the trees. They looked horrible, smeared with green and yellow slimes and thickly layered in mud. They raised their arms and stepped closer.

The voodoo doll laughed in triumph.

"This is her weapon!" I whispered to Audrey. *"An army of zombies ... doomed to obey her!"*

"She'll rule Arcadia forever!" Audrey whispered back. *"Queen of a land of undead dolls!"*

"I could barely fight you ... without hurting you!" I said. *"We can't hurt them! What are we going to do?"*

Audrey smiled.

"The magic is in the play," Audrey said.

That stopped me.

"That's right!" I said. "They're not real zombies, just pretend. Quick, what do we know about zombies?"

"Not much," Audrey said. "On TV, they're walking corpses, undead, and they eat brains ..."

"Perfect," I said. "She likes to insult people; I know just what to do!"

Smiling, I stepped forward.

"Hey, voodoo doll!" I shouted. "Do you really think we're going to fall for this?"

The voodoo doll frowned.

"You will fall before me!" the voodoo doll shouted.

"No, we won't!" I shouted, trying to hurry before the voodoo doll's army got any closer. "We didn't fall to your possessing us, as you'd planned, and we freed Audrey, against your plan, and this pathetic plan will fail, too!"

"Nothing can defeat my army of the undead!" the voodoo doll shouted.

I laughed at her.

"And you call yourself a smart doll!" I sniggered. "The plans of smart dolls don't fail one after another! Face it: you're the stupidest doll in Arcadia! You've got the smallest brain of any doll ever!"

"I'm the smartest doll that ever was!" the voodoo doll shouted. *"I'm a genius! I've got the biggest and best brain in Arcadia!"*

I smiled; *we'd won!*

"You're right!" I shouted, and I struggled to withhold my mirth. I stood tall and faced the terrifying zombie army, raising my voice so all hear. "You heard her, zombies! The voodoo doll is the smartest doll in Arcadia! She has the biggest ... and best brain anywhere! There she is, right in front of you, the sweetest, tastiest brain of all ... and what do zombies eat ...? Brains! There she is! Enjoy your feast!"

The voodoo doll looked surprised, and then snarled at us.

"Ignore her!" the voodoo doll shouted at her zombies. *"Attack them! Attack them all!"*

Yet every zombie hesitated, turning their slime-covered heads from side to side, looking from us to her. Finally, they oriented on her ... and started marching forward.

"No, not me!" the voodoo doll cried. *"Her! Them! The jumpers ... and the dolls ... not me!"*

Heedlessly, the zombie dolls converged upon her.

"Great, magnificent, tasty brains!" Audrey shouted. "There she is!"

"Delicious!" I shouted, encouraging them. "Licorice lobes ... perfect for eating!"

As the zombies closed around her, the voodoo doll tried to run one direction, and then the other. Finally, with no other choice, she ran ... toward us.

"Fan out!" I cried to all our dolls. *"Form a wall! Don't let her escape!"*

Behind us, the crowd of dolls spread out, forming a wide line between the swamp and the castle.

"No!" the voodoo doll cried as the zombies kept advancing toward her. *"You can't do this! It's not part of the game!"*

"Surrender!" Audrey commanded her.

"Yes," I said. "And tell us how to free the zombie dolls ... and our friends ... or we let them eat you!"

The voodoo doll glanced at the wall of dolls preventing her escape ... and back at the army of zombie dolls coming closer, their arms outstretched to her ... their mouths opening ... *hungrily.* Lastly she looked up at the wide sky overhead.

"Only rain can save them!" the voodoo doll shouted. "They're not dead, just dirty! It's makeup! Wash off the muck ... and they won't be zombies anymore!"

Audrey reached down and picked up the voodoo doll, turned around, and handed her to Mr. Magee.

"She won't escape from me," Mr. Magee sneered, and he snapped his wooden mouth open and closed a few times just to frighten the voodoo doll.

Audrey and I turned to face the approaching zombies. As one, we started to jump rope. Audrey invented a chant on the spot and I picked it up and recited with her.

> *"Rain! Rain! Come today!*
> *Wash the dirt and slime away!*
> *Clean our friends!*
> *End all ends!*
> *Finish this, our friends to stay!"*

Above, dark clouds appeared and rolled toward us, suddenly, and lightning flashed, followed by a fearsome roll of thunder. Yet it took some time for rain to begin from a previously clear sky. The zombie army marched ever closer, and our human friends soon reached the front of the line, their wider strides passing the smaller dolls. Although they limped, some dragging lifeless limbs, they crept forward.

We were forced to back up, and keep backing up.

The rain would come ... but would it come in time ... and hard enough ...?

Droplets began to fall. I felt them on the top of my head, at first so tiny that I wasn't sure if I were imagining them or not, but soon it began to rain in earnest. The first drops struck the zombies like hailstones, and they winced as if pained by the clean, pure water.

A downpour opened up. The zombies screamed and wailed as if being murdered, but this was a game, and they were already playing dead. The thin layers of slime and dirt washed off them, and they collapsed onto the wet grass. They writhed and flailed upon the ground, but slowly, as their slime and dirt makeup washed away, their screams stopped, and their eyes focused and looked around. Under the torrent of cleanliness, they fell as zombies, but arose as themselves, wet ... but free of possession.

Audrey looked back, saw Mr. Magee still holding the voodoo doll ... and screamed. The voodoo doll hadn't changed, but where once Mr. Magee's pale face had shined with pink cheeks and white eyes with black pupils, now his face and hands were the grained browns of polished wood.

"Don't worry," I said to Audrey. "He was never painted; his makeup just washed off. The hand puppets can fix him, and then he'll be as good as new."

Suddenly Mrs. Darby ran forward and embraced

Audrey, but I never got to see them smile; Mom ran up, grabbed me, and I was suddenly glad I wasn't a doll ... or she would've hugged the stuffing out of me.

"You did it!" Mom whispered excitedly in my ear. "I'm so proud of you!"

"I couldn't lose you, Mom," I said.

"Bless you both!" Great Aunt Virginia said. "Now let's get out of this rain ... before it ruins the dolls!"

Two days later, inside the castle, King Andy and Queen Anne summoned Audrey and I forward. We stepped proudly, our heads high, our smiles bright. I was wearing a long, golden gown, while Hilary was wearing a frilly pink gown, and we walked forward like a pair of fairy princesses ... armed with green and blue jump ropes.

We reached the steps before the dais, stopped and curtsied, and King Andy and Queen Anne rose and stood before us.

"We owe everything to Audrey and Hilary," King Andy said, and he bowed to us.

"We have gifts for you," Queen Anne said, and she snapped her fingers.

A guard came forward holding out a silver tray. From the tray Queen Anne lifted a pair of elegant rings, one with a real emerald, and one with a real ruby. She placed the emerald ring on Audrey's finger and I got the ruby ring placed on mine. Both precious stones were set on genuine bands of 14-carat gold.

"These treasures are real, and can be carried to your world," Queen Anne said. "I understand they're quite valuable there."

"You may keep them ... or sell them," King Andy

said. "With them, you could buy your dreams."

"I'm keeping mine," Audrey said, smiling and admiring how it looked on her hand.

"Me, too," I smiled.

"Really ...?" Queen Anne asked. "But ... what about your dreams?"

"We'll both get our dreams," I said. "There's nothing wrong with having dreams, whether they lead to a quiet life or a noisy one. The trick is to know what your dreams are, and remember that there're some things in life more important than dreams ... like good friends."

"Without friends, no dream is worthwhile," Audrey agreed. "Dreams are best when shared."

We reached out, took each other's hands, and smiled brightly.

All around us dolls cheered. Mr. Magee cheered the loudest, with his freshly-painted face perfectly redone. Many other dolls were also recently cleaned, dried, and repaired ... or waiting to be restored. Only one doll wasn't smiling; the voodoo doll sat helpless in the back, under constant guard by a dozen tin soldiers. The sailor doll had retied her threads and twine into knots no doll of Arcadia could untie, and a special iron prison cell was being cast just to hold her. The sailor doll was stuck in Arcadia, unable to return to his home, but he'd gladly moved into Sparkle City and spent every night dancing with hundreds of glamour dolls.

Audrey and I thanked King Andy and Queen Anne, then curtsied again, and turned and walked back through the crowd of cheering dolls. We slowly reached the end, near where Judy stood. She was fully-recovered, although still waiting for the rag dolls to make enough new fabric to replace her ruined dress. Smiling beside her stood Falcon, Muskay, Hiram, Princess Gracely,

Great Aunt Virginia, Mrs. Darby, and Mom. With a brief, shared glance at each other, we curtsied to them, too. This earned us hugs from all the adults, and we were delighted to receive them.

"We can't stay too late," Mom reminded us.

"That's right," Mrs. Darby said. "You're both behind on your homework, and Audrey has more than a week to make up."

"We'll study together," Audrey promised.

"And ... if we argue again, we're never going to let it ruin our friendship," I said.

"Arcadia has never been so protected," Great Aunt Virginia smiled at us.

The party lasted long, full of dancing and singing dolls, and the marionettes had baked cookies for everyone. Audrey and I had a wonderful time ... and we danced and sang with the dolls. Arcadia was free ... and now Audrey and I could share it forever.

THE END

ABOUT THE AUTHOR

Born in Tripler Army Medical Center, Honolulu, Hawaii, Jay Palmer works as a technical writer in the software industry in Seattle, Washington. Jay enjoys parties, reading everything in sight, woodworking, obscure board games, and riding his Kawasaki Vulcan. Jay is a knight in the SCA, frequently attends writer conferences, SciFi Conventions, and he and Karen are both avid ballroom dancers. But most of all, Jay enjoys writing.

Made in the USA
Columbia, SC
11 February 2024

31317884R00157